PROXIMITY

Visit us at www.boldstrokesbooks.com

PROXIMITY

by

Jordan Meadows

2023

PROXIMITY

ISBN 13: 978-1-63679-476-1

THIS TRADE PAPERBACK ORIGINAL IS PUBLISHED BY
BOLD STROKES BOOKS, INC.
P.O. BOX 249
VALLEY FALLS, NY 12185

FIRST EDITION: SEPTEMBER 2023

CREDITS

EDITOR: JENNY HARMON
PRODUCTION DESIGN: STACIA SEAMAN
COVER DESIGN BY INKSPIRAL DESIGN

Acknowledgments

First and foremost, I want to thank the entire Bold Strokes team for making this book happen. Thank you, Rad and Sandy, for taking a chance on me. Thank you, Jenny, for making the editing process clear and practically painless. I appreciate you all.

A big thank you goes out to my friends and family, who have not only put up with my obsessive writing but encouraged it. I particularly want to thank those of you who have been beta readers from the start. Mom, your enthusiasm and encouragement have meant the world to me. PJ, thank you for dreaming with me.

Haley, this literally would not have happened without you. You showed me it could be done, were a desperately needed cheerleader during our writers' retreat/road trip that led to my first novel, have continued to cheer me on, and are the absolute best brainstorming partner in the world. You are awesome and I'm so excited to see your first book come out. Soon!

Lastly, thank you. Yes, you. Readers are what really make a book, and I'm so happy you decided to read mine.

To my daughter. Without you, this wouldn't have happened.

PROLOGUE

I remember when Sabrina and I didn't always spend every moment together but wanted to. You're probably thinking that *every moment* is hyperbole. It's not. You're probably thinking, "Well, it can't have been that long a time, then, because who can possibly spend every moment with another person? I mean, people use the bathroom." You're wrong. Not about the bathroom part. Everyone poops, as the famous book reminds us. It's the *every moment* part you're wrong about. You can. And when lives depend on it, you will.

I was eight the day that my brother and I were sitting on the couch one Saturday afternoon watching a movie. Dad was home, but Mom was out. When Neil's nose started to bleed, I called for Dad. He came in and sent me for a hand towel while he had Neil try things like pinching his nose and tilting his head back. You know, the usual stuff one does for a nosebleed, and it seemed to be working at first, but then he bled through the towel and Dad got concerned. He called Aunt Sarah and asked her to come stay with me while he took Neil to urgent care. Dad and Aunt Sarah were the non-Family parents in our two families and had a bond because of that. So, that's who he'd have thought to ask.

Aunt Sarah was there in less than two minutes, Sabrina in tow to keep me company. They were fast because they lived in the same building, just two floors below us. As soon as they came in, the bleeding stopped.

"Well, guess the emergency is over," Dad said. "Sorry we bothered you."

"No problem," Aunt Sarah assured him. "I'm just glad Neil is okay."

"Can Sabrina stay and play since she's here and all?" I asked.

Sabrina nodded vigorously, and we both deployed our pleading eyes on the parents, who had no objections. We went off to my room to play. Neil came along with us, and Dad, presumably, cleaned up. I thought nothing more of the matter, to be honest, until Sabrina went downstairs to get her school bag. We'd played until Mom came home and said I needed to get my homework done. We'd decided to do it together. When Sabrina left, I stayed in the kitchen to chat with Mom and she started coughing.

"Mom? Are you okay?" I asked.

She waved her hand at me to indicate she was okay, but when she kept coughing and grabbed a tissue, it was red with coughed-up blood.

"Mom?" I asked, panicked.

"Joan," she coughed out, "go to your room."

I went, crying. Some kids might have stayed, clinging to their mom in fear. I was scared and very worried about my mom, but I did as she asked anyway. Because the thing is, I was a member of the Family.

Chapter One

Sabrina sighed at me from across the room. It was a sigh designed to get attention. I knew it well, as I knew everything about Sabrina well. Or at least, I was pretty sure I did. I'm sure she had some secret inner life. I did, too, but generally speaking, we were very familiar with each other's little habits. This habit of sighing for my attention was long established.

"Yes?" I asked. "Are we bored?"

She sighed again, theatrically. "Tragically bored. Let's go do something."

I closed my laptop. I'd been working on an online anatomy and physiology lab, which was a sucky way to do a lab, no doubt, but was better than not doing it, which was the only other choice, because I'd never get Sabrina in a room with cadavers. However, the fact was, I knew it would be impossible to concentrate once Sabrina had a hair up her butt, so I gave her my attention. "Fine. Like what?"

She shut her own laptop where she'd maybe been doing schoolwork of her own, but just as likely not. If I had to guess, she was either DMing Insta friends or working on a graphic design project or virtually traveling to some distant local. To be fair, she might have been working on either Spanish or German. She was taking both languages, and they were the only subjects aside from art that she bothered to give much attention to. She was on a fairly normal track where, at seventeen, she was a junior in high school.

I was currently in my junior year in college. Or, more accurately, I was in my third year of college, but I always took a big course load and could probably graduate this spring if I wanted to. This worked only because we did exclusively online school and had since midyear in third grade.

"I dunno. Shopping? Walking the High Line? I saw they've got an art installation going. Looks cool."

"High Line it is," I said decisively. I hated shopping unless it was for books, but since it was one of Sabrina's favorite activities, I put up with it sometimes. Given a choice, though, I was all about whatever was not shopping.

She grinned knowingly at me.

I picked up my phone and noted that it was one o'clock. "We should take our swim stuff so we can go straight to the pool," I said. I was the planner among us.

"Good idea." She got off the twin bed she'd been sitting on and started gathering her stuff. I tightened my ponytail, then got up from my desk and did the same.

We moved around each other with an ease born of years of working in close proximity. Sabrina was done first and stood by the door, waiting, boho bag over a shoulder. She gingerly patted her white hair while she waited, checking the spikiness level. Without discussion, once I had my sort of sporty backpack slung over one of my shoulders, we moved to the bathroom and took turns while the other stood just outside. In our younger years, we'd have just gone in with each other, but we'd decided somewhere around twelve that it was nice to have a few moments of privacy, even if it was only to pee. When one of us showered, the other still came into the bathroom so they didn't have to lurk in the hall, blocking traffic for however long it took.

We were at Sabrina's apartment that day, so there was no one to say goodbye to before we left. Both her parents were at work. We couldn't be sure that some other person wasn't within my zone of danger, thus the continued caution about proximity. Plus, it was all just ingrained habit now. After a few unfortunate events when we were young, we didn't take chances.

"Cookie or juice?" I asked as we rode the elevator down to the first floor.

Sabrina thought for a moment, then replied decisively. "Juice."

We could have gotten a cookie, and a good one, at the caf on the way out for free, but it was sometimes more fun to buy food out. We both had a liking for the concoctions at Juice Vitality. However, Sabrina had other reasons for wanting to visit besides juice.

"Paul won't be working, you know, it's the middle of the school day."

"I know," she huffed. "I can want the juice just for the juice."

"Sure you can," I teased. But she wasn't wrong. As I said, we both liked their drinks.

After the stop, we strolled up First Avenue toward the subway station, drinks in hand. Mine was a green smoothie that tasted mostly of pineapple. Sabrina's was also green, but a true juice.

Sometimes I wondered whether, had our lives have been more normal, or at least Family normal, our friendship would have petered out around middle school. We were pretty different people these days. I knew I'd have still wanted to be friends, although I'd have sat out the shopping and the synchronized swimming (at least back when we first started), but Sabrina was probably way too cool for me and would have moved on.

I paused at the intersection with Twelfth Street. "Mind if we stop at the Strand?"

Sabrina shrugged. "Why not?" We turned left instead of going straight on to the subway stop.

We both liked the bookstore but didn't necessarily like the same books. YA was easy enough, as we both were fond of reading fiction, but from there, it was a matter of waiting for one another again. Sometimes all of that felt like it took too long to bother with, but we were just out looking to fill the afternoon today.

The Strand wasn't too busy. After all, it was midafternoon on a Wednesday, so most people were at school or work. By habit, we went upstairs to YA first. That way, we could both browse for a while and each pick a book or two to take with us for entertainment. I started reading a book I'd picked, while Sabrina browsed the travel books, and then she spent long enough amongst the language books that I finally told her to just bring the current book she was looking at—an intro to Russian of all things—with her so I could finally spend some time in biology.

When I glanced at my phone to check the time, I said, "If we don't get going, we won't have time for the High Line before swimming." I half asked, which she was plenty able to read in my tone. *Do we want to stay at the bookstore for hours or actually go do what we planned?*

She shrugged, looked at the books she was carrying, and said, "I need to put most of these back."

"Same," I said.

We each left with one new book weighing us down. For me, it was a dystopian novel that Sabrina would probably read next, but she wound up with the rather large intro to Russian book. For someone who barely passed most of her classes, she had odd hobbies. "Weirdo," I teased. "At least I got one we can both enjoy."

She shrugged. "One we could get electronically from the library, probably. This, though, I need so I can do the worksheets in it."

I did get that. I preferred actual books for science myself.

We were almost halfway to the High Line now, so we didn't bother with a subway and just walked the rest of the way. We chatted some, walked quietly some. We spent all of our days together, so catching each other up was really never a thing we needed to do. However, we usually could find things to talk about— books we were reading, what some online work partner did or didn't do for a project, the other teens in the Complex (there were currently seventeen of us and they were our primary source of peer socialization), or just the general state of the world. But we also didn't need to fill every silence. That would be ridiculous for us.

We climbed the stairs at Fourteenth Street and started north. The High Line was always nice to stroll. Well, not always. On the weekends when the weather was nice, it was overcrowded and chaotic, but on weekdays it was often quiet, like today. There were plenty of people because the weather was good, but it was New

York. There were always lots of people around, so that was to be expected. It wasn't super crowded, though, and we were easily able to stay in range. By the third statue of a man, I'd had more or less my fill. A quick glance was more than enough for me, but Sabrina had whipped out a sketchbook at the first display and muttered about it being a good project for one of her classes, so I had a lot of time to kill. I sat on a nearby bench and practiced my meditation. Sabrina had to shake me to get my attention to move onto the next exhibit.

At the fourth display, after my cursory glance, I noticed a tree in its spring bloom behind it, and after a closer look, a ladybug walking across one of the new green leaves. I leaned in and watched it make its way, when I was startled by a stranger's voice quite close to me.

"Something more interesting than the art back there?"

I fumbled my book, ultimately dropping it in the dirt below the tree, and cursed. I bent down to pick it up, but someone beat me to it. "Sorry." The same voice came again from the blond girl with a bob who was handing my book back to me now. "I didn't mean to startle you."

"I won't insult either of us by lying and saying that you didn't," I told her, tucking the book away in my backpack.

She grimaced. "Yeah, sorry again. What were you looking at back there, though?"

I chuckled. "Just a ladybug."

"Must have been some ladybug." She smiled at me.

"You have no idea," I told her, straight faced.

"So…you're here for the nature, not the art, then?"

I shrugged. "I guess. I mean, I do like nature, but mostly I'm here with my cousin, who is really into the art." I swooshed my hand in Sabrina's general direction, and the girl turned to look at her. She was looking between her sketchbook and the statue.

"I see." She gave me a knowing look. "One of you is more into the male form than the other."

I laughed. That was subtle. "I mean, yes, that's true, but also she is really into art in general. What brings you to the High

Line today if not the statuesque male form?" I swept my hand dramatically toward the nearest statue. Apparently, that was enough to get Sabrina's attention. She glanced up at me, did a double take to see that I was talking to someone, checked her out, grinned at me, and gave me the thumbs-up. I rolled my eyes.

The girl I was talking to looked behind her again to see what I was rolling my eyes at, but Sabrina had already bowed back over her drawing. She turned back to me and raised an eyebrow. "Something I said?" she asked.

"No, just my innocent-looking cousin. But really, what brings you here today if not the art or the ladybugs?"

"Who says it's not the ladybugs? I'm mostly people watching. I've got some time to kill between my last class and the start of my Starbucks shift."

"Ah, one of those coffee artists." I nodded seriously.

"Ha! Not at Starbucks! But it's money, you know."

"Sure." Sabrina and I each did a few shifts a week at the caf in the Complex, as did all the teens in the building at some point. It was where most of our spending money came from, so I did know what she was talking about there. We also did shifts in the Complex daycare and some babysitting, both of which I enjoyed more, but sometimes you just did a job for money. "Joan," I said, holding out my hand to shake, like some weird formal person.

"Joan?" She more held my hand than shook it. "That's unusual these days."

"It's a family name." I was enjoying the not shaking, but it was also starting to feel long. I took my hand back. "And this is where you would typically tell me your name," I prompted.

"Oh, right. Social niceties and all. Clearly, what with my scaring the bejesus out of you and this need for prompting, I could use some schooling there." She grinned.

I grinned back, but reminded her, "And that name is…"

She laughed. "Ellie! Sorry."

"No worries. Nice to meet you, Ellie."

She glanced back over her shoulder at Sabrina, then turned back to look at me. "I don't want to seem presumptuous, but we've already established that I have no social skills, so…would you like to walk a bit? Your cousin seems wrapped up over there."

I sighed internally. I'd love to walk with this intriguing, cute Ellie, but fifteen feet from Sabrina was my limit. Should we break it, not only Ellie but anyone else in my general vicinity would be in serious danger. Normally, I'd just act like a weirdo who was attached at the hip with my cousin, who was also my best friend. It's not abnormal for teens to have that sort of codependent relationship with a friend, so people bought it most of the time and I generally didn't care if they didn't. But I wanted Ellie to like me.

"I'd love to," I told her, "But we've actually got to get going to get to swim practice in just a few minutes, so I can't wander off." She looked disappointed. I didn't want her thinking I wasn't interested in getting to know her more. I was. But it'd be easier for me online. Also, I wanted her to lose the disappointed look. "We could exchange numbers?"

Her face cleared. "Sure! And then we could find a time to do the whole walking thing another time." She pulled out her phone, and I recited my number. She entered it and then sent me a text.

"Nice to meet you, Ellie!" I said.

"Same."

When it was clear she wasn't going to leave quite yet, I gave her a sort of awkward wave and went to tap Sabrina on her shoulder. "Time for swimming."

She looked at the old analog watch she wore and looked up at me, clearly about to protest. I bugged my eyes out at her and she sighed. "Yup, right. We should go."

She closed her sketchbook, put it in her bag, and we walked back the way we'd come. I turned to see that Ellie was walking away in the other direction and heaved a sigh.

"Did she leave? Can I go back to finish my sketch now?" Sabrina asked. She sounded aggrieved. Rightfully so.

"No! What if she comes back and realizes I lied to her? We have to leave."

Sabrina rolled her eyes, then stopped and looked at me. "Wait. Did you like her or not like her? What's this craziness about?"

I blushed.

"Oh, you liked her and didn't want her to know that we're conjoined twins without the conjoined part."

I gave an exaggerated shrug accompanied by an exasperated look. "Would you?"

"What does it matter anyway? You'll never see her again." When I didn't reply right away, Sabrina went on, uncertainly. "Right?"

"We exchanged numbers," I admitted.

"Oh."

We hadn't dated for obvious reasons. We were well aware of each other's types. Sabrina tended to like tall artsy guys with tattoos. I was into, well, Ellie types. Generally speaking, girls on the femme side of things. Curves were welcome. Ellie, in her fitted on the top and flared below the waist dress, certainly fit the bill. She was cute, confident, and curvy. The best of the Cs. But dating was…well, kind of out, really. You just didn't bring your cousin along on a date. Unless you were part of a culture where chaperoning was common, in which case, you probably weren't dating the same sex. At least not openly.

When I didn't reply, Sabrina put her hands on her hips and asked, "What's the plan here, J?"

"Um…I don't really have one? But I liked her and think she's cute and thought maybe we could text or something."

"And what happens when she wants to actually, you know, do something with you?"

"I could say that my parents don't allow dating except in groups?" I floated.

She scoffed, then paused. "Actually, that's not a bad idea."

"Right! You could bring someone, too, like maybe Paul, and maybe we could get some of the others to go out, so it wouldn't seem too weird."

"J, I hate to break it to you, but we're weird. She'll find that out sooner or later."

She was right. I mean, everyone in the Family was weird to some extent. How much and how easy it was to cover up varied. All the precogs, who were the most common, but whose abilities ranged from a brief glance at next Wednesday's weather to getting enough specifics about the future to help set the Family up financially, got by with presenting as having epilepsy. They all wore those medical bracelets. When they had a vision, they looked like they were having an absence seizure, so it worked out. It was one of the many reasons we lived in New York. They could all get around the city just fine without needing to drive, which was problematic when you'd occasionally, without warning, just check out anywhere from a few seconds to a half an hour or so.

Nevertheless, we were all encouraged to date and only dated outside the Family. We never married within the Family, even though some of the relations were of the eighth cousin variety. That way lay inbreeding. And eventually, people we wanted to marry were brought into the fold, so to speak. But we were also supposed to keep our powers under wraps until relationships were on the *and now we should get married* sort of level. Even then, it was done very carefully.

So, there was no way I could explain to Ellie why I could never be apart from Sabrina. It was either find a way to hang out with her that included Sabrina but didn't expose our secrets, or not hang out.

"Yeah, okay, but later," I said. "It might not go anywhere anyway."

"Right. Particularly when neither of us can duck away to a quiet spot to help things go places."

I sighed. She was right. Still, this was all much better than living in isolation. At least for me. Sabrina could live a normal life easily. Her ability was super easy to hide. She dampened other people's abilities. It was just extreme luck on my part that we were born in the same generation, figured it out, and she was willing to basically cleave to me for life. We had a person living in isolation right now, up on the tenth floor. Linda was in her fifties and was used to living in isolation to the point where she was more than a little agoraphobic. She could, in theory, leave isolation with Sabrina, at least from time to time, but she hadn't been interested. She and I had a video chat sort of relationship, and I can tell you that I didn't want that life. But I sometimes thought I should voluntarily accept it to free Sabrina.

"You know," I said, reviving an argument we'd had before, "I could talk to the Council, see about getting set up in one of the isolation apartments. I wouldn't have to stay there always, but you could go to school or at least on a date."

"We don't want to give them any ideas," Sabrina replied darkly.

It's not that the Council was evil. But it was true that the Family could be a little...harsh when dealing with wayward powers. They killed a little girl named Martha in the eighties once they figured out she was giving everyone around her cancer. Her range grew after they tried her in isolation, probably out of the mental terror of suddenly being isolated from literally everyone at the age of eight. There wasn't even video chatting then, so she could only talk to people on the phone. From what we were taught in Sunday school, it was a blessing when they finally decided she should die peacefully. So, I did get it that Sabrina didn't want to set any sort of precedent for me needing to be locked up or worse. And I loved her for it. Still, I was very aware I was depriving her of a normal life. And very aware that if we hadn't, by a miracle, been not only age mates but friends whose powers developed together, I'd be living a life (or not) like Linda's.

Chapter Two

After synchronized swimming, we went to my place to eat dinner. I say *my place* but we were each equally at home in either apartment by now. We just referred to them by *mine* or *yours* for ease. In actuality, we floated back and forth according to convenience, mood, and schedule. We also did sort of go through phases. When we first became inseparable, we'd been working on a massive Barbie house in my room, made from materials we collected—delivery boxes, packaging, old clothes—that took up an entire wall of my room. Up in my room (our apartment was a couple of floors higher, so up), we had bunk beds. We spent a lot of time in my room in those days. Now we were less enamored with the bunk beds and often slept in Sabrina's room where we each had a freestanding bed. But in my room, our Barbie house of old had been replaced with a couch, so it was a comfortable place to hang out in during the day. Schoolwork was done in either spot, depending, again, on mood, who was home, and where we'd slept. We had desks in Sabrina's room, but that couch was pretty comfortable.

"Hi, girls," my mom greeted when we walked in. "How was swimming?"

"Good," I said, which was funny because I was very much not into synchronized swimming when we first started, but Sabrina had taken gymnastics in the Before Times and needed something physical to keep doing. Synchronized swimming seemed like a good bet, as long as we both did it, because we would be kept close to each other all the time. Still, we stood out as being unusually tied at the hip even over other best friend pairs on the team. After a few years, though, I found I was as attached to continuing swimming as Sabrina, which was important, because I had to work hard to keep up with her.

"Fine expect for the fact that Quinn can't hold her body position to save her life," Sabrina said. "I thought we'd drown practicing her lift over and over again."

"Well, I'm glad to see you made it through." Mom's eyes danced with amusement. "Dinner in fifteen."

We went to dump our stuff in my room and flopped on the couch, pulling out our phones. I dithered over how to reply to the message Ellie had sent earlier.

332-546-7870: *Hey, it's your friendly High Line stalker here. (grinning face)*

It was cute and a little dorky, maybe. I'd been mulling over my response all through practice and the trip home.

"Tell her your mom told you never to get involved with stalkers," Sabrina said, peering over her shoulder.

"Hey, eyes on your own phone," I scolded, not really meaning it.

"Please. You clearly need help."

"I was thinking something like 'At least that makes a change from cyber stalking.'"

"Like I said, you need help." Sabrina rolled her eyes. "Besides, a little cyber stalking never hurt anyone. You should check people out before getting involved."

"That would mean more if you'd ever been involved," I said, fiddling with my phone.

Sabrina laughed. "Okay, okay, we're both clearly novices in this field. Let's pull on our knowledge from books. How about…"

She trailed off, looking thoughtful, but before we got any further, Mom called us out to eat.

"Neil is coming home this weekend," Mom said as we all dished up. "He wants to bring Theresa."

"Seriously?" I asked. "Isn't he a little young for that?"

Neil was away for his freshman year of college. He was going to a small liberal arts school in Connecticut, so it wasn't too far for weekend visits. And maybe bringing a girlfriend home would be normal for most, but Family members generally didn't do sleepovers in the Complex until they were serious. And then it was the start of easing them into joining our diabolical cult.

Mom shrugged. "Sometimes when you know, you know. Neil knows the deal. If he thinks it's time for a visit, then we know he's serious about Theresa."

"What do you think, Mark?" Sabrina asked, fork poised with a bite of lasagna on it.

"I mean, you gotta start the indoctrination sometime, right?" Dad joked.

"But you were, like, a decade older than Neil. I mean, he just seems young to be bringing home a potential spouse," I protested.

"Okay, then, we'll know not to expect your wife until you're— what?—in your thirties? Does that seem right?" Mom teased.

"Ha ha. I don't know when, but I'd like to think I'll be at least in my twenties! I mean, Neil is literally still a teenager." I exchanged a look with Sabrina. She shrugged.

"Fine. I guess I'm the only one disturbed by this." I tucked into my dinner.

It's not that we couldn't have regular friends over. We could. Although the longer they were in the building, the more likely they were to experience oddness, so generally we didn't do sleepovers. As for Sabrina and me, we just didn't really have outside friends. Normal people thought we were weird for not ever being apart. On our synchronized swimming team, for example, we were friendly with people, but everyone assumed we were just one of those pairs of friends who didn't make room for others. That wasn't completely true, though. We did have friends in the building. Anyway, other people who weren't in our situation did have outside friends and even had them over sometimes.

"You two are on cleanup duty tonight," Mom said. "I want to get back to the studio for a while."

"And I'm meeting Greg for drinks," Dad said.

While we washed dishes, we discussed the Neil and Theresa situation some more.

"I do think he's young to be thinking marriage, but I also think your mom is right that when you know, you know—you know?" Sabrina said.

"Ugh. That was horrible."

Sabrina grinned unrepentantly. "Really, though. If he loves her and she's the one for him, isn't it better to know now rather than go ten years dating before he learns it won't work?"

I shrugged. "I guess." Part of the process of bringing someone home was a bit of light mind reading (or, okay, maybe not so light—I mean, someone was rummaging around in your head), which was Linda's job. That's why she was in isolation. For her, isolation was voluntary, sort of. She read the thoughts of anyone near her, and that made it more than a little difficult to be around people. She was very useful to the Family, though, for vetting potential spouses, as well as other things, like business dealings.

"Okay, but back to the important matter at hand. You've left poor Ellie on read for hours now. You've gotta reply."

"I know," I groaned. "But I still don't know what to say."

"You could lean into the stalking thing and be like, *How'd you get this number? I'm alerting the police.*"

"No way. If she didn't read it as a joke, then what? No, no, no. I can't do this. I'm out." I tossed my phone onto the bed across from us. It was the bottom bunk, which I slept in when we slept in this room.

Sabrina got up, took the two steps to the bed, retrieved the phone, and handed it back to me. "You do want to do this. Just reply. It probably doesn't matter what unless you send her a nude or something. She initiated, and obviously wants to talk to you."

I sighed and typed. I hit send before I could second-guess myself, then threw the phone again.

Sabrina looked at me, clearly surprised. "This is not like you at all. You're usually all mature and disgustingly levelheaded. You must really be into her. What did you say?"

"Should I provide you with a schedule to make the stalking easier? Or shall we pick a time and place for your stalking convenience?"

"See? That's cute. You're fine."

I groaned.

CHAPTER THREE

Our alarm went off early the next morning because we had a shift in the cafeteria. We were quiet in the mornings, just going about getting ready for the day in well-worn patterns. I tended to wake up a little on the slow side and Sabrina woke up grumpy until after her first cup of coffee, so we just did what we needed to do without even really looking at each other. On caf days, Sabrina got her coffee down there, so it wasn't until after the elevator ride and procurement of that first cup that Sabrina was ready to talk. By then, I was awake myself. I was not a coffee person, so while she sipped on her cup of caffeine, I knocked back an orange juice. Hard core.

We weren't the first ones there, so Sabrina was able to pour herself a cup of coffee without having to make it first. The morning shift workers were trickling in with a mix of early morning moods, from cheery to unpleasant. The caf was staffed by a core team of adults who worked part- or full-time and were the consistent ones who kept the place going long term. Then there were the teens in the building. We started working a couple shifts a week at fifteen or sometimes younger. Some of us had jobs outside the Complex, but we all had to put in at least a couple shifts a week for a year. Sabrina and I had started working at thirteen for pocket money and out of a need for regular socialization outside our core families. Labor laws are flexible when you're working for *family*.

As people got themselves beverages and slowly started putting on aprons and hair nets and stuff, there was some sleepy conversation.

"I'm so tired," our best friend Heather yawned out.

Sabrina yawned back at her. "Stop it, you're infecting me."

"At least you can go back to bed after this. I've got to go to school." Heather sipped her coffee.

"Yeah, right. Like I don't have schoolwork to do," Sabrina said.

The truth was, though, that sometimes she did go back to sleep.

Sabrina and I got to work chopping veggies for the egg and veggie scramble that was on the morning's menu. Others around us were cracking eggs, setting out the various help yourselves items, including fruit, various bread items by the toaster oven, oatmeal toppings, cereal, and a variety of milks for the cereals and coffee. These were things we always had. The hot dish varied.

Travis walked by, drinking his first Coke of the day. "Ladies," he said.

"Travis," I acknowledged while Sabrina ignored him.

"Hey," Sabrina whispered to Heather. "What ever happened with him and Valerie?"

Heather leaned in to whisper back. "They broke up. She finally realized he was scum."

Travis and Heather went to the same public high school. Valerie was a friend of Heather's who'd ignored her advice and started dating Travis. The three of us found him insufferable. He was cute (I could tell that objectively, even though I was not attracted to people of his gender persuasion, generally) and cocky. Luckily for us, his year of working in the caf would be up soon and he was unlikely to continue.

"Apparently, he never wanted to do what she wanted to do, and she got tired of going to watch him play soccer and then going to parties with his soccer playing friends. So, it's over." She did a mock cheer, then pulled a sour face. "But he's moved on and is dating Ashley already. At least she's not a friend of mine, so I don't feel too bad about it."

"Speaking of dating," Sabrina said, bumping me with her elbow, "this one here wants to date."

"Well, it's about time, girl!" Heather said loudly enough that we drew a look from Andrea, the day's supervisor. When she saw we were still actually chopping like we were supposed to be, she smiled a little and went back to cooking the first batch of veggie scramble. She was my favorite supervisor for a reason.

"It's not like it's easy for us," I protested.

"No," she acknowledged. "So, what's the plan?"

"The plan is to go on a group date. So…you in?" Sabrina asked.

"We need more people so it doesn't seem as weird that Sabrina and I have to go on a first date together. We're going to tell our dates, provided they accept, that our parents only let us group date."

"Sure! But I don't know who I'd bring. I'm a single gal, you know." Heather pouted at us a little.

"Just bring a friend or something. Heck, it could even be Marcel," I said. Marcel was a Family friend of ours, and clearly not someone any of us could date.

Heather wrinkled her nose. "Ew. I mean, we could invite him and a date, too, but I can't even pretend-date him." Not dating in the Family was seriously ingrained.

"I take it you haven't *seen* yourself with anyone?" Sabrina asked.

"You know I never *see* anything useful," Heather said.

She was a precog, but her power was sporadic and not very useful. She'd told us she just caught flashes that were difficult to parse out.

"Neil is going to be home this weekend, if we set something up for then, he and Theresa could come," Sabrina suggested.

"Neil is bringing home a girl?" Heather shouted.

This time when Andrea looked around, she said, "Okay, ladies. That's enough veggies. Heather, go work on the line. Sabrina and Joan, go start on dishes."

Heather gave us a look. "This conversation isn't over." She went to freshen up the food offerings.

Sabrina and I moved to the dish line where early comers had started leaving dishes in the window and got to work, settling into our usual rhythm. We were responsible for collecting the dishes and putting them in the washer, which operated on a conveyer system. We loaded a rack, rinsed the dishes, and sent them through. After a couple racks' worth, we moved to the other side to unload the washing rack onto the wheeled rack where they finished drying and then were conveyed to the line for use. Normally, a two-person team would have one person feeding dishes and the other at the clean end, but we were special. Ha.

After a few minutes of loading, Sabrina said, "Okay, so ask your girl about Saturday."

"She's not my girl. I've barely met her."

She tsked that away. "Fine. Still, ask her."

"Fine, I will, but then we're going to Juice Vitality after school to see if Paul is working and you have to ask him."

"No problem." She tossed her head, pretending a confidence I knew wasn't completely there. "He's into me, I know it." She pushed a rack in, and we moved around to the other end.

"He totally is." I paused. "But we've got to really knuckle down on school today before then, because we've got that daycare shift tomorrow and then synchro. So, no distractions."

"I'll agree to that as soon as you've texted Ellie."

"I can't text her in the middle of the school day! She'd think that was weird."

Heather popped her head in through the window. "I'm off to school, but don't think I've forgotten that you owe me the Neil story."

"It's not that interesting!" I called after her, but I don't know if she heard me.

"You're stalling. You think people don't text each other during the school day? Heather has probably already sent us a harassing text about Neil. Sad that crush could never be acted on."

"Like she'd ever admit it was a crush." Neil was her Family in both the big- and small-F ways. Heather was our second cousin or so. We didn't bother tracking these things exactly because you just didn't date Family, no matter what degree cousin they were. While crushing on your best friend's older brother was perfectly normal behavior usually, that was just not something we did around here.

"And who knows, maybe she really did just think of him as a cool older brother."

"Sure." She rolled her eyes again. "So, again, once you've sent the text, I promise to be good all day."

That was a promise she couldn't keep, but she probably really intended it. I sighed. "Deal."

❖

"Okay!" I shut my laptop and turned away from my desk to face Sabrina. "It's time."

Sabrina shifted a little. "It's early yet," she protested.

"Dude. It's four thirty. If we don't go soon, his shift will be over."

"If he's even working today."

"He's worked every single Tuesday we've gone in. I think we know his schedule by now."

Sabrina had been uncommonly quiet and presumably productive. I'd gotten a lot done between fretting about how the group date would go. I'd sent Ellie a text right after our shift that morning, and she'd said yes to a bowling date on Saturday. Why bowling? I don't know. Somehow it seemed better than a movie, and like it'd be easier for Sabrina and me to stay close over something like going for a walk. I'd explained that it had to be a group date, so we were still nailing down times, and she'd said she could go any time after eleven, when her Starbucks shift ended. That had led to a whole day of sporadic texting.

One text from Ellie read: *My history teacher just said something about the French Revelation when he meant French Revolution. I'm thinking—strip club name? (thinking emoji)*

Joan: *Definitely. (laughing emoji) They can serve eclairs at the buffet.*

Ellie: *Do you have a lot of experience with strip club buffets? (monocle emoji)*

Joan: *Only in movies, but as for eclairs...*

Ellie: *(laughing emoji)*

I was in a good mood. I'd gotten a lot of schoolwork done and was smitten with Ellie. Sabrina, though, still had her big ask in front of her, and sympathetic as I was, we needed to get a move on. "Come on. It'll be better after."

She rolled her eyes. "From your vast experience?"

"I mean, from my experience of today, yeah. I appreciate you pushing me to send the text and now I'm going to push you to ask Paul."

In a rare moment of vulnerability, she said softly, "What if he says no?"

"Then he's missing out. You're awesome. Plus, I'll forever boycott Juice Vitality. Or at least until he doesn't work there anymore."

She laughed a little. "Forever is a long time. Okay, let's do this."

We got up and I followed her out the door. We always moved from our desks this way, because hers was closer to the door. It was just one of the many ways we moved around each other without much thought, but Heather had told us it looked like we shared a mind. Sometimes it felt like we did. We were closer than literally anyone aside from conjoined twins. If we hadn't figured out how to function together, well, I'd be living in isolation, so my incentive was high.

Sabrina fidgeted with her phone just a little as we rode the elevator down. Most people would think she was the picture of calm, but I knew better. I racked my brain to think of something to distract her. Suddenly it came to me. I burst out singing song lyrics about getting the words wrong. I pointed at her.

As predicted, she crossed her arms and glared at me. "Excuse me, but you're the one who gets the words wrong."

"No way," I argued, completely erroneously. It was true, but I knew I could needle her with the line, and sure enough, here she was thinking about something else as the elevator dinged for our arrival on the ground floor. "I always know the lyrics. You're the one who always gets them wrong."

"Ahem," she said, as we crossed the lobby. "Beg to differ. I swear you'd get 'Happy Birthday' wrong if you weren't following my lead."

"Ha. At least I know the words to 'Truth Hurts.'"

"Because we both do."

"I'm pretty sure I nailed them first."

"Sure, sure, if by first you mean well after I did."

Now we were outside and near the end of the block. All we had to do was cross the street and then we would be there.

I started singing the first line to "Truth Hurts" but said *kid* instead of *bitch* at the end while we waited for either the light to change, or enough of a break in the flow of cars to make it across.

"Oh. My. God. Stop singing the Kidz Bop version, or I will end you."

"Pretty sure I'm the killer around here," I joked. "Let's go." There was a break in traffic and pedestrians were on the move.

I opened the door for her once we were across the street. "Madam." I swept my arm indicating she should go in, then followed swiftly after her even though someone else tried to go before me. It was rude, but not as rude as making them bleed all over the place. However, once we were inside, we uncharacteristically paused and let the woman go ahead. We always knew what we wanted to order, because we always got the same things, so we usually just marched right up, but Sabrina had paused briefly, probably gathering herself after seeing Paul at the register. He hadn't noticed us, as he was actually busy doing his job, but he smiled big when he caught sight of us after the woman ahead finished placing her order.

"A Tropical Green Smoothie and a Vitality Green Juice, for the witch," he said, waiting for verification before moving to ring it up, just in case it was a day for branching out.

Sabrina put her hands on her hips. "Ha ha."

It was funny that she was named after *Sabrina the Teenage Witch* and was kind of a magic user, although, of course, Paul didn't know that the latter was the case. Aunt Sarah had thought it would be a funny inside joke and liked the name either way. Uncle Todd, my mom's brother, had protested, but eventually gave in. Sarah said if she was going to join this secret Family and live with the rules imposed by doing so, she should get her way about something as small as a name, especially when it was so apt. Little did they know that there would be a reboot and all of a sudden there would be a lot of little Sabrinas running around, but here we were.

"What are you two up to today?" he asked, as he rang us up. "It's not a synchronized swimming day, is it?"

Like I said, we'd talked a lot.

"No. We're just hanging out. Needed a pick-me-up after a day of hitting the books."

"Ah. Cómo van tus estudios?"

Ever since he found out she liked languages, he used his high school Spanish on her. She gamely said, "Bien," and switched back to English, because she'd found his Spanish was pretty limited. "How was school?"

A customer came up behind us, wanting to order, so he shrugged and said, "School is school, you know? Fine." Then turned to his next customer.

"You're going to miss your chance," I whispered after we stepped aside. "Do you want me to ask?"

She huffed. "No, I've got this."

There were a few people in a row he took orders from, so while the last of the mini rush finished up, our drinks were called by one of his coworkers. We collected them and sort of edged back over to Paul. I hung back as much as I safely could, which we tried to keep to about ten feet for safety, so it wasn't super far.

"So, hey," Sabrina said, "if you're not doing anything Saturday afternoon, a group of us were going to go bowling, if you wanted to come."

I snuck a peek at his face, and he looked super pleased. "Yeah, sure, sounds cool."

"How about you give me your number so I can text you the deets?"

That was smooth of her, I thought. She set her drink down and pulled out her phone, entering the number he recited. "Cool. I'll text."

"Cool," he said.

She scooped up her drink and made her way to the door without looking at me. While I'm sure she knew I'd follow, that was a little unusual. We typically double-checked that the other was paying attention before just making a move to leave like that, but clearly she was a little flustered, so it was good I was paying attention.

Once we were outside and back across the street, she stopped and looked at me with a grin. "Okay, I'll admit you were right about this."

"Oh? Wait, can you tell me in detail about me being right? Let me just hit record on my phone."

"Ha ha. You were right that it would feel better after. Of course, if he'd said no, you'd have been wrong, and you had no way of knowing."

"Other than having eyes and ears? You two have only been flirting with each other for the last six months. I was pretty sure the only reason he's never asked you out is because I'm always there."

She sighed. "Yeah, well, that's not going to change, so he'll just have to man up if he wants to hang with me." She put her arm through mine, so I switched my drink to the other hand. "We're a package deal."

Just because that was true didn't mean I didn't feel guilty about it.

CHAPTER FOUR

N eil!" I jumped up off the living room couch where Sabrina and I had been sitting, waiting for Neil to show. I gave a quick look behind me to make sure she was coming (she was), then ran to give him a hug. "Hi!"

"Hi, favorite sister of mine," he said with a grin. Then turned behind him. "This is Theresa. Theresa, this one is Joan. And that one,"—he pointed to Sabrina—"is Sabrina." To Sabrina, he said, "And how is my favorite sister doing?"

She slugged him in the arm and said, "Great. How's my favorite brother?"

It was an old joke from when we were kids and I was in a fight with Sabrina and Neil. He once said, "Well, she's my favorite sister!" and I'd replied, "She's not even your sister!" and Sabrina had said, "Am, too! In all the ways that matter. What? You don't think you're my sister? I hate you!" I'd felt horrible and wanted to run away, but I couldn't. So, I just stood there crying. Neil stomped his foot and ran out. I knew Sabrina wanted to go with him, but she couldn't, so she stood there glaring at me until I finally said, "I'm sorry! Of course you're my sister!" She'd said, "Damn right! I'm everyone's favorite sister." Which, of course, she was my favorite, because I didn't have another sister, but then I started crying again because she was right. She was also Neil's favorite sister. She was fun and cool, and I was way too serious. I'd curled up in a ball on the top bunk. She'd stood there, probably wanting to leave again, but there we were. After a while, Neil came back and I heard them whispering. I was up there thinking about how they were whispering about how much they hated me and wanted me to go live in isolation, but then they both climbed up on the top bunk with me and made a cuddle sandwich. "We've decided that we're all everyone's favorite," Sabrina said. "Yeah," Neil agreed. "We're all favorites." The relief I felt was epic. "All favorites," I whispered. I don't remember why we were fighting in the first place, but each detail of the fight itself is imprinted in my brain. Anyway.

"Hi, Theresa. It's nice to meet you," I said.

Sabrina opened her arms and said, "Bring it in! We've heard so much about you!"

Theresa gave her a hug, saying, "Good things, I hope."

"Of course," we both hastened to say.

"Mostly," Neil teased her.

"All good," I assured her. "Come on in."

They were each carrying a backpack, and Sabrina and I took them and put them in Neil's room while they greeted the parental folks. We'd been holding dinner for them, so we sat down to eat almost right away.

We had heard a lot about Theresa, so we knew she was an engineering major, like Neil. They'd met in one of their intro to engineering classes. While he was mechanical, though, she was going biomedical, which sounded cooler to me. They played D&D with friends every Saturday. She was the one who got him into that. We'd played games growing up, but not role-play ones. She was from Wisconsin. They'd started dating in the fall but had gone home to their respective families for Christmas. Over spring break just a couple weeks ago they'd gone camping with friends. They'd applied for internships for the summer in the same places and were both hoping to land ones with Google. Mom and Dad had met her when they went up for parents' weekend in the fall, but it had been a new relationship then. Now, though, here she was, which meant Neil was super serious. Like, get down on one knee serious. I wanted to make her feel welcome, but I also felt weird and tongue-tied.

"No problems with the bus?" Dad asked.

"Nope. It was a smooth trip," Neil said. "We finished season two of *Schitt's Creek* and you guys were right. We're invested now."

"Right? At first, you're like, *No, these people suck*, but then you're sucked in," I said.

"No way. They were adorable from the very beginning," Sabrina said staunchly.

"Seriously? I mean, they were pretty awful," Theresa said, bravely, I thought, as she was new here.

"Well, now you're my favorite," I told her.

"I was replaced super quickly," Sabrina said, mock pouting.

Mom and Dad just looked at all of us fondly. They hadn't watched the show, even though it had been out forever.

"Next season is the best because Patrick," I said.

"Don't tell us! No spoilers!" Neil protested.

"Fine, fine. Just get watching," Sabrina said.

"Some of us have lives, you know," Neil said. "We don't all get to just sit in our bedrooms all day."

"Okay, listen. First of all, we do not just sit in our bedrooms all day," Sabrina said. "We work, we have synchronized swimming—"

"Sometimes we go get juice," I put in, "which sometimes results in dates—"

"Or visit the High Line, which also results in dates." Sabrina crossed her arms.

"Wait. You guys have dates?" Mom looked at us intently.

"Um…yes? Had we not mentioned this?" I bit my lower lip a little.

"No. We definitely would have remembered that information," Dad said. "When is this date? What are you doing?"

Theresa looked a little alarmed at the questioning. I could see her point. We were seventeen-year-olds and seemingly plenty old enough to be dating.

Mom gave Dad a significant look, with a slight head nod at Theresa, and he stopped the interrogation. In a jaunty tone, he said, "Have fun, of course. Just keep us in the loop." He took a bite of taco salad.

"Actually, it's a group date and we were thinking you two might want to come." I looked at Neil and Theresa. "We're just going bowling tomorrow afternoon. It'll be us, Ellie, Paul, Heather and Maria, and you guys, hopefully."

"Heather is dating someone named Maria? I thought she was into guys," Neil said.

"She's pan," Sabrina said. "And I think Maria is just a friend, maybe?"

"So, not really a date. More of a group hangout." Neil looked a little self-satisfied. He was generally a good person, but sometimes enjoyed being right a little too much.

Theresa gave him a look. "We'd love to join in, right Neil?"

"Oh, yeah, sounds fun."

The fact was that we needed as many people as possible who knew the deal so they could help ensure Sabrina and I stayed close. Neil knew that, but I still wanted to get him by himself at some point to tell him that was part of his job. Although Mom and Dad would probably also tell him. I sighed a little. Now we were going to have to have a talk with them about the plan. It wasn't that we'd been hiding it per se, just that they were going to have feelings about it.

The conversation turned to school, talking about classes people were taking and a little bit about building gossip. From what Neil said, he must have told Theresa at least a little about the Complex. He was pretty open about us all being related around here. He'd probably told her he'd grown up in a commune of sorts. It was what most Family members told their potential life partners.

After dinner, Sabrina and I cleared the table and cleaned up, while Neil and Theresa did the whole conversation-with-the-parents thing, but then we came back and rescued them.

"We're thinking a game," I announced as we walked back into the dining room.

Theresa looked at me and smiled, then looked at Neil, who was looking back at her. She answered for them both. "Sounds good. What games have you guys got?"

We all played Apples to Apples, but when Neil suggested Cards Against Humanity next, my parents excused themselves. I was starting to see what Neil saw in Theresa. She was outgoing, but not overwhelming. She had a keen sense of humor and she fit in smoothly. Actually, aside from being techy, not language-y or artsy, she reminded me a lot of Sabrina.

After the game, we watched a few episodes of *Schitt's Creek* with them, but by the end of the third one, Theresa was yawning hard.

"I think we have to call it, guys," Neil said, arm around Theresa. "This one has an eight a.m. lab on Fridays and never lasts late Friday night."

Sabrina looked aghast. "Why? Why would you do that to yourself?"

"It was the only time I could fit the biology lab in and still get all the other classes I wanted. Believe me, it wasn't by choice." Theresa snuggled in closer to Neil. "He's right, though. If we try to watch another, I'll just have to watch it again later because I'll be asleep in about five minutes."

She yawned her way through the five-minutes part, causing me to yawn. I covered my yawn with one hand and put the other up like a stop sign. "You have my permission to go to bed. Otherwise, I'll be over here matching you yawn for yawn."

She chuckled and stood up. Neil stood up after her, sticking as close to her as I did to Sabrina.

We hugged them both good night and I tried to catch Neil's eye, to let him know I wanted to talk, but he trotted off after Theresa.

"She's great," Sabrina said, looking after them.

"Yup," I agreed. "I like her a lot."

"Do you feel better about him bringing her home?"

I shushed her. "Let's go to your place and talk there."

We stopped off in my bedroom and picked up our bags with our laptops and books we were currently reading and stuff that generally shuttled back and forth with us. When we came back out, Neil was in the hall.

"Did we need to talk?" he asked. "I understand the assignment for tomorrow."

"Good," I said. "I did just want to touch base about that." I looked around, trying to figure out if Theresa was in the bathroom or in his room.

"She is in bed, probably asleep or close." He answered my unspoken question.

"Come in for a minute," Sabrina said, backing back into my room. We sat on the couch and he sat on the lower bunk.

"So…dates," he teased. Then sobered. "But really. How is that going to work? Have you told them or do they think you're weird?"

Sabrina and I looked at each other. "Paul definitely thinks I'm weird," Sabrina answered. "We go in there all the time, always together. He's commented on it, but he also said yes to hanging out tomorrow."

"And Ellie has no idea what she's getting into. We seriously just saw each other on the High Line the other day and were vibing. We've only texted since."

"Okay, so what's the game plan?" He leaned forward, ready for scheming.

Sabrina looked back and forth between us, but I leaned forward to answer. "I'm thinking we get two lanes side by side. Sabrina and I are in the same spot in the lineup. You go with her while Heather goes with me. The two of you help to speed things up or slow things down as necessary so that Sabrina and I always go up to bowl at the same time. We don't have to be exactly in tandem, but if we're in the seats at the same time and up in the bowling area at the same time, it should work."

He leaned back. "Okay, okay, that should work."

Sabrina agreed.

"What have you told Theresa?" I asked.

He shrugged. "The building is a loosely tied family commune situation. About you two? Just that you're super close. I would have told her more, maybe, but we have to go meet Linda on Sunday." He pulled a face.

"Yeah." I paused. "So, like, this is the girl you're going to marry? I mean," I held my hands out to him, "don't get me wrong. She seems awesome, just…it's a lot. Are you sure?"

"I mean, sure enough I want to be more honest with her about what our future would look like if she stays with me. It's not that I'm ready to get married tomorrow, but we're really serious and it seems not fair to have her hang around if she isn't into the idea of living here." He gestured around the building. "I couldn't risk having kids elsewhere what with…"

He trailed off. It was ingrained in us that Family kids had to be raised here, but if you were from a line of precogs, maybe you'd be willing to take a risk. We probably had some Family members out there who'd been raised away from this. Sometimes some precogs got flashes that would indicate that was so. However, if you had someone like me in your near line, you would not be cavalier about a child of yours coming into their powers away from this structure.

"And you think she'll buy in?" Sabrina asked.

"Maybe. I've told her some about growing up here and the community we all have." He shrugged. "She seemed…not appalled."

"That's a start." I leaned forward and patted his knee. We all knew this could be complicated. There were stories of potential partners freaking out and being *helped* to forget what they knew before being sent on their way. Or sometimes this first weekend was enough. I'd heard that some people just felt weird in the building, even though I didn't know how it was much different than any other, except that we all knew each other to some extent and there was a community meal option.

Of course, my chances of getting even that far with anyone were slim at best. It would be hard to progress in a relationship when your cousin was never more than fifteen feet away. I really liked Ellie, though. I was aware that I hardly knew her, but all my previous crushes had been celebrity crushes or someone inappropriate like a teacher. I just…really wanted to try.

"And so is going on a date," he said.

"We're all making huge steps!" Sabrina half shouted.

"Hey! Don't wake people up, favorite sister." He got up. "I'm going to go check on her. Sleep well, favorite sisters."

"Are you two both sleeping in your twin bed?" I asked. "That doesn't seem conducive to a good night's sleep. You guys could sleep in here."

"We sleep in one twin at school. I spend most nights in her dorm because her roomie changed dorms at the semester and no one moved in."

"Why'd her roomie move out?" Sabrina asked.

"Probably because I spent most nights there." Neil winked.

We laughed.

"Rude," Sabrina said.

"We're going downstairs," I said. "See you in the morning."

"But not too early," Sabrina added. "You two keep that deviant waking up early stuff to yourselves."

"Riiight, and when was your last breakfast shift?"

"Day before yesterday." Sabrina waved that away. "Distant past. I don't make a habit of it."

"Sure, and what about the early morning shift we did in the daycare yesterday?" I teased.

"You guys need to stop arguing semantics. I'm sleeping in tomorrow and that is that."

Neil and I held our hands up and pretended to back away. Of course, I didn't back very much.

"You two!" She huffed and stomped her foot.

Neil laughed. "I'm so glad to see you two." He pulled both of us in for a hug. "I'll see you whenever Sabrina is ready to grace us with her presence."

CHAPTER FIVE

I stood next to Sabrina and shifted from foot to foot.

She elbowed me. "Stop. You're making me nervous and I've been chill."

I crossed my arms. "Really? And who needed calming down in order to even ask?"

"Shh! There's Paul." She turned away from him, presumably so she didn't look like a creeper watching him come. Her glowing white hair worked like a beacon, though, and he made his way unerringly toward us. It was left to me to wave at him when he got close. Only then did Sabrina turn around and greet him, cool as a cucumber, at least outwardly.

"Hi," she said. "You made it."

"I made it." He turned and did a group greet. "Hi, all. I'm Paul." He waved both tattooed arms at everyone.

"Paul, this is our brother, Neil, and his girlfriend, Theresa. Coming down the street there are Heather and Maria." She pointed behind him where, sure enough, they were walking toward us. Heather had opted to meet us at the bowling alley, because she and Maria had decided to meet at the subway station. "We're just waiting on Ellie and then we'll go in."

The reminder that Ellie hadn't arrived yet made me shift again. Was she going to stand me up? But then in a flurry of arrivals, she came up behind me while I was watching Heather and Maria join the group. We went through all the introductions, which was awkward in its own way, but sort of smoothed over the awkwardness of seeing

Ellie in person again. We'd been texting all week, but it was weird to see her.

She was wearing another dress in a similar style, fitted on top, showing her curves, then flared below the waist. This one was pink and grey. I supposed that was her style, and I did not object at all. I just hoped she didn't mind my lack of style. I'd dressed medium up, which meant brown jeans and a button-up short-sleeved shirt.

We moved in a group into the building, Heather and Neil being slightly awkward in their attempts to keep Sabrina and me close, which helped us not seem as awkward out there by ourselves being weird. There was a short line at the counter. We joined the line and waited.

"I like your dress," I said to Ellie.

"Thanks," she said. "I like your pants." Then she blushed. Her skin was fair, so it really showed. It was super cute.

"So, we're teaming up, right?" Sabrina said. "I get Paul on my team, of course." She looked at him and he signaled his agreement. "And I call...Neil."

That was low. Neil was the best of us Family kids, but Heather wasn't bad, and both Maria and Theresa were unknowns. Maybe Theresa couldn't bowl at all and Maria was decent? If so, it would be okay. Wait. Ellie and Paul were unknowns, too. Maybe Ellie was a ringer. I turned to her. "Can you bowl? Like, I mean, are you any good? Sorry. I mean..."

She laughed. "I'm not good. I think I've bowled three times ever."

I took that in and turned to Heather to raise an eyebrow. She grinned at me. That could mean any number of things, but I choose to believe that it meant that she had had this discussion with Maria, and Maria could indeed bowl. "Are we wagering anything?"

The non-Family members were looking like they were concerned for their safety, but Neil, Heather, and Sabrina looked thoughtful. "The choice of after," Sabrina said after a moment.

It was our turn at the counter. We asked for side-by-side lanes and sorted out shoe sizes and such. During the hubbub, Ellie whispered to me, "Should I be worried? I had no idea you guys were…serious about bowling."

"Don't worry. We're more serious about betting than bowling. And Neil is too good compared to the rest of us. I'm just trying to get us a good deal here," I said softly to her. "You're in good hands."

"I hope so."

We gathered shoes and went to our lanes to put them on. A couple of people had to go exchange for a different size, but not Sabrina and me. When Paul was one of the ones who had to go exchange, we took the opportunity to go looking for balls. I invited Ellie to look with us. She looked a little askance at my shadow, but didn't say anything about it.

"I'm not even sure what weight ball or anything," Ellie admitted as we perused.

"Maybe eight pounds to start?" I suggested. "You can always switch it out if it doesn't work."

"What do you bowl with?"

"Ten."

Sabrina was doing me the favor of just tagging along quietly, not drawing attention to herself by speaking.

I stuck my fingers in the finger holes of a ten pounder that looked like it might be close to right. They slipped around, so I left it. "The most important thing is a good finger fit, though. You want to be able to slip your fingers in and grip, but not so tight that you can't slip them back out with relative ease." As soon as I said it, I heard what I'd said. I turned away in embarrassment and tried a different ball.

"Um…" Ellie said, clearly suppressing a laugh. "I think I found one."

I turned back. "Great!" I exclaimed with a bravado I wasn't feeling. "I…" I was about to say that I hadn't found the one, but then my brain suggested that she was saying something that wasn't entirely about bowling balls. That couldn't be, though. We'd known each other five days and had spent less than twenty minutes in each other's physical space. She was holding a ball. "I need to look a little more. Do you want to take yours back to the lane and I'll be there in a minute? It's probably heavy to carry around."

She turned to walk back. I looked at Sabrina. "So, um, turns out I suck at this."

"I don't think you're as bad as you think you are. Come on. Let's find a ball and get back before people think we're weird."

"Barn door. Horses. You know the saying." But I turned back to the job at hand.

Once everyone was back with balls and fitting shoes, I returned to the subject of the wager. "Winning team decides what we do after?"

"Good wager," Sabrina said.

"Okay, then. Since you guys have Neil, we get a twenty-point handicap."

"Ha!" Neil said. "That's ridiculous."

"It's not and you know it," Heather put in.

"Ten points tops." Sabrina crossed her arms.

I put my hands on my hips. "Per game."

She squinted her eyes at me. "What if you end up with a ringer?"

"That's a chance you'll have to take," I said. Heather nodded at my side.

Sabrina looked at Neil, who half shrugged. She turned back to me. "Seven points per game. Final offer."

"Eight," I said.

"You know that's reasonable," Heather said.

"Fine." We shook solemnly. "Let's bowl."

"We have to put names in and stuff, but I take your point," Heather added the last bit quickly, sliding into the seat to add names to the computer. "Okay, normally I'd say we should do silly names, but a lot of us don't know each other, so maybe real names today?"

Our team went with real names. But Sabrina, who'd commandeered their team's console, did not share Heather's outlook, so we ended up playing Joan, Ellie, Heather, and Maria versus Bess (for Elizabeth from *Madam Secretary*, which was a post Sabrina aspired to hold), Banksy (apparently Paul was a graffiti artist), King ("As long as we're being aspirational," Neil said), and

Serena (Theresa had been a pretty serious tennis player when she was younger, but gave it up after a series of injuries in high school).

There were some awkward moments where Sabrina and I were trying to keep in sync, but Neil and Heather did their parts, so it wasn't as bad as it might have been otherwise. Theresa turned out to be decent, despite not much experience. Apparently all that work on her hand-eye coordination was a boon. Ellie was as much of a novice as she'd said but was very game about it all. Paul was a little better and equally game. Maria, though, Maria was a marvel. After her second strike on the second frame, Heather said smugly, "She's in a league."

"Oh, ho!" I said. "The game is afoot!"

"We're not solving a mystery, Sherlock," Sabrina said.

"No, but what we are going to do after is going to be up to us," I said.

She huffed at me, but her disappointment was short lived. Not that they won, no. With the handicap and after two games, Team Real Names squeaked out a six-point victory. But Sabrina was not one to linger in negative emotions and managed to enjoy herself.

After we were done high-fiving and celebrating, she said, "Whatever we're doing next, I've got to go to the bathroom first. Anyone else?"

"Yeah, I could go," I said, nonchalantly.

No one else joined us. I guess it wasn't true that girls always peed in a pack. I had to admit to being relieved not to be peeing next to Ellie. We dropped our shoes off on the way. When we rejoined the group, everyone had returned shoes, but Paul was missing.

"Bathroom," Neil explained shortly.

Theresa ended up deciding she should go, too, so it was a few minutes before the gang was all reunited, but since none of them were on the winning team, Team Real Names took the time to decide what to do next. We settled on picking up pizzas and taking them to Washington Square Park. It was a lovely spring day out.

We split into couples while walking, which was a little tricky because usually Sabrina and I walked side by side, but she settled right in front of me, so I could keep a close eye.

"You and your cousin are really close. Or is she your sister? I thought you said cousin on the High Line, but Neil said something about her being your sister and he's your brother, right?" Ellie asked as we strolled.

"Right. Sorry, we've made this whole thing seriously confusing. She's my cousin, but we basically live together, so we all just decided we were siblings at some point."

"Why do you basically live together? I mean, not to pry, but is there an issue with parents?"

I shook my head. "No, nothing like that. We just live in the same building and do school online together and everything, really, but both our parents are great." And they were. Mom had called a meeting that morning that involved all four of them and the two of us. We talked about the dates and how they wanted us to have as normal a life as possible, but we really needed to be extra vigilant. They'd given their blessing for the date when we explained the plan. "How about yours? Do you get along with your parents?"

We approached a street where at least the four in the lead could have made the light, but they stopped to wait, earning glares from other New Yorkers out enjoying the lovely weather, but not so much that they weren't wanting to keep up that New Yorker pace. We ignored them like the teenagers we were.

"It's just my mom and me. She's great, but we're more like roommates. She had me pretty young and my dad was never in the picture, so we've kind of grown up together. That whole *Gilmore Girls* thing. It's been good, though. I mean, we like it this way."

"That's pretty cool. I get along with my parents and all, but they're definitely parents, not roommates."

The light changed and we started walking again.

"Are you a junior or a senior?" Ellie asked.

"Um, I'm a junior, but in college." It seemed even worse to admit that I was close to done with all the courses needed for my bachelor's degree.

"What? I thought you were seventeen!"

"I am. I graduated early and I'm doing online college courses."

"Why online? Why not in person?"

"My parents aren't really ready for me to leave home yet." That wasn't a lie. "Maybe next year." That was a lie. Sabrina and I would never be in the same classes again or go away to college. If I didn't do school online, there would be no school. And if I did all Sabrina's classes with her, they'd be either repeats or something I was completely uninterested in. Not to mention that she'd have to take language classes far below her abilities for me to have a chance. It never failed to depress me to think about it. "If I hadn't skipped ahead and stuff, I'd be a high school junior, though. You're a junior, right?"

"Yup. Senior year is right around the corner."

"And I know I hate this question, so I probably shouldn't ask it, but do you know what you want to do after high school?"

We arrived at the pizza place and ended up deciding to send two people in to do the ordering. After a discussion of who liked what, the two ended up being Neil and Theresa because Neil was the pickiest and Theresa was vegetarian and wanted to see if there were any options in the veggie arena. The rest of us Venmoed them our shares of the cost and walked the two blocks to the park where they'd meet us.

There was a table available when we got there, but it only had three chairs. We maybe could have rounded up some more, as they didn't appear to all be in use, but that seemed like too much trouble, so we just settled down in a loose circle in the grass.

"So, Maria, you're a big bowler, then," Paul said.

Heather linked arms with her. "She is. I did good, right?"

I could practically feel Sabrina wondering if this was a date, just like I was. We'd have to discuss that later.

"Where do you go to school?" Paul asked her.

With that question, we turned to talk of schools, which meant we got to have the fun conversation about Sabrina and me homeschooling yet again. Ellie gave me an odd look when Sabrina explained she was doing high school while I admitted to college work. "I thought you said you two did school together," she said.

"We do, as in we're in the same room, but, yeah, we aren't doing the same classes."

I could tell she wanted to ask about that setup, but Heather cut in to ask Paul about school, saving us for the moment, at least. Paul was a senior and not planning on college. He wanted to take a year to see if he could make a living off of art. His parents had agreed they'd support him by letting him live at home for the year, but he'd have to make enough for whatever he wanted to spend on aside from room and board, so he might still be working at Juice Vitality to earn enough for art supplies. Or who knew, maybe he'd sell art to buy supplies.

Sabrina was looking at him admiringly, and I thought that situation could work for us. She could concentrate on art while I did school and then…what? I'd never be able to work in medicine. I couldn't even go to medical school. What was I supposed to do? Say "This is my emotional support cousin. She has to come to the hospital with me?" No. Besides, Sabrina was more serious about languages. She needed school for that. I was the one holding her back. I should really set my stuff aside and start learning languages so I could enroll in the same classes. She'd help me.

Ellie pulled my thoughts back to the here and now when she responded to a question Heather asked by telling her about an after-school program she volunteered for, teaching kids how to program.

"That is so awesome," I said. "What ages?"

"Mostly third and fourth graders."

"They can program?" Sabrina asked.

"It's simple stuff at that age, but yeah. The center has these robots, and the kids can program them to do a series of things. Like, walk forward two feet. Raise an arm. Turn around. Whatever. We set up obstacle courses as they get better, and they program the robots to do the course."

"That sounds fun," I said.

She turned to me. "You should come to the center sometime. They can always use volunteers, and I could show you the robots."

That couldn't happen unless Sabrina came, too.

"Maybe we could do it together, if you didn't mind me tagging along," Sabrina cut in. "Joan and I work a bit in a daycare center and we just love kids. Plus, those robots sound like the bomb."

Ellie smiled a little wanly. "Sure. The more the merrier." She didn't sound like she meant it, though.

"So, is that what you want to do for a career? Computers, I mean?" I asked. "Or teaching? Teaching computers?"

She laughed a little. "I hope I'll always volunteer with kids, but it's the computers I want to do for a career someday. I plan on studying computer science in college."

"Cool," Neil said from behind me. I turned around to see him standing there with a couple pizza boxes, Theresa by his side. I scooted even closer to Sabrina, and Ellie scooted with me. They sat down and put the pizzas in the middle. "Theresa and I both applied for internships with Google this summer. Do you want to work for Google?"

Ellie shook her head. "No, I'm looking for more work/life balance than that. Although an internship with them would be good for ye ol' resume for sure. I wouldn't want to work for them full-time, though. There's this tech company that is doing revolutionary things with four-day work weeks and sticking to eight-hour days. That's the sort of thing I want to be a part of."

"That sounds so great. What kind of things do you envision doing with your free time?" I asked.

"Stuff like the work I do at the center for some, but I also like to travel. I want to take weekend trips and explore. I also want kids someday, and they take time."

Sabrina and I had done some traveling. We did road trips with our parents—things we could have all sorts of control over—but picking up and traveling was not easy for us. It wasn't that I didn't want to go explore a new place over a weekend, but it was complicated. How could this ever work?

"I love to travel," Paul put in. "Even just a day trip. Or even just going to the end of the line on the subway and seeing what's there. We should do that sometime." He touched Sabrina's arm.

She made a noncommittal noise.

"Let's check out this pizza!" Neil interjected.

Our attention turned to the pizza, and conversation thankfully shifted. When a friendly but animated discussion about using football versus soccer nomenclature broke out—don't ask, I couldn't tell you how we got there—Ellie touched my knee and said, "Do you not like to travel or something? You looked strange when I was talking about it earlier."

"Or something," I said. "I like to travel, it's just that I haven't very much."

"That's something you could change."

It was, kind of. Sometimes because things were hard, Sabrina and I just didn't do them, but we could. There was no real reason we couldn't take the bus up to visit Neil over a weekend, for example. "I'd like that. Do you and your mom travel a lot?"

"No." She shook her head. "It's just that I want to. It's a goal. We do little trips, kind of like what Paul was saying—ride the subway to a new place and just walk around. We've never had a lot of money, so sometimes we've had to be creative."

"I know this is weird and kind of old fashioned in this day and age, but Sabrina and I, well, our parents don't want us to date unless we're in a group. What I'm saying is that I'd like to come to the center sometime, but she has to come with me. I know it's weird. And I can tell she wants to do a trip like that with Paul, but I'd have to go with her. Sorry. It's so weird."

"It is kind of odd, but if we have to do group dates to see each other, then that's what we'll do. But…if your parents are old fashioned like that, how do they feel about you dating girls?"

"Oh, fine," I blurted out without thinking it through. It might have been easier to say that they were old fashioned in other ways, too, but no. I was going to be as honest as I could be given the situation. "It's really just this group date thing. I've been out to them since I mentioned having a crush on Taylor Swift when I was twelve. They've always been cool about that."

"That's good. Taylor Swift, huh?" She smiled wryly.

I shrugged. "The heart wants what the heart wants, and my little twelve-year-old heart was a Swifty. Who was your first celebrity crush?"

"Mine was maybe more a character than a celebrity. I was

super into Lara Croft for a while after my mom introduced me to the Angelina Jolie movies when I was about that same age."

"I haven't seen those movies, although I've heard of Lara Croft. Sounds like I should really check them out."

"Yes, yes you should. There's this scene where Lara is floating around with these bungie cord things in white pajamas that's just—" She kissed her fingertips. "Perfection."

I'd watched that kiss closely, and speaking of perfection, it took me a moment to actually process what she'd said. When I did, I said, "Maybe we should do a movie night."

"That'd be awesome."

"If you were choosing movies for a movie night, what would you pick?" Ellie asked.

That led to a group discussion about movies.

It was after six when Maria checked the time on her phone and said, "This has been a lot of fun, but I've got to get home." That signaled the end. We gathered up pizza boxes and crammed them into a trash can. I really didn't want my time with Ellie to come to an end and I would have walked her to her metro stop rather than going to the more convenient one to get back to the Complex, but it wasn't up to me, or at least not exclusively. All the Family kids plus Theresa were going to the same stop as Paul (lucky Sabrina, that date also seemed to be going well, judging by all the little touches). Maria and Ellie were going elsewhere.

"I had a good time," Ellie said when it became clear we were going different ways.

"Me, too. Thanks for coming."

"Thanks for asking."

The others were standing behind me, waiting. If only I could have told them to go on and I'd catch up. "I guess I have to get going."

She glanced behind me, then back. "Seems so."

I didn't know if I should go for a kiss or offer a fist bump or open my arms for a hug. Ellie settled it by squeezing my arm and turning to go. "Text me," she said over her shoulder.

I nodded dumbly.

"Come on, champ," Neil slung his arm around my shoulder. "You'll get the kiss next time."

I slugged him in the side, but not with any power behind it. Paul was still with us for crying out loud. Speaking of, he was turning to start walking, clearly expecting Sabrina to go with him, so I freed myself to fall into line right behind Sabrina again. Neil and Theresa started walking behind me. Heather darted around them to join me.

"How was your…date?" I asked her. "Was it a date?"

"I'm not sure," she admitted. "I was thinking friends, but then it kind of had a date vibe, but maybe it was just because we were with all you people."

"Do you want it to have been a date?"

"I think maybe I do. How was your date? It seemed to be going well."

"I really like her."

"That was pretty clear."

I lifted my hand to my face to half hide it. "Was it that obvious?"

She put her hand on my arm. "No. Just, you seemed to be vibing. She was there with you as far as I could tell."

"That's good. But back to you and Maria. I haven't heard you talk about her much before."

"No. The friendship is kind of new. She's in my French class and we got randomly paired up for an in-class assignment a couple weeks ago. We had to talk about hobbies and she mentioned bowling. We've been talking some since, and when the bowling thing came up, I thought she seemed like a good plus one." Heather looked pleased with herself.

"Indeed," I said.

At the metro station, we all stood awkwardly nearby while Sabrina said goodbye to Paul. He was brave anyway, though, and went for the kiss. It was a brief touch of the lips that probably didn't mean much to him, but was Sabrina's first kiss. I couldn't wait to talk to her about it later. I was also a little jealous.

Even on the train home, we couldn't talk about some of the things I wanted to talk about, like were the gyrations we'd gone through to keep Sabrina and me close super weird and obvious, or had we pulled it off? I suspected a mix. We were able to talk about some stuff, though.

"So, sealed with a kiss, huh?" Heather said, leaning to look around me at Sabrina. We were sitting in a row on a sideways seat.

Sabrina tossed her head. "You know it."

"And?" she asked.

"It was nice."

"Just nice?" Theresa asked from across the way.

"What's wrong with nice?" Neil asked.

We all stared at him.

"What?" he asked.

Theresa patted his arm. "Nice is like hugging a family member."

"Oh." Neil looked like he was rethinking some past events, but maybe I was reading into his slightly pensive expression.

"Better than nice," Sabrina said, drawing our combined attention back to her.

"Okay, now we're talking," Heather said.

"It's just…" Sabrina glanced at Theresa, then said, "I think a more private kiss would have been nicer."

I pointedly did not glance at Theresa and said, "Sure."

Theresa said, "That'll come."

Nobody said anything to that. The rest of us knew it wouldn't come.

"Next stop is ours," Neil said to Theresa.

We got up and moved to the doors.

"Sorry," I whispered to Sabrina.

"Don't be. I chose this."

"Yeah, when you were eight and couldn't foresee how this sort of thing would play out."

"We'll talk about it later," Sabrina said with a nod to Theresa standing in front of her.

I agreed.

CHAPTER SIX

Breathe in for one, two, three, four, five, breathe out for one, two, three, four, five, six," Gamma told us. Well, not just Sabrina and me, but the whole group. Our grandmother, Gamma to us, was our Sunday school teacher that week. She was a frequent teacher, but it did vary. Because she could control mood, she'd gone way down the path of meditation and yoga and stuff. She said it was really important to control her own mood so that she didn't put everyone in a bad mood. As with anyone who was perceived to be able to mess with your head, she wasn't the most popular person around. Even Mom and Todd were a little wary of her. But since Sabrina's power had come into effect, we'd never been manipulated by her, so she was just Gamma to us. In turn, I think we were some of her favorite people in the Family.

I followed her instructions, working to calm myself. We were taught these things from a young age because they had an impact on our powers. I hoped that putting in this work would make it so I could control when I made people bleed, but it was hard to practice when making a mistake meant injury or death. Still, I always practiced and really worked at it, hoping.

Sabrina was less disciplined because she said she was just a dampener. What more did she need to try to control? If she was around, other people couldn't do their thing. If she wasn't, life as usual. Sabrina's power would be considered a hindrance in some respects if it weren't for me. She told me more than once that she was happy to be my twin because it made her feel like she had a useful power. I'd told her that she would be very useful to anyone who had a problematic power. It seemed the Counsel agreed with me more than her because they'd asked her about the possibility of donating some eggs for the Family fertility clinic already.

Really, though, for most of the Family, we were a menace. We couldn't be around if my mom was doing her art because then she couldn't sculpt the metal with her powers. We made it so her dad, Todd, or any precog we were around couldn't see. Sometimes I thought that Heather was one of the few people who spent extended time with us because her powers were so weak that it didn't matter if Sabrina dampened them. And if we messed up, I'd probably kill people. So, that was fun to have hanging over our heads all the time. We were lucky, really, that the Family put up with us. Me, in particular.

Anyway, back to breathing.

Gamma guided us through a loving kindness meditation after the breathing. When we were done, she opened it up for discussion.

"How does everyone feel?"

Answers varied from chill to bored. This class was all the teens and some of us were, as teens are, snarky.

"All valid," Gamma said. "Does anyone have any particular feelings about the others in this room? I mean," she hastened to add, "have any of your feelings changed as a result of the meditation?"

"I feel a little less like punching Travis," Sabrina said.

"Ha ha," Travis said, as if she were joking.

Jess, a newly minted thirteen-year-old, said, "I feel a bit more comfortable."

It's not that we didn't know her or she us. Of course we did. We all knew all the kids in the Complex, but stepping up to the teen group was new for her, and I could see how she would be shy about it. The fact that she was willing to share was a stronger indication of her level of comfort than the statement itself.

"And how about for everyone in the Complex?"

Shrugs and nods.

"And beyond?"

"Why do we do this anyway?" Travis called out.

"Good question, Travis. Can anyone answer that?" Gamma looked around at the seventeen assembled teens. Because I knew her so well, probably better than anyone aside from Sabrina, I knew she wasn't as sanguine about him asking as she presented. He annoyed her as much as he annoyed Sabrina and me, but she was all either peace-and-light or stern taskmaster. She was in peace-and-light mode, but I could hear an ever so slight edge.

"So we don't unleash holy hell on the normies," Sabrina said. "Not that that's a skill of mine, but you know. So those who could be don't become supervillains or something."

"What? With our killer precognitive abilities?" Travis scoffed.

Idiot. With me. With people like my mom who could use her powers of metal manipulation to hurt people. With, yes, precogs, who could use their abilities not just to help us live comfortable lives but to accrue more wealth than we could ever use without helping anyone else so we could be billionaire assholes. Of course we needed to learn compassion for others, and that meant all people, from an early age. It was my personal opinion that that was part of the stigma against marrying within the Family. In addition to possibly becoming inbred, we would be that much more distant from the regular people. Even the term *normies* was considered slightly pejorative.

"Come on, Sabrina. Normie?" Heather said. "Do you want people calling your mom normie?"

Sabrina rolled her eyes. "Fine, although I don't think she'd care, but fine. To rephrase, so we won't unleash holy hell on people outside the Family."

"We do want to make sure we're using language that keeps us sympathetic, yes, but back to the why question. Sabrina is at least somewhat correct, right? We don't want to start thinking of ourselves as substantially different from non-Family members. Aside from unleashing *holy hell*, as Sabrina so eloquently put it, the first step in that is just believing ourselves to be different, right? But are we?"

"Duh," Travis said.

"Not that much," I argued. "I mean, the sorts of athletic feats someone like Simone Biles can do are probably further from the average person than the things you, for example, Travis, can do."

Travis, for all his hubris, was a precog who every so often and under no control whatsoever could get a few-second glimpse into next week, much like Heather. Precognition was by far the most common ability. In fact, in our class of seventeen, that was the power twelve people had. One person had some control over wind, about enough to fly a kite on an otherwise calm day. Two, sisters, could do some interesting things with water, like change its phase or manipulate the manner of flow. They were something like third cousins of mine. Our line tended to produce people who could manipulate specific materials. Then there were Sabrina and me.

"At least I'm safe in society," Travis said.

"If you think being an asshole is being safe," Sabrina shot back.

"Sabrina!" Gamma said. "Enough. Travis, you, too. These are exactly the sorts of things we should be meditating about. I want everyone to practice the Loving Kindness meditation every day this week. Sabrina and Travis, I specifically want you to think of each other when you get to the *someone who is problematic* phase. You'll each go visit Linda on Saturday."

Travis scoffed, but when Gamma pinned him with a look, he settled. The fact was, he had a point. Seeing Linda was really only significant for him. Sabrina would go see Linda, me in tow, but Linda couldn't read her mind, so it was just for show.

"Okay, we're going to wrap up for today. I'm posting new buddies. Come check and then go find your buddy or buddies."

Each teen was paired up with a younger kid, and we had to spend at least a half an hour with them as part of Sunday school in order to foster community. With Jess's recent promotion, there were twenty-nine kids twelve and under. It seemed we went in waves with progeny. Five of them were under three and didn't have buddies yet, which left twenty-four kids to partner up with nineteen teens. Every time someone aged out of kids or teens, there was a shuffle. Younger teens were often paired up with older kids. Sometimes if a kid had recently come into power and it matched an older kid's power, they were paired up. Having worked in the Complex daycare and done a fair amount of babysitting in the building, we knew all the kids pretty well. I was pretty open, aside from hoping against a couple that were either hyperactive or just a little bratty.

"Girls," Gamma said when we walked up to her desk. "How are you?"

"Good," we chorused.

"I think we should have lunch soon, don't you?"

"Yes," I said at the same time Sabrina said, "Yeah."

"I hear we have things to discuss."

Sabrina and I exchanged a quick glance. Great. That meant someone had told her about our dates.

"Looking forward to it, Gamma," I said.

She looked amused. "I'm sure you are. You two are paired with Isabella."

I cocked my head at her. Why were we getting just one kid when there were two of us and the kids outnumbered the teens?

"Isabella showed her power just last night, and I made a few adjustments to the register."

Now I was really curious.

"She's reading minds. So far it's sporadic, but some peace may be just what she needs while we wait to see if she'll be able to control it or…" We all knew what the other option was, and it was a horrible fate for an eight-year-old. "I'll also be working extra with her on her meditation, and if you girls can make yourselves available if she needs a break, that would be ideal. We're going to go to homeschooling for her, and we may need you two to be open to becoming a pod of three."

Oh hell. Poor Isabella. How did this even happen? Her mom was from the line of mostly water manipulators. Things happened, though. Sabrina's dad was a precog, Gamma's power involved power over minds, and yet my mom and Neil could manipulate materials. Sometimes someone just popped up with no warning. That was why we had to be on our toes with the kids. Poor Isabella. This was a tough road. But also, poor Sabrina and me. Were we really going to be saddled with a nine-year-old now? I mean, if it was just a lot of the time, fine, but were we going to have to take her on our dates now, somehow keeping all three of us together? That would mean no more, fuck, anything. No more dating, no synchronized swimming, no more any hope of me just buckling down and following Sabrina's language path. Like she could take a nine-year-old to college classes with her. Fuck! But maybe Isabella would be able to get it under control, so she only read minds when she wanted to. It was a long shot. Most mind readers ended up in isolation. And by most, I meant all of them I knew of in the history of the Family. But for now, it was sporadic, so I shouldn't be panicking yet. I looked at Sabrina, convinced the same thoughts were going through her head. Sure enough, she looked a little green around the gills.

Gamma must have read our thoughts. "I know this will be really hard on you, but consider how hard it is to be a mind reader and how valuable that skill is to the Family."

The unspoken part was that my skill wasn't valuable at all. Fuckity fuck fuck fuck. If they decided Isabella was more important to keep healthy and happy than me, and that three was too big a unit, I'd be in isolation and Sabrina would be ordered to become a unit with Isabella. Why had it never occurred to me before that this sort of shit could happen?

When Sabrina and I had coupled up after it was clear that I was making people bleed and she could stop it, Gamma and our parents had sat us down and explained that either we could choose to always be together or I could go up to isolation. They'd explained how lucky I was that this was even an option. It took no thought then. Sabrina and I were already the best of friends, and the idea of getting to be together always seemed wonderful. As we'd grown and things had become inconvenient at times, we kept choosing each other over the alternative. There'd never been an order to pair up. It was our choice.

It had never occurred to me that another dangerous power would pop up or that we'd just be told we had to expand our pod if one did. Dangerous powers, at least the ones that were immediately dangerous without a chance to control them, like me, the girl who gave people cancer, or the fire starter who manifested by there being flames everywhere, were rare. Once every few generations sorts of rare.

Even mind readers weren't an every-generation thing. Linda was the only one alive now before Isabella. Before her, we hadn't had one for several years, which made bringing new people into the Family tricky. This was good for the Family, but not great for Isabella. Or for us.

I looked at Gamma. She was very influential on the Council, and she loved both of us very much. Would she really let this happen? Maybe. She was also staunchly Family over individual. Fuck.

She put a hand on each of our shoulders. "We'll discuss this later, girls. How about lunch tomorrow? Hopefully things won't have progressed too far by then." Meaning hopefully we wouldn't be bringing Isabella with us. "For now, go find Isabella and remember how scared she must be feeling."

We would. It wasn't her fault that this new ability would possibly cause our world to come crashing down around our heads.

CHAPTER SEVEN

We turned and went to the youth hangout room adjoining our classroom. The rest of our class had already gone into the room ahead of us. It was a fairly big space with some couches, a couple of tables for games or snacks, and a ping pong table. Isabella was sitting on the floor in a corner, head down on her knees. Her closest Family friend, Sydney, was looking at her from her little group of three, looking worried. She must know. No one else seemed to be paying her much attention, so the news must not be widespread yet or they'd be paying attention so they could stay away. People who messed with minds in any way weren't generally popular.

We walked over and sat on either side of her. That was weird in and of itself. We usually sat next to each other—rarely did we let anyone split us.

She looked up, red eyed. "Hi," she said quietly.

"Hi, Isabella," I said. "I'd ask how you're doing, but that's a silly question, isn't it?"

She nodded.

"Has it been bad yet?" Sabrina asked.

In a really soft voice, unlike Isabella's usual exuberant self, she said, "Not too bad, but I heard what Mom thinks about Dad. And I…" She sobbed a little. "It was only a little bit."

I put my arm around her. "If it was only a little bit, maybe you didn't hear everything she thinks." I could imagine what that snatch might have been to make her feel so sad. "I'll tell you that occasionally I think very uncharitable things about Sabrina, but she's still my favorite person in the world."

Sabrina laughed a little. "It can't be worse than what I think about Joan sometimes." She lowered her voice. "Every now and then I think that she should just go to is—" She cut herself off abruptly, probably realizing that wishing me to isolation wasn't going to be comforting right now. "Go to the salon to get her hair done. Have you seen how boring it is?"

Isabella looked at me and smiled a little. Sabrina had landed on just the thing. Isabella was a fashion-conscious little thing. She reached up and lifted my ponytail. "You could stand to have a style that wasn't this," she said.

"Maybe I'll let you give me a makeover," I said. "You can be my little fashion guru."

A playful look stole across her face. "You need it."

"Hey!" I put my hand to my heart, all mock outrage. "I didn't think it was that bad!"

She looked at Sabrina and they both laughed. "It is, right, Sabrina?" she asked.

"Oh, definitely."

"For crying out loud. Are you two just going to incessantly gang up on me?"

Sabrina gave Isabella a mischievous look. "Maybe."

Isabella looked at me and cocked her head. "Maybe."

"Great."

We joked around with her for a while until she was much more relaxed. Her body language changed. Now her legs were flopped out in front of her, back resting against the wall, a smile coming easily. People were starting to leave when I got an idea. I waved Sydney over.

"Sydney, do you want to hang out a little longer and play a game with the three of us? I'm going to text Neil and see if he and his girlfriend want to come down and play, too. Maybe we can order takeout or something. What do you girls think?"

They both looked excited about the prospect of spending time together and skipping the Sunday caf lunch. Not that the food was bad, but Sunday was a little boring because all the kids were in Sunday school, so help was low and we usually just had cold sandwiches.

I looked at Sabrina, thinking I should have run this by her before offering, but she looked okay with it. I pulled out my phone and texted Neil. I noticed there was a text from Ellie, too, suggesting we do that movie night we'd talked about, if I was free. I wanted nothing more, but things were really complicated now. I didn't answer.

Neil texted back that they were in, and we moved over to one of the now empty tables and picked a game to start. After we picked an American Girl game, which was a favorite of Isabella's and Sydney's, Isabella said, "I'll be right back. I need to go to the bathroom." She started to walk away, then turned around looking worried. "Do...can I go by myself?"

"Oh, sweetie. Yes. You're fine. Unless you want us to come," Sabrina told her. "You probably won't even hear anything in the few minutes you're away, but you can decide."

Isabella looked a little worried, but said tentatively, "I'll go on my own."

We were left alone with Sydney, which was awkward because I really wanted to ask Sabrina about maybe doing a movie night. "Sydney, do you want to go let your parents know what you're up to? We'll wait to get started until you come back. Maybe you could stop by and tell Isabella's parents, too? If you don't mind."

"Okay!" Sydney popped up and took off. "I'll hurry!" she called over her shoulder.

I turned to Sabrina. "I know we have a lot to talk about, but for now, I have a quick question."

"I'm not letting you go into isolation," she said flatly.

"Thank you, but that wasn't the question. What do you think about a movie night tonight? Ellie and I talked about watching *Tomb Raider* and she's texted. I know this shouldn't be my focus right now, but somehow it's at the top of mind."

She thought about it. "Okay. Here's the plan. Tell her you have to babysit, so Isabella will be there and that I have to be there, too because of the stupid group date thing. We can see if we can get anyone to join us. Maybe Paul even. Shit. This is all bad timing, isn't it?"

"The worst. I think I'm concentrating on this so I don't have to concentrate on the larger picture of our lives possibly blowing the hell up. Also, if I do have to go into isolation, I'll have some memories to hold on to."

She grabbed my hand, looking fierce. "We're not going to let that happen."

Isabella came back, looking happy. "Didn't hear a thing!" She looked around. "Where's Sydney?" The quiver in her voice indicated that she suspected Sydney had changed her mind about hanging out with the mind reader.

"She just went to tell her and your parents that you guys are spending the afternoon with us. She'll be back."

Isabella looked relieved.

Neil and Theresa walked in.

"Hey, guys," I said. They'd spent the morning chatting on the tenth floor so Linda could read Theresa, and I was super curious about how it went. Neil looked happy, so it probably had gone well. I couldn't ask what I really wanted to know in front of Theresa.

Neil gave a tiny thumbs-up off to the side away from Theresa, so that told me something. We'd have to talk later, though. God, there was a lot of that. I was sure Neil was burning with questions he couldn't ask, too, considering the text I'd sent. He gave Isabella a curious look, but then just said, "Hey, Isabella. Doing okay?"

She blushed a little (did every kid in the building who was attracted to males have a crush on Neil?) and said shyly, "I'm okay."

I don't know what he'd told Theresa on the way down, but she didn't ask any follow-ups. She just said, "Since no one seems to be introducing us, I'm Theresa."

"Hi, Theresa, nice to meet you," Isabella said politely.

"I think we need to pick a different game," I said.

"Why?" Isabella asked, looking a little crushed.

"There are going to be six of us, and this game is just for four."

"Oh, right." Isabella turned to the games, which sat on a shelving unit just a few feet away from our chosen table. "Clue?"

We agreed and started setting up. Sydney was back before we were done.

"I'm hungry," Sabrina said once we were set up. "We should order food before we start. How do people feel about Thai?"

Everyone agreed readily enough, but it still took time for everyone to pick what they wanted and to order. Sabrina was doing the ordering and she knew what I liked, so I took the opportunity to reply to Ellie.

Joan: *I'd love to, but I have to babysit and even though Isabella will be there, I still have to have group it, so I have to have someone else, too. Sabrina says she's up for Tomb Raider. I know that's lame. Sorry.*
Ellie: *I'm sorry I don't get to have alone time with you, but I'll take what I can get. Besides, I like kids. What time?*

We set a time and then I signed off, explaining I had to play a game with Isabella.

She sent back the emoji with the smiling face and three hearts. Was that for me? For the idea of playing a game with a nine-year-old? I wasn't sure, but I liked it.

"Goof." Sabrina elbowed me.

"What?"

"You're grinning like the cat that got the cream. I take it Ellie said yes?"

"She did." I was very aware of the smile on my face. I knew it opened me up for teasing, but I couldn't help it.

"Another date with Ellie?" Neil asked. "Wow. My little sister is growing up."

"Hush." I glanced at Theresa, embarrassed that she'd think I'd never had a girlfriend at seventeen, even though it was true. "We all know I'm the more mature one, anyway."

Theresa laughed a little. Isabella and Sydney, though, were

super interested in me dating and who was Ellie? Eventually we started the game.

We played and ate and played some more until Neil and Theresa had to go to catch their bus. We put the last game away and all got on the elevator together. Neil pushed the button for floor seven and Sydney pushed it for six. Sabrina, Isabella, and I looked at each other.

"Let's get off on five," Sabrina said. That was her floor. The three of us could have a frank discussion there without worrying about Theresa overhearing. When we got there, Isabella held the door while we said our goodbyes.

"It was really great meeting you." Sabrina gave Theresa a hug.

"You, too," Theresa said. She turned to me. "And you."

"It was great. I hope to see you soon." I hugged her.

"You should come visit at the school. Get a taste for college life," she told me.

"That would be cool," I said, thinking that the possibility of that was getting further and further away by the day.

We both hugged Neil.

Isabella let go of the door and gave each of them hugs, too. I quickly stopped the door to stay on Sabrina's floor and we finally exited, calling out goodbyes.

The three of us trooped down the hall to Sabrina's place and went in, saying hi to her parents on the way, who were sitting on the couch watching a movie and looked a little surprised to see Isabella with us, but greeted us all warmly.

I looked at Isabella and made a questioning face, looking for permission to tell them. They'd know soon anyway. The news of Isabella's power clearly hadn't gotten far yet, but it was only a matter of time. Isabella gave a little nod.

"Isabella will probably be spending a lot of time with us at least for a while," I told Todd and Sarah. "She's starting to get her power, and it looks like mind reading."

Both of them had a flash of sympathy, replaced quickly with a more neutral expression. Todd got up and offered Isabella a hug.

"Welcome, Isabella. You girls let us know if you need anything and we'll figure it out."

Anything like an extra bed crammed in our room. Although we'd bypass that need if Isabella just took over my bed.

"We're going to go have a girls' chat in my room," Sabrina said. "But we'll let you know."

We all sat on Sabrina's bed, backs against the wall.

"What happens now?" Isabella asked.

"What have you been told by…anyone?" I asked. "What happened, exactly?"

She took in a deep breath. "Last night I was saying good night to my parents and Mom said, well, she didn't really *say*, but I thought she said it. It didn't sound like her voice exactly, but it was her, and how would I have known if she didn't say it? So, I thought she said, 'I hate him so much.' And I was like, 'Mom, who do you hate?' And she looked at me like…" She started to cry. "She looked at me like I was a monster or something and then I knew. I knew I'd read her thoughts because…"

She trailed off, but I knew what she meant. We all knew powers were coming. We all knew mind readers were difficult to be around. It was like when my mom coughed up blood. You just had a moment where it dawned on you that you had a power and, in our cases, that power sucked. Sure, hers was super valuable for the Family, but for her, it sucked. I put my arm around her again.

"What happened then?" Sabrina asked.

"Mom said it was time for bed. She tried to cover like everything was fine, but I knew it wasn't fine. It was hard to fall asleep." She sobbed again. "When I woke up, Mom was there, but Dad wasn't. She said I should go to Sunday school, and I'd be told what was going to happen. So, at Sunday school, Fred was teaching."

Fred was on the Council and was also the Family historian. You'd think that would accord him some sort of title or something, but we all just used first names in the Family. My guess was that her mom had called, well, Gamma, probably, and Gamma had told her to send Isabella to Sunday school and go from there.

"Anyway, Fred said that I was going to homeschool now." She choked up, but pushed on, "I guess I homeschool. Do I live with you now?" Her lip quivered.

For fuck's sake. A lot had been dumped on us. Were they scrambling today trying to figure shit out? Gamma had said the mind reading was intermittent, so she wasn't going to be with us full-time. In fact, she'd just told us to spend some time with Isabella, nothing about the long term. Maybe we were supposed to have sent her home by now. You'd think someone would have told us all the deal.

"What do you want to happen?" I asked her. "Eventually, that might not matter. But for now, it seems you're not required to live with us. I mean, eventually, the Council may decide or you may decide that—what I mean is, what do you want?"

She started crying again. "I want my mom and dad! But what if they don't want me?"

Fuck this mess. Fuck this being dumped in our laps.

"I'm sure your mom and dad want you, sweetie. Let's face it head-on, shall we? You're allowed to be by yourself. No one has said you're tied to us. You can just go home and see what's happening. If you want, we'll go with you. Either way, in about an hour, Joan's friend Ellie is coming to watch a movie, and we'd like you to be there."

"Okay. Can we…can we go see my mom?"

So, we went to see her mom. When we got to her door, she seemed unsure if she should knock or just go in, poor kid. I knocked.

Isabella's mom, Lynne, opened the door, looking red eyed like her daughter. "Isabella!" She gathered her daughter into her arms. "How's your day been, honey?"

"Fine," Isabella said, small voice making a comeback.

"Really?" Lynne held her at arm's length. "I thought you might need a day with Sabrina." She glanced at Sabrina there. "But I've been worried. Sydney came by to tell me your plans, and I thought maybe that was best. Your dad…" She trailed off.

Isabella looked worried. "What's happening with Dad? Did he leave?"

"Come inside, honey. You, too, if you want to," she said to us. "Let's not have this discussion in the hall."

We all stepped into an apartment that was an identical in layout to Sabrina's because both Sabrina and Isabella were only children, so their families each lived in one of the two-bedroom apartments, but of course the décor was different. We stopped just inside.

"Do you want us to stay, Isabella?" Sabrina asked.

Isabella looked at her mom. "Mom?" Her voice wavered as she waited to see if her mom was going to be scared to be alone with her.

"It's up to you, honey." Her mom took a deep breath. "I want you to know, and I'm sure you'll see, that I love you very much. I also am not perfect and sometimes I think things I'd never say. Do you understand?"

Isabella looked down but nodded. "Do you hate Dad?"

"Oh, honey. That's something we need to talk about, but first let's decide if these two are staying."

"I want to be alone with you, Mom. No offense," she tacked on in our direction.

"None taken," I said, hands up. Frankly, it was a huge relief. I was so not ready to be a trio.

"Remember the movie at six," Sabrina reminded her as we made to leave.

"Although if you would rather stay home, I'll make your apologies," I said.

Isabella and her mom looked at each other. Finally, her mom said, "How about if we let you know?"

We agreed and gave Lynne Sabrina's phone number. That was a conscious choice, at least on my part. There might come a point where I was out of the picture.

Shit, shit, shit.

CHAPTER EIGHT

Sabrina and I went like shots back to her place. We wanted to be alone to talk about everything that had happened. We didn't even have to say that out loud. We just went to the elevator and pushed the button for her floor. Her parents, though, were sitting in front of a paused movie when we went through. They asked us to come and talk to them for a minute.

"I called Gamma," Todd said.

"And what did she tell you? Because there's a lot we don't know," Sabrina said.

"She told us about Isabella, which we knew. We asked what the plan was and she said Isabella is going to homeschool and will start spending time with you two when she needs a break and maybe permanently." Both he and Sarah looked rightfully worried.

"That's about what we know," I confirmed. "We spent most of the day with Isabella, and she may be coming back to hang out with us this evening. Her parents..." I didn't want to disclose that it seemed they were maybe having problems. That was their business, so I censored my thought and instead said, "Are figuring out coping. We'll see how it goes."

"We were just going to go talk about it all. We haven't gotten a chance to do that, really," Sabrina said.

They both still looked worried but gave us hugs and let us go. It made me realize we hadn't checked in with my parents. One thing at a time.

When we were in her room, Sabrina and I both just stopped and stood staring at each other for a while. I don't know how long, but I felt like we were reading each other's minds. Telling each other without words how scared we were, how worried for Isabella, how this all fucking sucked. Then we were in each other's arms, crying.

"It'll be okay," Sabrina said between sobs. "We could run away."

"We can't."

"Why not?"

I didn't really have an answer for that. Was it just a sense of Family loyalty? Then my brain kicked in. "How will we support ourselves when we can't be apart? No one will hire us as a twosome."

She sighed. "We could, I don't know, open an in-home daycare or something."

"Let's think about that, but maybe we should focus on figuring out our next move here." I sat down on my bed, and she sat next to me.

"What moves do we have if we're staying here?" she asked, helplessly.

Honestly, I didn't know. "Maybe just be as supportive of Isabella as possible while encouraging her to spend time on her own?"

"How is inviting her to the movie night in"—she checked her phone—"forty minutes going to help with that?"

"I don't know. I'm just...trying to juggle everything." I slumped.

"I know." She patted my leg. "So much for one thing at a time. Okay, so if Isabella doesn't come and it's the three of us, that's going to be…"

"Awkward as hell," I finished. "Let's invite Heather."

She started texting.

"So, I think we should offer to let Isabella do her schoolwork with us but encourage her to spend evenings with her parents this week," I said, musing aloud. "Then there will be breaks for them, but they might learn to live with it."

"Seems fine, I guess."

Her phone buzzed. "That's Lynne. Isabella is going to come to the movie."

"Is that good or bad?"

"Who knows? But we've got things to do."

❖

A half an hour later, Isabella, Sabrina, and I met Ellie in the lobby. God, we were weird.

"Hi!" I waved.

She waved back. "Hi."

"So, um, this way." I indicated the elevator and we all trooped over.

"Ellie, this is Isabella. Isabella, Ellie."

"Hi," Isabella said confidently. For all she'd had a really bad twenty-four hours, she was an outgoing kid.

"Hey," Ellie said back. "Ready to watch a female action hero kick some butt?"

"Hell yeah!" Isabella answered. "Is that what we're doing? What's this movie about?"

Ellie explained a little as we rode up to my floor. I liked how she was with Isabella. She was relaxed and treated her like a person. She clearly was comfortable around kids.

My parents had agreed we could have the living room for the movie watching. Before Ellie came, we'd gone to the bathroom so neither of us would have to, which would be weird again, and we'd put chips and a few drinks out on the table so people could help themselves without us having to both go to the kitchen, and we'd figured out where we could stream *Tomb Raider* and cued it up on the TV. We all sat down on our very large couch.

"Heather is joining us, too," I said just as there was a knock on the door.

"Come in!" Sabrina called, but I guess Heather didn't hear her because she didn't. What was she thinking, making us come to the door?

"Isabella, would you go let Heather in, please?" I asked.

She hopped up and ran to the door, opening it for Heather. She came back with a weird look on her face. I was hesitant to ask why. Maybe she was flashing back to something that happened earlier in the day, maybe she had another flash of mind reading, but I shouldn't ask questions that might be hard to answer in front of Ellie.

"Okay!" I clapped my hands. "Let's get this show on the road!"

About halfway through, Ellie whispered to me, "What do you think? She's something, right?"

I could see what she saw in Lara Croft, for sure. She was pretty hot and very capable. Of course I liked those things. And the scene with the bungees? Poetry in motion. However... "She's not really my type."

She looked at me, aghast. "How can she not be?"

I nudged her with my elbow. "'Cause you are."

"Oh." She looked a little surprised, but very pleased.

I could feel Sabrina distinctly trying to not pay attention on the other side of me. I took hold of Ellie's hand anyway. She turned it and laced her fingers with mine. We went back to watching the movie.

It was about ten minutes later that my mom came in. She'd been in her studio. Ellie dropped my hand, but I picked hers back up again. She looked at me. "It's okay," I said softly. She interlaced her fingers again.

"Hi, girls, don't mind me. I'm just getting a bite from the fridge and then I'll get out of your way."

I strongly suspected she'd have just stayed in her studio if she hadn't been dying of curiosity about Ellie. Her arrival and greeting were enough that Dad came out of their bedroom. I sighed and paused the movie.

"Mom, Dad, this is Ellie. Ellie, this is my mom, Megan, and my dad, Mark."

"Hi, Ellie. It's nice to meet you," Mom said.

Dad echoed her. "Nice to meet you."

"It's nice to meet you, too," Ellie said.

Then they cleared out as promised and we went back to the movie.

We paused again when Isabella said she had to go to the bathroom.

"Anyone else need anything?" Sabrina asked, slightly grumpily if you knew her as well as I did. It had been a long day.

When everyone shook their heads, I pushed play and we were able to finish the movie.

We chatted about the movie for a bit after, but it had been a seriously long and stressful day and it wasn't long before I said, "I hate to kick you out, but it's a school night and I should get Isabella to bed."

Isabella gave me a slightly affronted look. It was only seven forty-five, but she played along.

"Oh, okay." Ellie glanced at the others, then said, "Walk me out?"

Ah, hell. I was still trying to decide what to say to that exactly when Isabella saved me. "Yeah! Let's all go!"

That was totally not what Ellie had in mind, but what was she going to say? I was supposed to be babysitting anyway. It probably seemed like Isabella was trying to put off bedtime. What was weird was that we literally all rode down in the elevator together.

Isabella asked questions all the way down. When we got to the lobby and walked to the doors, I mouthed, "Sorry."

Ellie shrugged. "Text me later?"

This time, I hugged her. I was still too shy to go for a kiss, particularly with everyone standing witness. Sigh. She left.

I turned around to find everyone right behind me, of course.

"Isabella, are you ready to go home for the night?" I asked.

She nodded with a little hesitation, but she nodded.

"Has anyone said what you're supposed to do tomorrow?" Sabrina asked.

"Just not to go to school. Mom said the Council is going to enroll me in an online program, but I don't think I start tomorrow?"

"Do both your parents work away from home?" I asked.

"Yeah. Dad is an electrician and Mom does something for the Family, but not at home."

Sabrina and I looked at each other. It really seemed that

everyone just expected us to watch after Isabella without having come out and said so.

"Ask your mom when you get home if there is a plan and then you can text us on her phone, okay?" Sabrina said. "If there isn't a plan, meet us at ten in the youth room. We have a shift in the caf in the morning."

Isabella chewed her lip. "Okay."

We all trudged to the elevator banks once again. Before the elevator arrived, a couple joined us to wait for it. Corina was the Family member of the couple. Her power was fire starting, but luckily only when she wanted. There'd been a kid named Frank back in the 1920s who was an uncontrolled fire starter. The story was that he was in his bedroom when suddenly it burst into flames. He ran out into the hall to escape it, but the fire followed. He went back into his room and jumped out the window, presumably to save his family and, perhaps, the Family as well. It being the twenties, the Family was able to cover up the death and pass it off as just a fire. We didn't know Corina well, but we exchanged hellos, as was only polite. They looked at Isabella curiously. Word had probably started to get around. They and Isabella got off. They looked back at Sabrina, and when she didn't follow, hurried down the hall to their apartment. We could see Isabella hang her head as the door closed.

CHAPTER NINE

O kay, tell me everything," Heather said as soon as the elevator door slid shut.

It was a sign of the day that I didn't even know exactly what she was asking about.

My phone started ringing. It was Gamma.

"Hi, Gamma," I said.

"Joan. I've called to tell you about plans for this coming week."

"Okay."

"Are you on the elevator? I just heard a ding."

"Yes."

"Why don't you and Sabrina come on over, then?"

"Okay," I said, pushing the fourth-floor button. "Be there soon." I hung up after she said goodbye.

Sabrina said, "Sounds like the tell-all will have to wait."

"Tomorrow on caf duty, then," Heather said.

We stopped on floor eight for Heather, then rode back down. While we waited, Sabrina said, "Gamma plans or Council plans?"

"I'm guessing Council."

"Me, too."

We exited the elevator, walked to Gamma's door, and knocked.

"My girls," she said. She opened her arms for a group hug. "Sounds like you two had a very full day."

She let go and swept her arm wide, indicating we should come in. "Sit down and make yourselves comfortable. Tea?"

"Yes, please," I answered for both of us.

We moved to the dining room table, which was adjacent to the kitchen, so we could talk while she made the tea. We didn't drink tea anywhere else, but there was something about Gamma's tea that got us. Sure, cream and sugar helped, but we'd tried making it for ourselves and it was never the same.

Gamma poured boiling water into her teapot, which I presumed had her mix of tea already in there. She must have started prepping as soon as she said to come to her place. "I've spoken with Lynne and know you spent most of the day with Isabella. I also know a few things you don't. I was elected to talk to you two girls. We'd like Isabella to spend her school days with you two, but evenings and nights with one or the other of her parents."

Sabrina and I exchanged a look that Gamma caught and addressed. "Yes, separately. Apparently the thought that Isabella heard was about a long-growing issue. For now, Paulo is going to stay in a studio on three. Both he and Lynne are nervous, as I'm sure you can understand, about Isabella reading their thoughts, but they both love their daughter and want to spend time with her. We shall see how that goes. For now, we're hoping she is able to gain some control, and not using her power won't help with that, so we'll build in break times with you two and times she will be around others." Gamma brought the tea tray over and slid it on the table. "Give that two more minutes before you pour."

That echoed pretty closely what Sabrina and I had been thinking when we thought it was all on our shoulders. Except that part of our thoughts were that it would be easier for us to continue to be a twosome rather than a threesome.

"We were thinking the same," Sabrina said.

"Well, good. I hope you girls knew this wasn't on you to figure out. The Council has been in meetings all day, deciding and delegating. Right now Greg is filling out forms to enroll Isabella in the very same program you two started in. We're hoping to expedite things and have her going by the end of the week. We already called Ryan and had him order her a laptop."

Greg was a Council assistant, and Ryan was a tech guy who'd

married into the Family. The Family employed a fair number of Family members, born or married in, who all worked on the third floor, aside from caf employees down on the first floor. I knew some obvious jobs—we had a medical clinic, and there were assistants for the Council. Some of them took care of Family finances. There were definitely some tech people, Ryan being one of them. I don't know what all they did, but if you needed help with your phone, tablet, or laptop, you could go talk to them. I supposed they'd maybe developed and now maintained the intra Family chat app we had? And then there were others that did…stuff. I wasn't sure what.

"Of course, if little Isabella gets to a point where she is hearing everything all the time, we'll have to make adjustments, but we'll cross that bridge if it comes."

"Gamma, will that bridge mean Joan or Isabella in isolation?" Sabrina asked, reaching for the teapot.

Gamma gave a nod of approval for it being time to pour, then evaded the question. "The Council will come to a decision on that. Believe me, we will take all your needs under consideration."

"But not as much as the Family needs," Sabrina muttered, pouring for me, as well.

"Don't mutter. I will make sure we take all needs into consideration." Gamma patted each of our hands with hers.

I doctored my tea as I thought about what that would mean. It probably wouldn't be enough, having Gamma at least a little on our side, but one could hope. Although, did I really want to send a nine-year-old into isolation just to save myself? Probably not, but there was also Sabrina to consider. Truly, being saddled with someone half her age was a really different ask than with a same-age best friend.

"But let's talk about tomorrow. I still want to have lunch with my girls, and there are things for us to discuss that should probably happen away from little ears. And I know you two probably need some time to yourselves this evening after the day you've had. Also, the Council has decided to consider your time with Isabella work time, so you'll no longer be working in the cafeteria. You'll get paid for the hours you're with Isabella. Tomorrow is a little different because we want to give Andrea at least that long to shift her schedule around. You'll also stop working in the daycare."

I'd guessed that was the direction we were going in, but it was still a bummer. I was pretty attached to those kids. So was Sabrina.

She lowered her teacup. "Do we have to stop?"

Gamma considered. "Maybe not. Actually, Isabella is going to go help in the nursery tomorrow until you two are done with your cafeteria shift, and then again while we have lunch. Maybe we could work out the three of you spending time in the daycare at least once a week. Would that help soften the blow?"

I looked at Sabrina for confirmation, then answered for both of us. "That would be good."

"Okay. That's settled then. Tomorrow, cafeteria for breakfast, then Isabella and schoolwork until one, then lunch with me, and then back to Isabella and school until her parents are off. I have many questions for you girls, but we'll talk tomorrow. Your parents have been told all this, so you won't have to explain things."

"Okay, Gamma," I said, somewhat defeated.

She patted my hand again. "Be of good cheer, my girls."

I appreciated her signature sentiment, but my future looked uncertain at best. I picked up my tea and finished the cup.

"I see you two are done with your tea. I'll let you go commune with one another. I'm sure you need it."

CHAPTER TEN

We told Heather everything about the new arrangement (she was unhappy we were leaving the caf and said she might, too, then, as she'd served her year and we were what made it fun over bearable), about how things were going with Ellie (although she'd been there for all the in-person parts), and about our feelings and concerns about it all (she commiserated).

We didn't exactly do school after the shift. Instead we played games with Isabella.

"Okay, what was that weird look on your face last night?" I asked. "When you let Heather in?"

"I don't think I should say," she said.

"I guess that means you heard something," Sabrina said.

"Yes," Isabella said.

"Was it about one of us?" Sabrina pressed.

Isabella made a zipping motion across her mouth and mimed throwing away the key. "I don't think I should tell secrets."

"That's fair," I said, even though I was burning with curiosity. Sabrina and I exchanged a look promising to speculate later.

"Has it been happening more?"

"Only three times altogether so far. I think people have to be thinking pretty loudly for me to pick it up. I saw my dad last night because he came home to tuck me in, and I heard him thinking very loudly that he loved me. I also heard him thinking that he wanted me to know that."

"That sounds nice," Sabrina said.

"It was." Isabella opened her plastic diary-shaped game piece and pulled out the cards we'd given her. "Guys! These are all bad!"

"We work with what we've got," I said. We were playing this old American Girl game where you gave the other players cards with things written on them you thought they'd like. They ranked them and you got points for how well yours ranked. Sabrina and I knew each other so well that we were winning. It wouldn't be long before we'd know Isabella just as well. So far most of what I knew about her was that she was into fashion and she played the violin.

After the game, Isabella went back to the daycare and we went up to Gamma's.

"Gamma! You ordered Indian for us! You're the best." Sabrina kissed her on her cheek.

"I know my girls," she said, indicating we should take our seats. "Now, tell me about your dates."

We told her and she was very interested. She looked a little happy for us and a little worried. I confessed that I had worries about how Ellie was taking me and Sabrina being a unit. "I want you girls to have all the experiences. But I worry, too. How has Ellie been today? Has she seemed…all right?"

"She's been a little short," I admitted. I'd texted her a few times and she'd replied, but she hadn't regaled me with anecdotes from her day like she usually did.

"It's a tough row to hoe," Gamma said. "My advice is to double down on telling her your parents won't let you be alone together, but that you realize it's strange."

I sighed. She was right. I should say something to Ellie instead of just ignoring the discomfort I was sensing from her. I'd always known that building a romantic relationship with someone was going to be a challenge given that I couldn't be alone with anyone or away from Sabrina, but it was even harder than I'd imagined. It would all be so much easier if I didn't care about Ellie. I was going to have to think of something to say to her that would at least show I knew it was weird, but I wanted it to work.

Gamma turned to Sabrina. "And when are you seeing your Paul again?"

Sabrina shrugged. "It seems like a back burner issue now."

"I believe that double dates are your ticket. Set up your next get-together, my girls. Make it happen."

Sabrina reared back in surprise. "Gamma!"

"There may not be many opportunities in the future," she explained darkly, which did not bode well.

We went down to daycare to pick Isabella up. She could have just met us, of course, but we didn't know what time we'd be done with lunch and she didn't have a phone, so we just went and got her. We stayed for a bit and played with the kids who were awake. It was nap time for the littlest ones. Then we decided to go hang out in Sabrina's room for the afternoon. Isabella asked if we could go by her place and pick up her violin so she could practice while we did our schoolwork.

"I'm impressed you want to practice when you basically have a pass to do whatever you want today," I said.

She put her hands on her hips and gave me a look that told me she thought I was being the height of stupid.

"What?" I asked.

"It's *violin*. It's not, I don't know, math. You have to keep up. Besides, I don't feel right if I don't get some violin in every day."

"I feel the same about language." Sabrina put her fist out to Isabella to fist bump.

I felt a little left out. I liked school and I loved biology, but I'd also happily take a day off. I wished I had a thing that was all consuming like that. I supposed I didn't ever go a day without reading. If nothing else I had to read at least a page before sleep, but Sabrina was the same way and she had languages, too. And even though she didn't talk about it, she also had art. I was sure she at least doodled every day.

Making the point to myself about feeling fine with missing a day of schoolwork, I spent the afternoon texting Ellie, or trying to get myself to, at any rate. I spent quite a while fiddling with my phone and thinking about if it was fair to her. Eventually, I decided this was just a teenage thing for her. She'd move on and forget all about me, but for me, this might be my only chance at romance before isolation for the rest of my life. Finally, I sent this text:

Joan: *Hey. Listen, I'm sorry if things seem really weird when we're together. I know this probably doesn't make sense, and why wouldn't I just go around my parents if I want to see you? But there are reasons I'm not allowed to say. What it comes down to is that I have to have Sabrina within fifteen feet of me all the time. It's not that we're codependent, although we probably are because of being together all the time. I can't explain why and this probably seems really weird, but you should think of us as conjoined twins, really. If that's all too weird, I understand. I wanted to lay it all out, though, and tell you I really like you and if you can see your way past this very strange thing, I'll like to continue to see you. That's all.*

Then I set my phone aside and tried my best to do a set of math problems while I waited for a reply. It was a couple of hours later and almost time for Isabella to go back home when she replied.

Ellie: *You're right, that's weird. I won't lie, I think that's really out there. But I like you and knowing that, well, we can try. I do have one question, though.*
Joan: *Yes?*
Ellie: *Does it mean kissing is out?*
Joan: *God, I hope not.*
Ellie: *Okay, so then you pick the next movie? Or maybe Sabrina (winky emoji)*
Joan: *Or Paul. If we invite him, Sabrina will also be occupied.*
Ellie: *That sounds like a solution.*

There was a pause.

Ellie: *So today at lunch...*

And she launched into a story about the dating life of one of her friends who was going back to a girl who'd cheated on them. We both agreed they were making bad decisions.

I told her about lunch with Gamma and the morning with Isabella. I even recorded a short bit of Isabella playing her violin. Once she moved on from scales, it was actually lovely ambient background music, even if the one piece she was working on got a little repetitive.

Eventually, Ellie had to go work a shift, so I put the phone down.

"How are things with your girlfriend?" Isabella teased.

"She's definitely not my girlfriend," I said.

"Why not?" Sabrina asked.

"Because no one has said anything about being girlfriends," I said.

"I'm not sure it needs to be said," Sabrina opined. "If you are seeing each other romantically, I think it might just happen."

"Oh. So, is Paul your boyfriend, then?"

"We've only gone out once," Sabrina said with dignity.

"Well, let's rectify that. We could go on a group date this weekend," I suggested.

"Can I go?" Isabella asked.

"It's a date, so no," Sabrina said.

"I was there for last night's date," she pointed out.

"Still no," I said. It was plenty weird enough having to have Sabrina close.

She pouted a little, then said, "You should invite Heather and Maria, though."

"How do you know about Maria?" I asked.

"Oh!" Isabella put her hand to her mouth.

"So," Sabrina teased, "I guess that means we know what Heather was thinking about when you let her in last night."

Isabella crossed her arms. "I didn't mean to tell!"

"We know." I patted her knee. She'd clambered onto my bed next to me in order to tease me in closer proximity. I'd abandoned my desk while I was texting with Ellie.

I picked my phone back up, saying, "I'll text Heather."

It took a few hours before we managed to get everyone's responses and times that worked, but we eventually set a date to walk in Central Park that included Sabrina and Paul (who also asked to see Sabrina sooner, so we set up another movie night for Thursday—Ellie was coming, too), Heather and Maria, and Ellie and myself. Isabella begged to come to movie night, and we told her we'd think about it, but she'd gone home and we were back from synchronized swimming by the time we got everything set.

By the next morning, Isabella had her computer and was officially enrolled in the online academy. Sabrina and I took turns helping her figure out what she was supposed to be doing while the other one did their own schoolwork. This, of course, was in between texting Ellie, Paul, and Heather. It was a good thing that as of last week I'd been ahead in my classes because I sure wasn't getting a lot of homework done this week.

Heather put in her notice for the caf and was planning on applying to work at a consignment store where she and Sabrina both liked to shop. She was hoping for an employee discount. Everything was changing.

Meanwhile, the movie date was set. We'd set up a group chat for the six of us and Paul had suggested *The Breakfast Club*. None of the rest of us had seen it, but it being one of those iconic films you hear about, we decided to go for it, particularly since it seemed our tastes in movies varied a lot.

By Wednesday, Isabella needed us a little less when it came to figuring out what she was supposed to do, and I caught back up on my own work. The question of Isabella coming to movie night was answered when her mom said no. It was nice we didn't have to. She'd continued to have very sporadic bits of mind reading and it had to be a loud thought, so both she and her parents were getting more comfortable. It was also nice that we got to keep going to synchronized swimming.

My parents allowed us use of the living room again on Thursday evening, and we were ordering pizza. Everyone was coming over at five thirty because Isabella went home at five and we were thinking it was possible we'd make it a doubleheader if we started early enough. Having told Ellie that Sabrina had to stay near, I was feeling less stressed about seeming normal.

The movie night was a huge success with the couples all snuggled up. It seemed Heather and Maria had moved out of the friend zone. They all stayed until nearly ten, but not because we watched another movie after watching *The Breakfast Club*. Instead, we started talking, first about the movie, then other movies, and on to other topics from there. At one point, Ellie and I had a side conversation.

"So, which one are you?" she asked.

"From *The Breakfast Club*? Um, probably Anthony. I'm kind of a nerd."

"Kind of? You're totally a nerd, doing college already. And I suppose you've got that cute nerd thing going, but luckily for me, you aren't a dude."

I laughed. "Luckily. How about you?"

"I don't know that I'm represented. What category do you think works for the middling-popular, middling-academic, cute, fat lesbian programmer?"

"Well, first of all, I'd double down on the cute part. And I don't know that you're middling-anything, but I hear you. I'm not sure which character you are, but I can tell you that the category you fall into is my type." Then I blushed.

"Aww. That's so sweet." Then she turned tilted her head up and, oh my God, it was happening, kissed me.

It wasn't long, my first ever romantic kiss, but I felt the tingle sparked by her lips touching mine all the way to my toes. For the next ten minutes, I felt like I was just going to float right off the couch. The only thing grounding me was her hand in mine.

The six of us rode down to the lobby to say goodbye to our dates and surprised Taylor, a twenty-five-year-old precog, who started to step into the elevator when the doors opened only to be met by our crew, each of the couples holding hands. Her face went from sleepy, to surprised, to pleased. I guessed she was a fan of love. She stepped back to let us out, then stepped inside.

At the door, I made a move, initiating the second kiss. As the others were also kissing goodbye around us, it didn't feel that strange to kiss in front of people. This time, we kissed just a little longer, moving our lips together. There was no tongue, though. Should I have initiated that, too? Or was that her move? Or were we really not quite there yet?

After we watched them leave, we boarded the elevator once more.

"So," Sabrina said, "good night, right?"

"A really good night," Heather said.

"Did you kiss with tongue?" I blurted out and they both stared at me.

"Um, yes, a little?" Sabrina said.

"No," Heather said. "We kind of kissed cheeks, in fact."

"What about you?" Sabrina asked.

I shook my head. "How fast does kissing tend to progress, Heather?" She was the only one of us with any dating experience.

"Oh, sure, because I'd know with my three ever dates?" She thought for a moment. "I guess five now, because this was definitely a date, which means that Saturday was a date, too, I guess. You guys are practically dragging me kicking and screaming into dating here."

Sabrina rolled her eyes. The elevator dinged for her floor. We stepped into the doorway to hold it open. "You have dated, though, and I presume there was a kiss or two in there somewhere?"

Heather sighed. "Yeah. With Preston, it was way too much, too fast, which is why there was only one date. He really pushed." She shuddered a little and I wanted to hug her, but she wasn't much of a toucher generally. "With Nayte, he actually shook my hand at the end of both dates. I think the fact that neither of us pushed for a kiss speaks for itself." She shuddered a little again and I wondered what could have been so bad about a handshake or two.

"Do you want to really kiss Maria, or is this another miss?" I asked.

She didn't even think about it. "I want to kiss her." She pumped her eyebrows playfully. "Maybe Saturday!"

"See how grateful you are for us dragging you kicking and screaming into dating?" I teased.

She laughed. "Let me go home, you weirdos." She made shooing motions, so we cleared out and let the elevator go on up.

CHAPTER ELEVEN

I willed the train to move faster. Why had I agreed to leave the Complex at one instead of twelve forty-five like I'd wanted? We'd just missed a train and now we were going to be late, and I hated being late.

"It's fine. We'll be five minutes late at most. Most people don't even consider that late," Sabrina said, reading my mind.

"Ellie does. We talked about it. We both like getting places early."

"Text her then and throw Heather and me under the bus."

I held up my phone. "No signal."

Heather reached across Sabrina and patted my arm. "Sorry, Joan. She'll still be into you, though."

I huffed.

Finally, we got to our stop and exited the train. I made for the exit.

"Slow down. You're going to lose me." Sabrina spoke in a voice she rarely used. I stopped dead and looked back. Sure enough, she was pushing between a couple of people, Heather behind her. It was almost really bad.

"Sorry," I said.

"Just…you know."

"I know."

I let Sabrina lead after that.

We were seven minutes late, but not the last to arrive. Paul wasn't there yet.

"Sorry we're late," I said to Ellie and Maria as we approached.

Ellie turned to me and tutted a little, mostly mock disappointed. I suspected there was a little bit of the real deal in there, too.

"It's their fault." I pointed a thumb at my two fellow Family members.

"Hey!" Sabrina said.

"You told me I could throw you under the bus!" I protested.

"Not, like, in front of me like that."

Ellie laughed.

"What have you two been up to over here waiting?"

"Talking about how strange it is that you guys live in the same building and travel in a pack," Maria said.

"Yup. Weirdos," Sabrina verified. "Has Heather told you about us being a kind of commune? I mean, you should get the full weirdness here."

"Seriously? A commune? I thought communes were typically out in the country or in other countries or something," Maria said.

"Seriously," I said. "Somewhere way far back, we're related to a handful of people who were the building's developers. Descendants live in the building for a percentage of income. We have a communal eating situation for breakfast and lunch. It's a whole thing."

Ellie cocked her head at me. "You just keep getting stranger and stranger."

I took a little bow.

Paul arrived, apologizing and saying he'd gotten held up at work. If he was coming from work, it would have made sense for him to come with us, but I could see why Sabrina wouldn't have suggested it. He didn't know about our need to be close, and public transportation was a good way to make that obvious.

"Shall we stroll, then?" Heather asked. "I want to go by the dog statue."

That was as good a destination as any, so off we went. I heard Maria asking Heather more about our commune as they started off in the lead. I let Sabrina and Paul go next, then Ellie and I followed. I was feeling like I wanted to keep Sabrina in sight after the near accident at the subway station.

Ellie followed suit with the commune question. "So, how does it work? I mean, how do you prove you're a descendant of one of the original developers?"

"Oh, there's a kind of HOA thing that keeps track of birth records and stuff. Basically, if you want to keep the line going, you have to register your kids when they're born. People do, though, because it's a really good deal." Really it wasn't hard to track because we all lived in the building when we had kids, but that seemed too weird to explain, that no one chose to live elsewhere. "You can live in a decent apartment off of a teacher's salary or even for free in certain situations, like you're in college or something. Of course, there are people overpaying for the decent apartments, too, but they don't mind." Or if they did, it didn't matter. That was the public story of our building, and it was close to true. People really did pay a percentage of their income to the Family. But we also had a huge trust, so if someone slacked it was really no big deal. Not that people tended to. If they didn't go to school or have a job outside the Complex, they were employed by the Family.

"That's kind of amazing, actually," she said.

"Socialism at work. Kinda." More than kinda. We had our health insurance through the Family and everything, so we were a mini socialist society, but those were details I didn't need to share.

"So, will you continue to live…there when you grow up? Does your building have a name?"

"We call it the Complex. And yeah, I will. Definitely." Possibly in one of the eleventh-floor isolation units.

"How does it work when you get married?" she asked, then blushed.

She didn't need to worry, I didn't think she was popping the question. "Your spouse moves in and you get a bigger apartment. If you have more than one kid, you get a bigger apartment again."

"What if your kids aren't your bio kids?"

"It still counts." That didn't happen, though. We didn't marry people who already had children or adopt from outside the Family. Having kids without powers around was considered dangerous in terms of our secrets getting out. If I, by some miracle, had kids someday, they'd have to be my bio kids or bio kids from a Family member. It used to be that if you couldn't have bio kids, then you were childless unless there needed to be an intraFamily adoption. That did happen on occasion, accidental pregnancy where the mom didn't want to have an abortion or death of the parents or, very occasionally, an abuse or neglect situation. With our communal style of living, that sort of thing was rare, but if it did happen, it didn't go unnoticed. Now we had our own sperm and egg bank. Family members, particularly those with strong, useful powers, were encouraged to donate. The subject had already been broached with Sabrina. While her power was rather a nuisance for most people (for example, she couldn't hang out in my mom's studio while she worked), it was clearly good in situations like mine or Isabella's, or for anyone with an *oh shit* power. "Do you want to have kids someday?"

"I do, yeah, someday. I think I'd like to carry, too. I've always thought being pregnant would be cool. My mom says she thought it was really awesome, even though it was also hard at times. How about you?"

She could carry if it were my egg. I scoffed at myself. That was a future that wouldn't happen. "I love kids."

"But do you want your own? I mean to raise, not bio necessarily."

"I do." I'd never get the chance.

"You seem a little sad. Is there something about kids that makes you sad?"

I shook it off. "No. Really. Kids are great. We...I work in the daycare at the Complex. I love kids."

"Then we have working with kids in common, it seems."

"Indeed. They can be funny little things, though," I said.

She laughed. "That's for sure! There was this one kid..."

We were still talking about the funny things kids did when we got to the statue. We paused and chatted as a group for a bit about pets. Some people in the Complex had pets, but we never had. Heather had a cat. Only Paul had grown up with a dog out of our group.

When we moved on, Ellie and I ended up in the middle. She

took my hand, which was an awesome idea. As we strolled on, I was thinking about kissing her again. Would we wait until the end of the date? Could I just turn to her and kiss her?

We walked and talked about this and that, but my mind was on kissing. I'd enjoyed it very much. What if I didn't like tongues? What if we never got to tongues and I never found out if I liked tongues? The feel of her hand in mind was warm, comforting, grounding, and slightly exciting, but the feel of her lips against mine was exhilarating.

We stopped on the Bow Bridge and leaned on the railing, watching the boats navigate the dirty water. I leaned into Ellie a little. "I hear this is supposed to be romantic."

She looked around. "It is a sweet bridge. You just have to ignore the fact that the water is questionable."

I looked at her and admired how an ear poked out of her bob. Without thinking about it, I lifted a finger and stroked the shell of her ear. She shivered a little.

"Sorry," I said.

"No, I liked it," she whispered. She turned to me. Everything aside from her faded. I couldn't look at anything except her sweet round face with her bright blue eyes looking right at me, all framed by her blond bob. I lifted a hand again, this time to tuck her hair behind her ear. We leaned toward one another and our lips met. We were kissing again and it was everything I remembered. I hadn't realized quite how sensitive lips were until mine were pressed against hers. I felt light-headed with pleasure. When her tongue touched my lip, I gasped, surprised, but delighted. Still, that ended the kiss because she pulled back to look at me questioningly. "Was that all right?"

"Very all right. Good. Great, even."

She grinned.

"Okay, lovebirds." Heather tugged on my sleeve. "Let's let other people have a turn on the bridge."

I held my arm out so Ellie could thread hers through mine, and we followed Heather and Maria off the bridge.

The first sign that something was wrong was when Ellie lifted her free hand to her nose. Then a lot of things happened fast. There was blood on Ellie's hand, bright red and scary. It could have been just a nosebleed. People do get them from natural causes, even when I'm around. But then Heather whipped her head around and looked at me with alarm. She was coughing. Shit. Maria turned to look at her in concern and I saw blood trickling out of her ear. I turned and ran back, leaving Ellie behind. Sabrina was standing where we'd stopped, back to us, completely wrapped up in Paul.

My heart was beating a thousand beats per minute, but I calmly said, "We're moving on now. And do you by chance have a tissue?" I was horrified when Sabrina turned to me and I noticed her eyes were red, like the small vessels in them had bled. I quickly looked at Paul, who had a trickle of a nosebleed, too. Holy shit. It seemed that my power outdistanced Sabrina's.

The coughing had already stopped behind me, but Ellie was still holding her nose. Likely the bleeding had stopped, but she might not have realized it yet. From what I could tell, Maria hadn't noticed anything was really amiss aside from the coughing fit. Heather was distracting her from Ellie by loudly saying she'd choked on her own spit.

Sabrina turned and looked at me, eyes wide with alarm, an echo of Heather earlier. "Um, no, sorry." She also spoke calmly. Sabrina saw me looking at Paul and she turned to look. When she looked back, her eyes were a little wider. Paul used his hand to wipe his nose and didn't bother looking at his hand, so Sabrina took his hand, wiping the back of it as subtly as she could.

"Let's go find a bathroom or something," I said.

We walked up to join the others and I looked nervously at Ellie. "How's your nose?"

"I think the bleeding stopped," she said. She had a thoughtful look on her face. "I'm fine."

"Oh, good."

Back in formation, we walked off the bridge, but not before I noticed a duck floating in the water below us, blood in the water around it.

CHAPTER TWELVE

S o that was bad." Sabrina stated the obvious when we were safely back home and sitting on the couch in my room.

"Yes."

"And your power reaches farther than mine." More obviousness.

"Yes. Sorry." Her eyes were still red.

She waved that off. "We have to be more careful."

"Maybe more dates here on the couch where even if we get, um, distracted, we won't suddenly drift apart."

She buried her face in her hands. "I'm so sorry. I was so involved I didn't notice you move."

"It's equally my fault. I was so wrapped up in Ellie that I didn't notice you weren't following."

We both groaned and leaned our heads back against the couch.

"We're stereotypical stupid teenagers, all hormonal over our first kisses," I said. "I thought we were better than that. More mature."

"Clearly not," she said.

I turned my head toward her without lifting it. "Do you think Paul noticed anything?"

"Other than the nosebleed? No. How about Ellie?"

I hesitated. "I think she knows something is weird."

"Why?"

"She gave me a look. And she was right next to me with

Heather in front of us, so she noticed Heather coughing, and may have noticed Maria's ear bleed. And I suspect she saw the duck."

"What duck?"

"Oh, fuck, you didn't see the duck?" I did that purposefully.

"What fucking duck?" She was actually slightly irate.

"I'm pretty sure I killed a duck. I saw a dead duck float out from under the bridge. The water was pink around it."

"Oh fuck." She paused. "What do you think autocorrect would make of this conversation?"

We laughed. It was probably hysterical laughing, but it helped break some of the tension. "It's never duck," I said when we slowed down and we were off again.

"But this time it is," she said. More laughter.

When we calmed down, I leaned my head on her shoulder. "I'm sad about the duck, though. I feel bad."

"At least it wasn't one of our friends."

"Fuck." That thought really did scare me to my core. But Sabrina giggled a little and I couldn't help but join her. God, we were awful.

This time when we sobered, I said, "We should experiment."

"How?"

My phone buzzed and I picked it up. "I'm not sure yet, but I bet we can figure something out. Knowing my power works on animals…" I trailed off, looking at my phone.

"What?" Sabrina asked.

"Ellie knows something is up. She just texted saying, 'So, about the bleeding…'"

"What are you going to say?"

"Hell if I know." I dropped my head back against the couch again. I whispered. "I told her about the fifteen-feet rule."

"Seriously?"

"She knew something was weird and I wanted to keep seeing her, so I had to admit to part. But now…"

"But now. Now you have to make a decision."

"Yeah, basically it's A) never talk to her again, B) spill my guts, or C) let Gamma and Linda work on her. Fuck."

"That sums it up."

"Well, C is fucking out."

"Okay." Sabrina was so my ride or die and I loved her for it.

"And I really, really don't want A."

"I get that."

"We kissed again and…" I trailed off, thinking about the magic moment just before the terrifying moment.

Sabrina looked a little dreamy herself. "Kissing is pretty much all it's cracked up to be."

We spent some time comparing notes on our respective kissing experiences. Then I pulled the conversation back.

"I'm going to tell her."

Sabrina sucked in a breath. "That's entering the danger zone."

"Like we haven't already?"

Sabrina ran her fingers through her short white hair, leaving it more rumpled than spiky. "True. At least she'd know to help us stay together."

"Besides, I think she's like halfway there already."

"That's a leap."

"Really? Why?"

She looked at me scornfully. "You really think that a normie's first reaction to the information that we can't be more than fifteen feet from each other and a little bit of bleeding is going to be, *Hey, this person has powers*?" She scoffed.

I scrunched my mouth over to one side and glared at her. "Then why would she bring up the bleeding?"

"Because she wants to know if you're freaked out that she had a nosebleed on your date?"

And, okay, that made some sort of sense. "You're not wrong. I'll just…" I trailed off, already starting to type a reply.

Joan: *Yeah, sorry you had a bloody nose. Are you okay?*
Ellie: *Dancing dots*
Ellie: *(monocle emoji) I'm fine, but I have questions.*

I held the phone so Sabrina could see. "See?" I demanded.

Sabrina did a half nodding, half shaking her head thing. "Ask what her questions are."

Joan: *Okay, go ahead and ask.*

The response came lightning quick.

Ellie: *Will you answer honestly?*

"Okay," I said to Sabrina. "See? She knows."
"Or suspects."
"Didn't we already agree that there were basically three options and that telling her was the one we were going for?"
Sabrina held her hands up. "I'm just wanting to be really sure before we step into the viper's nest here. If anyone finds out we've told, she'll get wiped, and we'll be in the shit. You'd probably end up in isolation."
"Like that won't happen anyway," I said sadly.
She put her arm around my shoulders. "I'm going to do everything in my power to prevent that."
"The problem is that it's not really in your power. We, like we discussed, as a unit are pretty much dependent on the Family." I hung my head.
"Okay, okay. Tell your girl. You're right. We're going to try to keep you out of isolation, but if this is the only time you get to experience dating, let's make it count."
I turned and hugged her. "Thanks, Sabrina." I straightened and typed.

Joan: *Yes. I'll answer honestly.*
Ellie: *Can we video chat? I want to see your face. Or I could come over.*

I looked at the time. It was only eight and it was Saturday night. I showed Sabrina the phone again and she nodded.

Joan: *Come over, then. Text when you're here and we'll come down and let you in.*
Ellie: *(thumbs-up emoji)*

While we waited, we gushed over our crushes like any teenager would do. We also texted a bit with Heather, who was crushing on Maria, too, and wanted to debrief about the park incident. We didn't tell her about Ellie coming over. The various different secrets were getting old.

When Ellie texted and we went through the living room to go meet her, my mom looked up from the show she was watching and said, "Going downstairs for bed?"

Having just thought about the plethora of secrets, I said, "Not quite yet. Ellie is coming over to hang out for a little bit."

She turned and really focused then. "So, that's going well?"

"It is."

"And she doesn't think this"—she looked between us—"is weird?"

"She does," I admitted. "But I just told her that was part of the package, always having Sabrina around, and she doesn't understand, but she wants to keep hanging out."

"Okay…" Mom said dubiously.

"She's waiting. We're going to go let her in." She was actually a couple blocks away when she texted, but I was done with this conversation.

We let Ellie in and she let me hug her but also seemed a little standoffish, and I couldn't blame her. Considering the conversation we'd just had with my mom, I didn't want to go back through there. Sabrina's parents were home. We could go to the youth hangout, but that was very public and someone could walk in or eavesdrop from the hall easily.

I stood and stared at Sabrina as all this went through my head. "Where do we go?"

She thought. "Good question."

I turned to Ellie. "We're trying to think of a place that will be private." As I was saying that, I was struck with an idea. I turned back to Sabrina. "Tenth floor."

She snapped her fingers and pointed at me. "Yes."

The whole tenth floor was also a hangout room. But people only went there so that Linda could read minds without people going into her apartment, so no one went there unless they had to. With Sabrina, though, Linda wouldn't even know we were there.

We rode the elevator up in silence. It would have been safe enough to talk with just the three of us in the car, but we all seemed to be waiting to talk until we were settled, which was pretty quickly after we got to the tenth floor, as the elevator opened into a large, comfortable sitting area. The entire floor was just this one room, and it was pretty cool, really. There were windows all around, and couches and chairs kind of scattered, but you could move them, too, so there was currently a couch pointed to look out right in front of a window. We maneuvered a stuffed chair next to it, and Ellie and I sat on the couch while Sabrina sat on the chair at a right angle to us.

I looked at Ellie nervously, not sure how to start. She looked between us, seemingly also nervous. It was Sabrina who finally said, "So, you have questions."

Ellie nodded, but it seemed she had perhaps lost some of her nerve on the trek over. She knotted her hands on her lap. Tentatively, I reach over to pat them. "We don't have to do this," I suggested.

She looked up at me with determination in her eye. "If we're going to hang out, then I think we do."

"Okay. Ask away, then."

She took a deep breath. "Okay. So, you two have to stay within fifteen feet of each other, right?"

"That's right," I said.

"And this isn't a choice, I think. I mean, it's not just that you are the most codependent best friends ever, right?"

"That's right," I said again.

"Okay." She paused. "I feel a little out on a limb here, but...do you make people bleed when you're apart?" She looked at Sabrina, then back at me.

"You're really close," I said, "but Sabrina doesn't make people bleed. She stops me from making people bleed."

Having suspicions was clearly different from having them confirmed. Ellie shot to her feet, hands to her head. "What? How? What the fuck? Just…what? How? That can't be true. How the hell do you make people bleed?"

"Shh," I said, looking nervously at the ceiling.

Ellie looked around, panic in her eyes. "What do you mean by shushing me? Are we being watched or something? Is something going to happen to me?"

"No, no." I held my hands up placatingly. "No. It's just that there's a woman who lives on the next floor up, and if she hears us there will be questions that will be hard to answer."

If anything, Ellie's eyes got larger. She whispered, "What about the people below? Is it…everyone in the building? Do you all?" She looked around, on the verge of panic.

I got up to comfort her, but she backed up and I patted the air placatingly again. "No," I said firmly. "I'm absolutely the only person in this building who makes people bleed." That was nothing but the truth. "And there is actually just an empty floor beneath us, so no one below can hear us."

The entire empty twenty-foot space between floor ten and floor nine was just there as a buffer zone with a leaded floor for extra protection. It wasn't even numbered. We didn't need to go into all that right now, though.

Sabrina was watching us, but not stepping in, clearly seeing this as my thing.

Ellie looked slightly less panicked. She whispered again, "Do they do something else?"

"Ellie, please come sit back down." I patted the couch beside me. "I promise you're safe." She was, unless someone found out we'd told. And then she'd still be safe, really, but she'd leave the Complex thinking we'd had a brief friendship and gone our separate ways. It wouldn't hurt her. It'd hurt me a lot, though.

She complied, but perched on the edge of the couch, clearly ready to make an escape if she needed to.

"Ellie, I...I care a lot about you. I think you know this. I think you're sweet and funny and awfully cute. This"—I gestured between us—"has meant more to me than you probably know." I blushed, as if this were the hard part to admit. "You're my first, um, girlfriend, if you don't mind me calling you that." I thought briefly. "I've never had a boyfriend, either I mean. I mean, I'm not into guys at all. Okay, that was off track. What I'm trying to say is that I like you a lot and that this means a lot to me. I'm telling you this not to make you uncomfortable, but because I want you to understand that what we're telling you here is a huge deal. We're just not allowed to tell. So you can't tell anyone. I mean *anyone*. Not your mom, even. It would be bad if you did. For me. It would be really, really bad for me. And kind of bad for Sabrina, but not really bad for you." I was babbling.

Sabrina cut in, "What Joan is saying is that you're safe. You don't have to worry about yourself. The worst that will happen to you is that you'll kind of forget, not everything, really, but most of this. For us, and for Joan in particular, the repercussions of us telling you could be bad if anyone found out."

"Would they kill you?" she whispered.

"No." I shook my head. I hadn't intended to tell her about the modification of her mood and thoughts to shape her memories, or that I could end up in isolation, but I'd certainly opened the door in that direction. Fuck. I was messing this up.

"What would they do to you?"

I sighed. "People with problematic powers get put into isolation. Forever."

Her eyes widened again. "They'd lock you away?"

"It would be a very cush prison, to be fair. It's a whole apartment and I'd have electronic contact with anyone in the building and access to the internet to an extent. All the books I could ever want. And I could get seriously into video games, and they'd buy me any system I wanted, but I don't really like video games so that seems unlikely. I mean..." I trailed off hopelessly. I was getting very sidetracked, thinking about my future cush prison. It would be awful, and it was probably going to happen one way or another, but I didn't need to tell her that part.

"And they'd mess with my mind?"

"Just a little."

She laughed hollowly. "Well, then. Just a little."

"You could just leave and pretend none of this ever happened," I forced myself to say. "If you never told anyone, that would be the end of it."

She shifted and then straightened resolutely. "I do care a good deal about you, Joan, even if you're not my first girlfriend."

Now I wanted to know what other experiences she'd had.

"But I'm mad with curiosity about what is going on. Does the whole commune have powers? What kind of powers? How does this work?"

I took a deep breath. As much as I wanted to tell her and take this whole thing deeper, it was hard to tell Family secrets when it had been drilled into me my whole life that our very existence depended on it. "I'm just going to take this from the beginning, okay? So a little of it might be stuff you've already guessed or I've said."

"Okay," she said.

"Okay, so the commune thing is a bit of a cover story," I started. "We sort of are, but it's more than that. Everyone born into the Family has some degree of some power, and we come into our powers when we're eight, give or take. I was exactly eight and super lucky that Sabrina was both my friend and came into hers either at the same time or before." I told her the story of the day we figured it out and about the Family in general. "So, anyway, that's why we can't be more than fifteen feet apart," I finished.

She sat quietly. "That's a lot."

"It is," I said, on pins and needles waiting for her reaction.

"Thank you for trusting me with this."

"You're welcome." It had been a super big leap, and I was glad she realized that.

"I think I'm both glad you told me and a little freaked out."

"That's understandable," I said.

She thought for a moment. "So, do you all marry within the Family?"

I reared back a little and noticed out of the corner of my eye that Sabrina did, too, that taboo was so strong. "No!"

"Then how do you keep it a secret from the people you marry if you never tell outsiders?"

"Oh, well, eventually we do. There are steps, all of which we've bypassed here. Theresa, you met her last weekend, is Neil's girlfriend, and the fact that he brought her home is the first step toward letting her see more and more who we are."

"What if she freaks out?"

"Well, that's the thing…usually there's some mind reading involved with specific questions asked to see if the person might be open or if it would freak them out. If they don't pass that test, the relationship is over and we're not supposed to say why. If they do, they come back and there're more probing questions and maybe a little lifting of the veil, so to speak. If then, once they know more, they freak out, then there are procedures…" I trailed off.

"The making you forget thing you mentioned earlier?" she asked.

"Yeah. In addition to the mind reading, Linda can manipulate thoughts a little and Gamma, well, Gamma can manipulate mood. So, between them, they can kind of massage the experience of dating the Family member until it doesn't seem like a big deal."

"That freaks me out more than a little."

I reached over to take her hand, hoping she'd let me. She did. "I'm sorry I've brought you into this."

She interlaced her fingers with mine and straightened herself again. "If you'd told me all this that day we met on the High Line, I probably would have run. I thought you were really cute, but I didn't know you. Now, though, I know you're thoughtful, considerate, open minded, and really smart. I want to be in your life. What can I do to make things easier?"

The rush of pure relief I felt left me slumped. I closed my eyes for a moment, feeling teary. When I recovered, I said, "Thank you." I glanced over at Sabrina, who was looking out the window, trying her best to give us privacy. "The main thing is to not do anything that would mean Sabrina and I would be too far apart, and if you notice that it might happen, like today, to say something."

"Is it only distance or do things like, I don't know, walls make a difference?"

"Walls don't seem to matter." Although that made me curious whether the leaded floor would make a difference or not. Not that we could test that out with the potential danger to bystanders.

"So, like, we could be on one side of a wall while she's on the other?" Her cheeks turned pink.

"Um, yeah." I felt my cheeks heat up, too.

"Okay, good to know. And you know for sure it's fifteen feet?"

"Well," I said, "we haven't really tested it because of the possible consequences."

"That seems like good information to have, though. If it's just a matter of a nosebleed, it seems worth experimenting."

"Ah, well, it could be worse," I said. "I made my mom cough up blood once. Once my brother threw up blood. That was…that was really scary. It was the day everyone put it together that Sabrina dampened my power. The internal bleeding can be pretty bad. Plus there's the duck."

Her eyes got wide. "You think you killed that duck that was floating?"

"Pretty sure."

"Well, then, there's the answer, you can experiment."

Sabrina, now that we were away from the relationship stuff and onto how to handle things, spoke up. "We were talking about that earlier, but we didn't get far because then you texted. I don't mean anything bad by that. We just got sidetracked, I mean."

"Okay," Ellie said, "then, let's tackle this problem. Do you make all animals bleed?"

"The only verified ones are humans and ducks, but I think if it affects both of them, we can surmise that it affects all animals, really. I mean, humans and ducks don't have that much in common genetically," I said.

"So, mice, maybe," Sabrina said.

"I don't want to kill mice." I hung my head.

"It'd be better to know what you're working with, though," Ellie argued.

"Yeah, it might be better to kill mice in order to keep people safer," said Sabrina.

"How will it keep people safer to know that I can kill mice at thirty feet, though?

"What if it's one hundred feet?" Sabrina asked. "Then even an isolation unit wouldn't work."

"Oh, that's fucking great. You're saying that if I can kill people at one hundred feet, then when they decide that Isabella needs you, they'll just kill me. I'm not sure I want to know that."

"Don't you want to know before you actually kill someone, though?" Sabrina cocked her head at me.

She was right. I'd rather just die than kill off Linda and everyone who happened to be on floor nine and above (unless the leaded floor worked) when Sabrina got more than fifteen feet away from me. "Fuck," I whispered.

"Wait. Wait. What? They'd kill you?" Ellie looked panicky again.

"They might if the alternative is me killing or seriously harming people, yeah. But if we know, it's possible something else could be worked out. Like maybe a cabin out in the middle of nowhere that…" But no. How would they deliver supplies? I guess if they put them far enough away and I collected them, it could work. What about whatever wildlife strayed into my kill zone, though? If my power extended more than thirty feet and if the Family decided Isabella was the priority, they'd likely kill me. Or if they knew it would be a death sentence, maybe they'd put Isabella in isolation instead so I could live and Sabrina and I could go on as we were. I honestly didn't know. Gamma, of course, would campaign for me and, frankly, Sabrina, but the Family came first. We all knew this. Fuck.

Sabrina must have been going through the same thought process because she said, "They might make a different choice if they knew that making me pair up with Isabella would mean a death sentence."

"What is that about? Pairing up with Isabella? Why?" Ellie looked between us.

"Isabella is a mind reader. So far, her powers are sporadic and there is hope that she'll get control over it," I said.

"Why would she need to go into isolation because of mind reading? I mean, I can see how people might not want to be around her, but it doesn't physically hurt anyone. Why would they isolate her?"

I glanced up at the ceiling involuntarily. "Mind readers find it hard to be around other people. I've never heard of a mind reader who could control when they heard, so they just hear too much and it's overwhelming." I pointed at the ceiling. "Linda lives up there and has since she was eight. She just started hearing everyone's thoughts and couldn't control it and it freaked her out. We've offered to take her out, but I suspect she has strong agoraphobia now and she declined."

"I imagine she does, being locked in up there since she was eight! How does she get food and stuff?" Ellie asked.

"There's a regular delivery via a dumbwaiter," Sabrina said. "And she can ask for anything she wants and generally gets it."

Ellie shuddered. "And they'd do that to Isabella?"

"Or me. Unless I'll kill people anyway," I said.

Ellie stared at me. "This is brutal."

"But necessary." It sucked that killing people was sometimes a necessity. But if it was one person or a lot of people, I did get why the Family made that choice. I just didn't want it applied to me, not when there was an alternative. The fact that they might anyway… Well, that was a lot to deal with. I pushed it aside to contemplate later.

"And this is why we should go test this out. You should see how far and if you can control it. If you practiced…"

Sabrina was right. People did get better at using their skills when they actually used their skills. Metal benders like my mother were dangerous, too. After all, we lived in a steel framed building. She'd discovered her power on a needle, so she'd had time to hone her control and skill before it got strong enough that she'd have affected the girders. So, if I could really practice, then maybe I could get control.

"You're right. The biggest problem I'm seeing, though, is how to keep you safe once we're fifteen feet apart, but not into the safe zone."

She mulled it over, then suggested. "We run. We go to fifteen feet, then just run in opposite directions. I might get a little nosebleed or something, but it wouldn't be bad."

With that, we switched into problem solving mode, coming up with ways to practice and to test my limits. The three of us talked it out, came up with possible problems, and then brainstormed potential solutions.

It was getting late when we got to a point where I felt like I was willing to try our plan. "Okay, Sabrina, let's do this next weekend."

Ellie said, "Wait. What about me? I'm a part of this now. I want to go, too."

My knee-jerk reaction was to say no way. I was not going to put her in danger, but then I realized she could just stay out of my even expanded possible range and be there before Sabrina and I parted. I looked at Sabrina, who shrugged her willingness. I turned back to Ellie. "Okay."

"Really? Just okay? I figured there'd be a battle." She grinned.

I shrugged. "I want to spend time with you, and I don't see why it would be dangerous as long as we take some simple precautions, so okay."

Her grin morphed into a smile. I leaned over and kissed her smiling lips. I didn't linger, though. Sabrina was sitting right there. As always, but she was just sitting there, paying attention.

"Okay, then," I said when I sat back. "It's a plan."

CHAPTER THIRTEEN

Sabrina leaned forward from the back seat between Ellie and me. "So, I had to turn Paul down for a date for this."

"Why didn't you just invite him?" Ellie asked.

I took my eyes off the road long enough to give her a *think about it* look. She said, "Oh, right. I guess you'd have had to tell him, then. And you won't be doing that?"

"No," Sabrina scoffed. "I don't want to marry the dude, just bang him maybe."

Ellie reared back.

I took a hand off the wheel to quickly pat her leg, then put it back. I could drive, but it wasn't like I got a ton of practice, living in New York, and I was a little bit of a nervous driver. Sabrina was no better a driver, and was easily distracted, so I was driving. "Don't worry. We don't have to get married. However, traditionally people don't find out about the powers unless that's where you're headed."

"Since we're keeping it a secret, you could keep it a secret that Paul knows, too," Ellie suggested.

"No." Sabrina shook her head. "I'm not that serious about him."

I felt Ellie look at me, then away.

I stared straight ahead at the road and said, "I'm pretty serious about you, but I'm not going to ask you to marry me. We're only seventeen."

Almost too quietly for me to hear, she said, "I really like you, too."

"Good, good, so everyone likes each other," Sabrina said. "I think we knew that last weekend when she spilled the beans."

"Way to let us have a moment, Sabrina," I said sarcastically.

"You two are nothing but moments," she said flippantly, and who could blame her? She was putting up with a lot with this relationship. "When are we stopping for snacks? Gamma gave us the credit card."

"For gas," I pointed out, but not too seriously.

"So, we buy snacks from a gas station, obviously," Sabrina said.

"Shouldn't we at least be buying some gas, too?"

"Sure. We can. Look—we're at half a tank, that's plenty of room for gas."

She wasn't wrong, so I pulled off the highway at the next service station. Given our limitations, we all stood around while Sabrina pumped the gas. She enjoyed it for reasons that were beyond me, then we moved the car and went in to look around.

"Get whatever you want. The Family is paying," Sabrina told Ellie.

She seemed reticent, but I reiterated that was true.

"But why?" she asked.

"Because when we went to Gamma to tell her our plan to experiment with my powers, she thought that was a great idea. She also agreed that summer camp was the place to do it to minimize risk, so she gave us permission to use a Family car and a Family credit card."

"Not, like, her personal credit card?" Ellie clarified.

"No. It's on the Family, and the Family is rolling in it," Sabrina said.

"When you went to tell her about this experiment…you didn't tell her about me, right?" Ellie asked.

"No, no. Of course not. I mean, I have told her about you. Like that…" I blushed. Should I not have told Gamma about Ellie? No. We were clearly girlfriends now, given everything I'd told her. "I told her that we were, um, dating. I didn't tell her about you coming this weekend or that I'd told you Family secrets. That would have gotten me in a lot of hot water, to say the least."

"I see." Ellie glanced at Sabrina, then back at me. She took my hand. "I told my mom about you, too. I mean, the dating part."

We shared a sappy look, which Sabrina broke by loudly rustling a bag of chips she'd picked up. "Time and place, people. Time and place."

We each chose drinks and an assortment of salty and sweet snacks. When Ellie and I both reached for black licorice, Sabrina rolled her eyes. "Gross. You two are made for each other."

Ellie and I smiled at each other. "Should we just get one to share?" Ellie asked.

I shrugged. "Sure. We can always stop for another bag on the way home."

Ellie pointed at me. "Good thinking."

Back in the car, Ellie asked, "Do you really have camp at this summer camp?"

"Yup," Sabrina said. We did. The kids had a two-week camp every summer, and there were Family weeks and weekends over the summer that were optional but encouraged.

"But it's also so we have options—a place to go in case of emergency," I added.

"What kind of emergency are we talking about?" Ellie asked.

"Anything from someone having a power that time in nature might help, to us all needing to hide out for a while due to a natural disaster," I said. "The Family likes to be prepared. There are enough cabins for everyone there, and everyone who can drive learns. Some of the precogs can't because they have too many episodes."

"You have precogs?"

"We may be getting into territory you don't really need to know," Sabrina warned.

I rolled my eyes. "Like it matters. In for a penny, in for a pound, really."

"Whatever," Sabrina said.

"So, precognition is the most common power. Precogs can see

into the future in bits and pieces. The more powerful ones see long sequences, but some people just see bits and pieces that aren't super useful. Precogs pass the easiest, because it just looks like an absence seizure—like they're daydreaming, but you can't break them out of it—when they're having a vision. But a precog without control and frequent episodes isn't safe to drive. Of course, all the non-Family spouses can drive. Anyway, even though a lot of teens in New York just don't get their licenses, that isn't an option for us, because it's one of the safety precautions for the whole Family. In theory, we can get people out of the city if necessary."

"In reality, though, if it were a disaster where everyone is fleeing the city, it'd be like *The Stand*. Have you read it?" Sabrina, still between our seats, shuddered. "We'd all get stuck in a tunnel or on a bridge."

"Yeah, New York is a death trap for the end of the world," Ellie agreed.

"So, this is cheery," I said.

"Says the person who kills just by being around," Sabrina said.

While it was the kind of teasing we did with each other all the time, I felt raw about it just then. Up until three weeks or so ago, we just joked. We were going to be an us forever and that was just how it was. I would go around killing people otherwise. Our lives might be strange, but we were living them and doing okay. Now everything was blowing up and I was feeling sensitive. Not to mention that we had a dozen mice in a box in the back that were destined to die or at least suffer today. Well, hopefully they wouldn't suffer too much. In addition to searching out where to buy feeder mice, we'd also done some research on pain meds for pets. I didn't know the details of how Gamma got the drugs, but we'd asked for her help because they were a veterinarian prescribed thing, and she'd produced them a couple days later. We'd be giving each mouse a treat with a mix of sedatives and muscle relaxers. Still. "Ouch."

"Really?" Sabrina asked.

I nodded, teary. "I think I can't handle the teasing considering"—I waved my hand in the air briefly before putting it back on the steering wheel—"everything."

"Okay," she said.

"Thanks."

"You guys are so good at communicating. I mean, I've never seen anything like it, and my mom and I talk about everything. Except what you told me," she hastened to add. "I haven't told even her, and I won't. But you guys just say what you need from the other and there it is."

"We've had to get good at it because we can't take breaks from each other," I said.

"Although sometimes we both put on our headphones and turn our backs on each other for a while," Sabrina said.

"We do do that," I agreed.

"I think it's partially this open communication thing that is why I told you," I mused.

Sabrina said, "That actually makes total sense. You don't know how to have a close relationship without open communication."

"And you do?" I laughed at her.

"I probably need open communication in a close relationship, too. I'm just not there yet. Plus, we're going to get you all trained up so that we can live our individual lives so when I find my life partner in Guam or something, I can have open communication without having to explain why my cousin has to be within fifteen feet of me at all times." She paused and when she started talking again, she sounded a little sad and a little resigned. "Or it'll be about Isabella, not you." She leaned her head on my shoulder.

"I'm sorry," I said, meaning that I was sorry that she was so valuable to the Family that she might not ever get to live her dreams, tethered to me or not.

She sighed. "It is what it is."

❖

"So sixty feet, then, I guess," I said, looking down at a mouse who was still alive, unlike the one at fifty feet, but bleeding. We were on the summer camp's game field, surrounded by trees. Just off down a couple of paths we could barely make out some cabins if we really looked. It would have been idyllic aside from the dead mice in cages.

"Although you seem to kill mice easier than people." Sabrina had red-rimmed nostrils and her eyes were bloodshot.

"Yeah, so maybe I'll only kill people who stay in the twenty-feet zone too long. Or, heck, maybe if they're there long enough, I can kill to forty feet," I said bleakly.

Ellie hugged me from the side. "We're going to figure this out." She'd stayed well out of range the whole time and was not bleeding.

"I don't know how, when I'm probably killing Sabrina slowly with each try," I said. This was our second go. We'd only put mice out to forty feet the first time, which was clearly an underestimation.

"Okay." Sabrina put her hands on her hips. "First of all, I'm fine. This little amount of blood isn't going to kill me."

"You don't know," I protested. "Who knows what's happening internally?"

"Wouldn't I feel it?" she asked.

"Not necessarily. What if you have blood in your stool, then what? We can't keep doing this."

"But you say that people can get control, right?" Ellie said. "How do they do that?"

"Practice," Sabrina said.

"But I can't practice," I said. I stood there, dejected for a moment. "We are also taught skills like concentration, focus, and that kind of thing through meditation and stuff."

"And you rock at it," Sabrina said. "So, yeah. You should sit down and meditate instead of running away, which is signaling to your body that you should be panicking, which is probably making things worse."

So, we set up again, this time with just one mouse forty feet out from where I'd be sitting. Ellie got clear and I went to sit down and meditate. It was really hard because I kept listening for Sabrina leaving, worried about hurting her. I made two more mice bleed and then we were down to three mice that I'd already made bleed, so it would be difficult to differentiate new bleeding from old.

"Well, that was a long drive for not much," I said, gloomily.

"And what do we do with these bleeding mice? Releasing them seems cruel, but I don't know what else to do with them."

"They're not bleeding anymore," Ellie pointed out, looking at them. "And they're moving around some. Releasing them is probably the best thing."

"But not near our food stores," Sabrina said, unusually practical. "Also, it wasn't for nothing. For one, we've pinned down that I have a twenty-foot zone, so that gives us a little more space."

"That's true. I hope our food stores are better protected than what these three little guys can get into, but okay. Also, we should give them the chance to wake up from the drugs a little. We'll release them on the way home," I said.

It was a two-and-a-half-hour drive and we'd left home at nine that morning. With a couple of stops on the way and then the experimenting, it was now one. "Should we get lunch on the way back or stop for gas station snacks again?" I asked.

"Do we have to leave right away?" Ellie asked. "It's lovely here. We should walk around or something."

So we did. Sabrina and I showed Ellie the cabins, including the one where we always slept in the bunk bed near the door. We'd used a Sharpie to draw a stylized *J* and *S* together in a way that couldn't one hundred percent be said to be our initials because technically, we weren't supposed to do that, but there were a lot of marks, so it was never exactly investigated closely. I say *we* but it was really Sabrina, as she was the artistic one.

We went to the lake, where we had a rock skipping contest. Sabrina and I had had a lot of practice, and I won number of skips with six, but Sabrina got furthest skip. Ellie picked up a big rock and tossed it underhand with both hands. "I guess that means I win biggest splash." We all laughed.

We went to the playground and swung on the swings, all trying to stay in sync, which sort of worked. Ellie surprised us by dismounting with an actual flip, which was pretty amazing and quite a surprise, considering that she was again wearing one of her signature dresses. When we'd left that morning and I commented on the fact that she was wearing a dress to the woods, she pointed

out that she was wearing boots with it, which was more than the
sneakers Sabrina and I had on, and she'd lifted the dress a little
to show black bicycle-type shorts underneath. That little lift had
been…interesting. Sabrina and I clapped and cheered, so Ellie gave
a little curtsy. It was very cute, so I kissed her.

Eventually, though, we had to go. We were getting hungry, and
I didn't love driving after dark. So we piled into the Jeep and drove
about twenty minutes before pulling over and releasing the mice.

"Good luck, little dudes or dudettes," I said.

We drove through a Taco Bell, because we were starting to feel
like we should be getting home, and ate on the road.

"So, next time," Ellie said, "maybe we should make it so you
can't hear Sabrina leaving. She could wait until you're super zenned
out and then sneak away. You should wear earplugs."

"Next time? I don't know. I really don't want to hurt Sabrina
anymore." I didn't look at either of them. "She won't know by
looking at me that I'm truly calm."

"You haven't really hurt me yet," Sabrina said.

I protested again. "We don't know!"

Sabrina sighed. "What if we take equipment to monitor your
state? Like, you know, those heart rate monitors and brain wave
things we use sometimes in meditation classes. Gamma would let
us borrow it."

So, we went back to brainstorming solutions for practice.

CHAPTER FOURTEEN

"So, we want to try monitoring my meditative state," I said to Gamma over Chinese takeout the week after our first experiments. "Can we take a heart rate monitor and one of those biofeedback headbands?"

Gamma thought for a minute. "Take one of the pulse ox rings and a biofeedback headband instead. You just put an app on your phone for both of them and the pulse ox will give you a little more information. This is really good, my girls. I think you can figure this out."

Her words gave me hope.

"Can you do us another favor?" Sabrina asked. "We don't want to tell our parents what we're doing…I don't even know why, but we don't. Will you tell them you have a project for us to work on up at summer camp and that it'll keep us busy for the next few weekends?"

"I can do that," Gamma said. "I think you should keep the circle small. I worry that the Council will get wind of your experiments and shut them down out of worry that you're endangering Sabrina when they have uses for her."

And that was the reason exactly right there. "I worry I'll endanger her, too." I hung my head.

Gamma patted my hand. "And that is why you two will take every precaution, because I know it's vitally important to you to keep her safe. The rest of the Council might not be so convinced. I think that meditation is the right track. Okay." She brushed her hands together twice. "I'll tell your parents you have a project and you can stay for whole weekends, then, but I'm a little worried about you two out there alone in case something goes wrong. Maybe you should let Heather in on the secret, if you think she's trustworthy."

We looked at each other, then quickly away, but Gamma picked up on it. "Girls? What have you been up to?"

"Nothing. Just, yeah, we were thinking about telling Heather but didn't know if it was a good idea. If you think it is, then okay," I rambled.

Gamma narrowed her eyes at us, but let it go. "All right, then. I'll tell each of your parents and Heather's that there's a project up at summer camp I want you three to work on and you'll spend the next three weekends up there. I want to hear about your progress every week. Call me if anything comes up over the weekends, as well. Use the landline."

Well, it looked like Heather was going to be coming along, too.

"Be of good cheer, my girls. I have faith in you," Gamma said as we left.

We volunteered in the daycare the next day, taking Isabella along. She wasn't careful about staying within the twenty-feet range, and when Ian was sobbing, she announced that he wanted Harper to give back the fire truck he had been playing with. Sasha, the primary daycare provider, gave her a funny look. I worried that either we'd be asked not to come back or that Isabella would be told she had to keep within twenty feet at all times. That wouldn't be too bad, except that we wanted to have our lunches with Gamma without bringing Isabella. There were things she didn't need to know. No sense in her knowing that her very existence as a mind reader meant the end of the world as Sabrina and I knew it, and that we looked at her as a ticking time bomb.

"So, we can't take Ellie anymore," Sabrina said later that night when we were alone in her room, each sitting on our own beds, facing each other.

I nodded gloomily. That did seem to be the case. I was sad about that, though. I'd really enjoyed having her along, but the only way we could take her now was to tell Heather that we'd told Ellie.

Goodness, these secrets were getting seriously tangled. "I already texted her. We're both pretty bummed about it."

"I know, but if we make you safe, then you'll get to spend all the time you want with your girlfriend."

"And if we don't, I'll never see her again."

"I'd call you a drama queen, but that's probably true. So, let's hang out with her as much as we can when we're in town. Or we can revisit the running away idea. Maybe she'd like to run away with us?" Sabrina mused.

"I think she likes her mom too much to go join the witness protection program."

"That's too bad." She paused. "I would miss people, too."

"Yeah."

"But I'd miss you more if you had to be locked away."

"You could visit."

"I guess I could. But with what we know about your range now...you wouldn't be isolated enough up on eleven. They'd have to build you a cabin out in the summer camp and airlift you supplies or something."

"While I'm out there killing any animal that strays in."

Sabrina got off her bed and joined me on mine. "That's not going to happen. We're going to get you trained."

I mused. "I have a question, though. If we think I can control this through meditation, then what happens when we sleep? I mean, we can basically turn off powers while meditating. So, when we sleep, are you still dampening? You fall asleep before me sometimes or I wake up earlier. Why don't I kill people then?"

"It's a good point, really," she said, tilting her head this way and that while she thought. "But I think meditating doesn't necessarily turn powers off. If it did, it wouldn't be a useful tool to control powers. Your mom doesn't go around bending metal in the middle of the night. Maybe mine is just always there, like a—I don't know—white noise machine that's plugged in and turned on. Your power, though, is more like your mom's or Neil's. Once they got control over their powers, they decide when to use them, and of course, no one is using a power while they sleep, just like people don't walk around while they sleep, just because they have that ability. But we always breathe, and mine is more like that."

"Some people do walk in their sleep. That's what we call sleep-walking," I said extremely pedantically.

She hit me. "You know what I mean. Luckily you don't seem to be a sleepwalker."

"If we're going with the breathing analogy, people can hold their breath or change their breathing patterns. What if you can turn yours on and off, too, if you think about it?"

"Maybe that's something to play with out at summer camp, too, but right now I don't think it's the most important thing."

"I guess you're right."

"You know it. So, text your girl. See if she wants to come over for a movie or something after practice tomorrow night."

I toyed with my phone. "Am I being stupid? I shouldn't be worrying about dating right now. Why did I even tell her? I should have just broken it off."

Sabrina huffed. "First off, you told her and that's that. Second, you're not being stupid. I've seen you two together. You just fit. She even took this whole thing more or less in stride and only wants to help. Plus, if—if!—you end up in isolation, you'll have had at least this."

Still feeling sorry for myself, I said, "Or now I'll know what I am missing out on whereas if I'd never met her, I might take better to isolation."

"Well, too late now," Sabrina said, then pointed at my phone and demanded, "Text her."

I did and we ended up setting two dates. She was coming over to watch *Salt*, another action film starring Angelina Jolie, apparently, on Friday after practice. And we were also going to go for a walk Thursday. I suggested a double date, but Sabrina said no. She said it was fun with Paul, but he wasn't endgame, so she was just letting it go.

"What about inviting Heather along, then?" I suggested. "Then you'd have someone to, you know, talk to and stuff."

Sabrina smirked "And leave you and your girl as alone as possible?"

"I mean, maybe a little," I admitted.

"Okay, just remember to tell her not to mention anything about stuff she's not supposed to know in front of Heather."

"I'm sure she knows, but I'll mention it."

❖

I texted Ellie.

Joan: *Sabrina and I are stopping for a juice on the way. We're picking one up for Heather, too. Want one?*
Ellie: *Sure. Surprise me.*

We were meeting back on the High Line, the original meeting place, for our walk. I was curious how it was going to go seeing Paul, but we avoided the issue by going in just before his shift was scheduled to start. Then we got the joy of each carrying two cups of juice/smoothies on the subway. Perhaps we should have planned a little differently, like, say, getting the juices at the other end of the subway ride. Finally, though, we made it where we found Ellie and Heather together.

Ellie smiled and gave me a kiss when I walked up. I was a fan of that greeting.

"Hi. Berry Colada smoothie or Green Dream juice?"

"I'll take the smoothie," she said. "Unless you want it."

"No, I'm good with either." I handed her the smoothie. Only then did I turn my attention to Heather to say hi and saw she was standing there, looking cross and worried.

"What's up?" I asked. I looked to Sabrina to see if she had any clue and she just shrugged at me. I looked back at Heather, who was holding the drink Sabrina had carried over for her. "If you don't want the PB Punch smoothie, you can have the Green Dream juice and I'll take the smoothie."

She glared back at me. "Come on, you two, we need to talk for a minute. Sorry, Ellie, we'll be right back." She grabbed my arm and started walking away, leaving Sabrina no choice but to follow. Just out of earshot, she turned to us and hissed, "You told her?"

You could have knocked me down with a feather. Why would Ellie have told? We'd just talked about how important it was that she kept the secret. I couldn't believe she'd have turned right around and casually mentioned to Heather that she knew the Family secret. I looked over my shoulder back to where she stood. I couldn't see the expression on her face from the distance, but her body language looked bewildered. She was facing us, free hand a little out, head cocked. She didn't have the look of someone who'd just spilled the beans.

I turned back. Sabrina was just standing there, mouth opening and closing, like she was trying to come up with something to say. I decided to bluff it out. "Why would you assume that?"

"I am not assuming anything, Joan! I heard it loud and clear!" And there was something about the way she said heard that made me realize what was going on.

"You're a mind reader," I hissed. I tried to whisper it and I also wanted to shout it, so it came out as a hiss. "Heather! How? What? You're a precog!"

Heather hung her head. "This is why I didn't tell people. I let everyone think I was a minor precog because even you think I'm a freak."

"No." I put my hand on her arm. "I don't. Of course I don't. I'm one of Linda's only friends, and we love Isabella. And for that matter, we hang out with Gamma. Who else does that? I don't think you're a freak. I'm just surprised. How have you…"

"Pulled it off? That's a story for another moment, with Ellie over there, waiting."

Sabrina crossed her arms, drink still dangling from one arm. "You're the one who dragged us over here while she's over there, looking at us like we're a bunch of weirdos."

Heather threw one hand up, the one not holding her smoothie.

"Fine! If she knows anyway, then let's bring her into this. I just am so used to secrecy. Wait. How much does she know? Does she even know that mind reading is a possibility? Will she freak out about me now? No, we can't tell her."

"What are we going to tell her about why you dragged us over here?" I asked. "No. Enough. She knows stuff and she's been good about not freaking out. She's a part of this. Also, she went with us last weekend and now can come again if we're open about this, so she's in." After my impassioned speech, though, I started to feel like it was stupid. No way was Heather going to agree to tell my girlfriend her secret, but I hid my self-doubt and put my free hand on my hip.

"Fine." Heather turned and walked back toward Ellie, leaving Sabrina and me gaping at one another before we hurried after her.

"We should go somewhere we can talk more privately," Heather said as soon as we all got back by Ellie. "There are things that need to be said."

Ellie tentatively said, "My place is closer than you guys'. My mom isn't home."

"Fine," Heather said again.

In a charged quiet, we made our way to Ellie's, with her and me in the lead and Sabrina and Heather following. Ellie lived on the third floor of a walk-up, so we trudged up the stairs in the same formation. Everyone was still carrying their beverages, even though they were a good forty-five minutes past being fresh at this point.

Ellie unlocked the door and gestured for us to come in. We entered into a small, slightly messy living room. There was a couch, a coffee table, and an entertainment center that doubled as storage. There were books and knickknacks in some of the cubbies, but there were also some cubbies that just held a collection of random objects. The coffee table held a couple magazines, an abandoned glass, and what looked like Ellie's homework. There was a blanket tossed haphazardly on the back of the couch and a sweater lying on it. When we walked in, a cat jumped up from the couch and ran off through an open door, presumably to a bedroom.

"That must have been Squish," I said.

"Yeah, he's shy." She'd told me that before, but I supposed it was for the benefit of the others. "Sorry about the mess."

"What mess?" Heather asked. "Just looks like someone lives here to me." She set her backpack down and sat on the couch.

Ellie picked up the sweater and tossed it through the same doorway as the cat. The couch was a three-seater, so Ellie sat on the floor. I felt weird about sitting on the couch with both Heather and Sabrina while she sat on the floor opposite us, so I joined her. Sabrina sat next to Heather.

"So…" Ellie said.

No one seemed to know how to start, and poor Ellie didn't even really know what this was about. "Heather knows you know," I said to her.

"What?" Ellie looked shocked, which wasn't a surprise, given how I swore her to secrecy multiple times. "How? Why? Did you tell her?"

I shook my head.

Heather sighed. "I understand that you know there are mind readers in the Family, right?"

Ellie nodded slowly. "Are you a mind reader? I thought…" She trailed off. She thought that there were only two, just like the rest of us.

"Apparently, Heather has been keeping some secrets of her own," Sabrina said. "So we're all kind of in the same boat, but the secrets are spilling over."

"What kind of analogy is that?" Heather asked.

Sabrina waved her hands. "It doesn't matter. Just tell us how you've kept this secret. How have you coped?"

"Have you just had control over it from the beginning?" I asked, thinking about Isabella and how that could happen with her, which would take some pressure off me, although if I could learn control, that would free up both Sabrina and me, so it was worth trying even if Isabella learned control on her own. Also, though, how had she possibly kept this a secret when she was eight when it came on?

We'd been friends for a long time, and she'd never seemed to read minds. Of course, she wouldn't around us anyway.

"Well, as with most of us, I was eight. I got lucky, I guess, because the first mind I read was Desiree's." She looked at Ellie and explained, "She's my older sister. She was twenty-one at the time. She came home for a visit, I hugged her and I said, *Who's Max?* Our mom was in the room and she looked at me curiously, but Desiree just said, *I'll tell you more later.* She turned to Mom and said, *Girl talk.* Honestly, I thought she'd said aloud something like, *I don't want to have to bring Max here.* Turns out, I'd read her mind. I've always had to touch people for it to work, so it's easier for me to manage than for Linda, I guess."

"But why didn't you just say you were a mind reader? You'd be, like, super valuable, especially if you could be out and about. I mean, you are super valuable," Sabrina said.

"Right, and how is being super valuable working out for you?" I asked. I looked at Heather and gave her a nod. "I'm just surprised you had the wherewithal to keep it to yourself at eight."

"I wouldn't have if it weren't for Desiree. She explained that it would be really hard, that lots of the Family wouldn't want me around because they'd be worried about me reading their minds. She also told me…"

When she didn't go on, I asked, "What? What did she tell you?"

"She told me we weren't actually biological full sisters."

"Did they use a different sperm donor than Desiree's dad?" I was confused. Desiree's dad, who had been the Family-born parent, had died in a car accident when she was ten. Their mom wanted another child, and because of the Family sperm bank, she could have one who was a full sibling.

"No. I mean, it was Dad, but they actually used someone else's egg. I don't think Mom knows. Desiree knows because of her power. She used to eavesdrop a lot when she was young."

"What's her power?" Ellie, who'd been listening to all this raptly, asked.

Heather turned to her. "She can alter visual perceptions. It's overstating it to say that she can become invisible or make something else invisible, but she can make it so it's easy to overlook her or whatever she's trying to get someone to overlook." She turned back to Sabrina and me. "She liked to try to see what she could get away with and she overheard some Council members who were pretty sure they were alone talking about trying to blend Dad's power line—altering perceptions and mood—with Linda's—mind reading."

To say I was shocked was a dramatic understatement. We'd been deeply ingrained with the idea that you didn't marry within the family because of inbreeding, so to hear that they were purposefully doing so and not even telling people was seriously mind boggling. Sabrina, though, clearly reacted with more anger than shock. "What the actual fuck? That's gross! And lying about it? That's really fucked up!"

"I know," Heather said simply. "Desiree didn't tell me all this at the time, but she must have been watching for my power to develop ever since hearing that conversation. She told me right away to pretend I was one of the unhelpful precogs. When my mom questioned me further at the time, I said I'd seen Desiree meet someone named Max the next week, and Des backed me up."

"Why haven't you ever said anything? That shit needs to stop," Sabrina said.

"You two always toed the Family line. I didn't think you'd be open to hearing negative stuff about the Council. You're so close with Jenny." Gamma's given name was Jenny, and she was also Heather's great-aunt. It was people with valuable powers who often ended up running the Council.

"I get where you're coming from. This clearly shows that we're open to questioning some of the way the Family does stuff." I moved my hand in a circle to indicate all of us. "I'd like to think, though, that if you'd told us this stuff, we'd have reacted the same before now."

"Sure," Heather said. "Maybe, but I didn't know that."

We sat quietly for a few moments, all absorbing these new revelations.

"So," I said slowly, "I think that what we need to do is get my stuff figured out so I'm not a liability, and then grow up and take over."

"Fuck growing up. Let's just take over," Sabrina said.

I had a little more complex feelings than Sabrina seemed to about how messed up or not the Family and particularly the Council were. We had a fairly good system. I liked being kind of socialist. I liked the collectiveness of the Family. I found this news offensive, though. And if they did this kind of thing, what else did they do?

"Yeah," Heather said. "Desiree says she'll never have kids. She doesn't want them growing up in a system that would do this to anyone. Also, they started asking her to donate eggs when she was a teenager. It's kind of fucked."

Sabrina and I exchanged a look. Sabrina finally said, "They've been bugging me about that, too."

There was another pause, then I said, "Sabrina, why is your dad a precog?"

"What do you mean? It's the most common."

"I know, but he comes from a line of manipulators. Mood, materials, presumably something to do with blood." I touched a hand to my chest. "Usually manipulators don't produce precogs."

Sabrina and Heather both sat up straighter.

Sabrina said, "Are you saying that we're not really cousins? That Dad isn't biologically Gamma's son?"

"I'm saying maybe not." Then I thought about it more. "Although manipulating actual physical things might be the part that's different. I mean, maybe it's more likely that a mood manipulator would produce a precog than a metal manipulator. Maybe it's my mom who isn't biologically Gamma's daughter."

We sat and pondered the possibilities for a few moments, then Ellie kind of raised her hand. "I know I'm not really a part of this, but I think it's messed up what they're doing. Strange things with breeding, sometimes killing people, isolating people, messing with people's memories...God, all of that sounds really bad when I say it like that." She stopped and considered. "But I think I really mean this next part. I also think the community you guys have and the way each Family member is supported—unless they're killed or something—man, I just can't get past that—is something I wish we saw in larger society. So, you guys just have to grow up, take over, and make the Family what you want it to be."

That echoed my thoughts so closely that I couldn't help but scoot closer and take Ellie's hand. "That's exactly what I've been thinking."

"And I still think we need to do it now," Sabrina said. "Before more people get hurt."

"But how?" I asked.

"We speak up at a Family meeting," Heather suggested. "With Sabrina there, near Jenny, she can't manipulate mood, so we just tell everyone."

"I suspect most adults know," I said. They both looked really disgruntled. I held up my hands, palms out. "I'm not saying we don't make changes. We do. We just have to get there. We have to get to a point where people will actually listen to us." I stopped and considered what I was actually saying. Was I really saying that we should wait to make positive change until we were some mysterious age that was old enough? Was that what I really believed? "Actually, no. I'm wrong about that. By the time we're to an age where we might be taken seriously, we might either be disillusioned or talked into accepting the status quo until some future unspecified time, or we might just withdraw nearly completely from the Family like Desiree. Okay, I think we should bring this up at a Family meeting and we can talk strategy and what we want to accomplish exactly later. But first, no one will listen to me if I have a wild power I can't control. Let's figure me out."

Sabrina gave a little whoop. "Okay! Let's fix the world!"

Heather said, "Or at least start with the Family." But she was smiling.

Ellie squeezed my hand and smiled at me. "I'm with you. Let's get you sorted."

CHAPTER FIFTEEN

"You did it!" Sabrina cheered loudly, startling me out of a deep meditation.

I pulled an earplug out. "You left?" I asked, excited when I realized what she was saying. "And no bleeding?"

"I did! No bleeding!" Sabrina was practically jumping up and down. Off at a distance, I could see Heather and Ellie jumping up and down, too.

I looked down at the mouse in the cage by my knee. It was definitely alive and still very white. That was such a relief, I nearly slumped when the feeling rolled over me, but then I caught Sabrina's excited mood and jumped up to hug her and dance a little, too.

"Okay, okay. Now we need to try the next phase," I said.

"Yeah, but tomorrow," Sabrina said. "We should celebrate and relax."

She wasn't wrong. It was Saturday and we'd driven up that morning, then I'd tried to meditate nearly all day. We had the monitoring devices, but still, when I'd hear Sabrina move, adrenaline would jolt me out of meditation, which aborted each effort. After several rounds of that, we decided to try earplugs. We hadn't thought to bring any, but Heather said that she was pretty sure there was a supply of them in the medical room, because she and her mom had been given earplugs once when they were sharing a cabin with another small family and the mom in that family snored to raise the roof. We'd used the keys Gamma had sent with us to open the room and search for the earplugs, which were there. Then we set back up.

It must have been super boring for Ellie and Heather, standing over one hundred feet away, watching the excitement of me meditating and Sabrina sneaking away. It wasn't super late, only midafternoon, but I was sure we were all ready for something different. I was stiff from sitting myself.

"I think we all need ice cream sandwiches to start," I said. We'd used the credit card Gamma gave us to pick up some supplies at a grocery store on the way up, in addition to our gas station treats. Granted, what we'd purchased wasn't much healthier, as we'd gone for ice cream sandwiches for snacks, frozen pizza for dinner, and pastries and orange juice (my pick) for breakfast. The kitchen was stocked with coffee for the others. We were planning on fast food for lunch or dinner on the way home.

Sabrina pointed at me. "Now you're talking."

As we walked over to the others, Sabrina slung her arm around my shoulders. "I'm so proud of you. My little girl, getting to be so grown."

I laughed. "Very funny. You're three months younger than me."

"But we all know I'm the mature one."

We both laughed at that.

Ellie and Heather met us halfway while we were still laughing, and there were hugs and high fives. They agreed with the ice cream sandwich idea. It was a warm spring day, making ice cream extra appealing.

We wandered the property while we ate, talking about how excited we were that I was making progress, and about the next phase.

"So, we agree, right, that once Sabrina has snuck away, we tell you so you come out of the meditation and then try to control the power?" Ellie said.

I nodded, but a little reluctantly. I didn't want to kill more mice. I didn't even have to say it aloud, because the others knew how I felt about it.

Heather said, "Better mice than people." Which was true, but also unhelpful. I wouldn't kill people if Sabrina and I just always stayed together.

Sabrina was more helpful. "Listen, we know that your basic way of being isn't making animals or people bleed. We know this because nothing happened when you were meditating. So, you probably do it when you're scared or amped up in some way." That was a polite way of saying that I'd been in a state of excitement about Ellie that day on the bridge in Central Park. "If you can stay calm, you won't kill the mouse. And you can stay calm, J, I know you can. You won't be in any danger of hurting any of us, so just focus on that. You can do it."

It was that sentiment that made me stop in my tracks. "I want to try it. Right now. I don't want to wait until tomorrow."

We turned and went back to the field. On the way, I said, "Wait. How are you guys going to let me know Sabrina is clear without startling me?"

"We could text you and you could have your cell phone on vibrate," Ellie said.

"We don't have cell service," I reminded her.

"Oh, right," she said. "Um…"

"How about we use a Bluetooth speaker to play soothing music?" Heather said.

"That won't work well with the earplugs," I said. "What if I put in my earbuds instead and then Sabrina plays music on them once she's clear? Also, why didn't we think of earbuds instead of wasting time looking for earplugs?"

Everyone kind of shrugged and made faces about that one.

"How far does Bluetooth reach? I think it won't reach sixty feet," Ellie said.

I laughed. "Okay, so first we need to do some Bluetooth testing. We're really great at planning, aren't we?"

Back at the clearing we found that the Bluetooth connection became unreliable around thirty feet. So, it would still be inside my danger zone if she pressed play on my phone from there. Also, with no cell service, we couldn't set up a chill song as my ringtone and have someone call. Eventually, we decided to set a ten-minute alarm with "Gypsy" by Fleetwood Mac as my alarm. I know, super old song, but it was my comfort song. If I hadn't gotten deep enough into meditation by ten minutes, Sabrina would just reset the alarm. If it went off, that meant she was in the clear.

The first try took one reset. I was excited about making progress and probably a little high on sugar, so it took some work to really settle my mind and body. But I eventually settled, and as the opening strands of "Gypsy" played in my ears, I did feel a slight jolt of anxiety, but then I let the calming strands of the song wash over me. I sank into it for a moment, then opened my eyes and reached for my phone to turn it off. I stayed in a semi-meditative state, where I really concentrated on each action as I was doing it and how it felt in my body. Once the song was off, I sat peacefully breathing for another moment. Then I heard the mouse move. That gave me the impetus to actually look at it and check on its well-being. I felt a slight spike of anxiety as I turned, and sure enough, the mouse started bleeding from its eyes and mouth. Fuck. But I could do this. I could! The mouse was safe when I was calm. I needed to stay calm. I needed to implement my tools for staying calm. I had them. And I suspected they had been working until I actually went to look at the mouse and see if it was okay. It was that spike. I needed to smooth that out. I was close. I felt it. It was that initial jolt of anxiety when I checked and saw the mouse bleeding that made the stress continue. But I would do this.

First, though, I hung my head and let myself feel sad for that little mouse. It wouldn't do to push that emotion down. I sank into that feeling until it passed. As it passed, I reminded myself that these mice that we'd gotten would have been snake food if not for us buying them for this. They had a much better chance of life with me than with the snake. I just had to chill out.

With my new resolve and calm, I waved to get Sabrina closer, then went to meet her, at which point Ellie and Heather joined us to hear how it went.

"First I want to say that I think, really think, I can do this." I held up a hand. "I don't want to hear sympathies right now. Right now I need cheerleading. That said, that mouse died, and I need another."

I looked at Ellie and saw resolution. "You've got this. I'll go set up for you." She hugged me, then went to remove the dead mouse and set up a fresh one.

"It didn't die right away after the alarm, I think. I think I can do it. I really do," I continued as she walked away.

"I know you can do it. You have always been able to do whatever you set your mind to, like graduate three years early, you nerd," Sabrina said.

"Or remember when you figured out that Travis was bullying Henry and you arranged to get him caught?" Heather said.

"That was all of us," I said. "But so is this. Thank you guys for your belief in me."

"It's not misplaced," Sabrina assured me.

They continued to build me up until Ellie came back. "You're all set if you're ready."

"I'm ready. I've got this."

I didn't kill the next mouse, even though we went two more times that evening. After that, we really wanted that pizza. We watched *Maleficent* on DVD in the theater room while we ate so that Ellie could keep feeding her mad crush on Angelina Jolie. We'd all seen the movie before—because of Angelina Jolie for her, and for us because we had a limited number of DVDs at the summer camp. We'd pretty much seen them all, so we did a lot of talking over the movie, including teasing Ellie about her crush. Although, to be honest, I think we all understood it, even though Sabrina was boringly straight.

After, we took sleeping bags outside and stargazed. Now that we knew our distances so well, Sabrina and Heather gave us nearly twenty feet of privacy. Ellie and I spread a sleeping bag out on the ground, then put one over the both of us. This gave us the opportunity to snuggle close in a way we hadn't quite before. We started out by pointing out stars and constellations to each other. Her mom was into astrology and had taught her some constellations, so she was better at finding them than me.

"So, are we compatible?" I asked.

"Well, I'm a Pisces, and you're a Virgo, so yeah, we're super compatible, if you believe in that sort of thing. You're here to even out my dreaming and I'm here to bring some dreaming to your structured world."

"You don't strike me as very dreamy, though. Programmers have to be logical thinkers, which seems pretty structured to me."

"Right? That's part of why I think it's kind of nonsense, but fun nonsense."

"And I feel really unstructured lately. Not that I'd say I'm a dreamer, either, but just lately everything seems like it's falling apart. I mean, meeting you and then Isabella getting her power has been such a catalyst for change, some good, of course, but some hard. Coming to terms with the Family being a little nefarious and all is definitely hard."

"It's that thing they always say about parents. It's when we're teens that we're supposed to realize that parents are actually just people with faults. In a lot of ways the Family is your parent."

"That's true," I said, turning to look at her. "You're pretty wise for being a dreamer."

She grinned and tilted her head a little in a sort of head-only bow. "Why thank you."

"So, what do you dream about?"

"Lately? You."

That was so shmaltzy, but I still felt a flare of excitement in my chest. I had to say something back. "Ellie…I…I dream about you, too," I finally got out. It was too soon to say I loved her, right? Although me spilling the beans about the Family probably meant that, right? Or was I just being a silly teenager?

We turned to each other and kissed, but it was more than kissing. This was my first ever make-out session. The moment where she parted her lips and touched my lips with the tip of her tongue made me tingle all over. When I opened my mouth to accommodate her and our tongues touched, well, that I felt in my groin. I soon lost myself in the kisses and the exploration of our hands, but when I realized what I really, really wanted could not happen less than twenty feet away from Sabrina and Heather, I pulled back.

"Too much?" Ellie asked softly.

"No. Well, yes, but only because of the fact that we have company," I said back, equally softly.

"Okay, then, tell me why 'Gypsy' is your comfort song."

She shifted and pulled me close, so my head was resting just above her breast. That was a little distracting, but I gathered my thoughts. "I first heard it, at least that I remember, when I was nine. It was back when I still hated synchronized swimming."

"You hated it?" she interrupted. "You always speak so positively about it, I honestly thought you loved it."

"I do now, but I didn't at first. I was doing it willingly because it meant a lot to Sabrina. She's way more into sports than I was. She'd been really into gymnastics before we discovered my power. She was so good that she was starting to spend a lot of time in the gym, and I'll be honest, I wasn't overjoyed about that. I missed her. Anyway, she willingly just gave it up, but there was a lot of brainstorming about how she could still be active. It was Gamma who came up with the idea of synchronized swimming. Luckily, we'd both taken swimming lessons and I did like the water. I was always happy to swim for fun, you know?"

"I like swimming, too, or did when I was a kid, at least. I liked to just go bop around in the water and dive for things and stuff."

"Right? It's very soothing to be weightless or go underwater and shut everything out."

"I always liked going underwater and then looking up at the surface and seeing the bubbles and stuff."

"Yeah, that's all really cool until you start synchronized swimming and you have to be underwater longer than is comfortable. Also, even when your head is above water, it's really hard work. Sabrina took right to it, between being comfortable in the water and being athletic. I had to work really hard to catch up. Sabrina was great about it, doing extra practice with me and stuff, but I was just so tired all the time and felt out of my league." I paused, remembering how difficult it had been.

"And this is leading to 'Gypsy' still?"

I nodded, again becoming a bit distracted by where my head

lay, there on Ellie's shoulder. I couldn't help but move my hand from Ellie's stomach upward. Then I caught myself. "Yeah." I cleared my throat. "So, at the time, Gamma was overseeing our homeschooling. We were too young to be left home alone, and all four of our parents worked. Actually, first we tried having my mom oversee homeschooling, because she is an artist and has flexible work times, but she does a lot of shaping with her power, and having Sabrina around meant that didn't go so well. So, Gamma, who also works, but it's for the Family and in the building—she either worked from her apartment with us or we took our laptops or workbooks or whatever to her office. Anyway, it's part of why we're so close with her."

"I can see that. It doesn't bother you that she's part of the Council that has made questionable decisions?" Ellie stroked my hair, which felt really nice.

"I mean, yeah, I guess. I just also…she's always been on our side, at least as far as I know. She's making this whole thing possible." I gestured around, indicating being at the summer camp. "She's really great. I wish you could meet her. Maybe someday."

Ellie nodded, an action I felt more than saw.

"Okay, so one day when we had practice coming up, I was already so tired and so overwhelmed that I just started crying over my math workbook, which was so weird because I loved math best at the time."

"Me, too! I mean, math was also my favorite subject in elementary. Really until I took programing in middle school."

"We're such girl geeks," I said, smiling.

"I know! It's great, right?" She kissed my head. "So, what happened when you started crying?"

"Gamma asked me what was wrong. I didn't want to tell her because I didn't want to make Sabrina feel bad. She'd given up so much for me, the least I could do was make synchro work."

"But, of course, she was sitting right there. What did she think of all this?"

"She got up and gave me a hug. She wasn't into school at all then because she didn't discover her academic love until we took our first language class in middle school, so really, any excuse to stop working was good for her." I chuckled a little and Ellie joined in, making her chest move pleasantly. "I tried to pull it together, but I couldn't stop crying. Gamma finally came over and asked gently if this was a headphone moment. You see, one of the things we worked out quickly is that we needed noise canceling headphones so that we could have at least some semi-private moments." I paused again. "Which is why I feel so stupid about not thinking of earbuds earlier today."

"There has been a lot going on. Stress will do that, I understand."

"Yeah, I guess. Anyway, Sabrina looked a little hurt, but when Gamma said she could watch an episode of *Glee* right then during the school day, she got over it pretty fast." I chuckled again. Again, Ellie joined in.

"Were you a *Glee* fan, too?" she asked.

"Sure. I mean, Santana and Brittany, right? It was probably the first hint that I was a lesbian. What was yours?"

"I think I always knew. I told my mom I was going to marry my best friend, Carrie, in preschool."

"Precocious," I said.

"My mom's best friend had a female partner, so that option was always there. You said your parents are cool with it?"

"Yeah. I mean, they were the parents who introduced us to *Glee*, so they knew pretty early on, too."

"How do you divide your time? Is there a schedule?"

"There was at first. We spent Sunday through Wednesday sleeping at my place and Thursday through Saturday at Sabrina's, but pretty quickly it became just wherever we felt like it. We spent a lot of time at my place because we were really close with Neil, and that's, of course, where he lived. Now we like Sabrina's room better for sleeping, at least, because we don't love bunk beds the way we did when we were little." More laughter.

"We've gotten way off track. 'Gypsy,' woman. You're supposed to be telling me why it's your comfort song."

"Right you are. Okay, so, Sabrina put on her headphones—we had big, over-the-ear noise canceling headphones at the time—and started her episode. Quietly, because noise canceling technology isn't perfect, I told Gamma why I was crying. She told me I was doing a good thing, keeping at it even though it was hard and I didn't like it. She didn't even tell me to suck it up because Sabrina was basically giving her life up for me, which was nice of her. She just said that I was brave and she was proud. She told me that when she was young, she had a song that she always listened to when she was sad and asked if I wanted to hear it. Of course, I said yes. And there you are. The song was 'Gypsy.'"

"It's kind of a melancholy song."

"I know, but that's part of why it works for me. It meets you where you are if you're feeling down, but it kind of takes off toward the end, so it also lifts you up. Since then, I've associated it with Gamma comforting me. She also made us tea for the first time after that. She said we were old enough to appreciate it. It didn't hurt that Stevie Nicks was pretty cute in the video."

Ellie laughed. "Sure, but she's wafer thin. I thought you liked your girls a little more full-bodied."

I wondered if Ellie was feeling like maybe I didn't like her curves as much as I'd indicated. "I do," I assured her. "But I also can appreciate the type of softness Stevie has. Like you, she's a dress enthusiast."

She laughed again.

"Do you have a comfort song?"

Ellie shifted a little. "Not like that. I mean, I don't have a song I go to when I'm feeling down or need soothing. I do have a song that I kind of consider my anthem, though."

"Oh? Do tell."

"It feels a little basic," she warned.

"There's nothing wrong with basic. Mainstream is mainstream for a reason. Don't worry, I'll think you're one of a kind no matter what the song is."

"'Run the World' by Queen Bey."

"That's a good song. Why is it your anthem, though?"

"I distinctly remember the first time I heard it. I was seven and I'd been going to this science camp. There were other girls in the camp, but the teacher was a man and he super-favored the boys. At the end of camp, we split into teams and did this little kid science Olympiad. We ended up splitting into boys versus girls. What the teacher didn't know was that us girls had been all going over to Ruby's house to study and do experiments in her kitchen. Her parents are both chemists, and they were super supportive. Anyway, we kicked the boys' butts and Ruby had us all over to celebrate the weekend after camp. She played this song and we ended up playing it over and over. I had it memorized by the end of the day. It's my pump-up song."

"That's really cool."

"Hey! Sorry to interrupt you lovebirds," Sabrina called over, "but we're getting bored over here. You guys want to go play a game?"

CHAPTER SIXTEEN

By the end of Sunday, Sabrina was walking away while I was just sitting calmly with my eyes open. The next weekend, Ellie planned to stay home, because Isabella was coming with us. Isabella was hearing more and more, which was distressing both for her and the people around her. Ellie said it was probably for the best because she needed to spend some time with her mom.

"What have you been telling your mom, anyway?" I asked Ellie when we went for a walk one evening, Sabrina trailing behind listening to music.

"That I'm spending time with you."

"And she's okay with that? Without even having met me? Overnight?"

"Sure. She trusts me."

Both sets of my parents, so to speak, were good people, and Sabrina and I had a great level of freedom as long as we were together, at least in part because if we weren't one place, it was assumed we were at the other. But even so, I don't know that they'd be happy about an overnight love interest. Although, with Sabrina as chaperone, perhaps they'd know they had nothing to worry about. "Does she know it's a whole group and we're sleeping in the same cabin all together?"

"I did tell her that. I told her basically what you guys are telling your parents. Your grandmother owns a summer camp and she's paying us to do some projects there."

"Will you need to produce money? I could work that out."

She stopped and put her hands on her hips. "Joan. You are not paying me for spending time with you."

"Okay." I put my hands up in surrender. "I see what you mean. That does sound bad."

She turned and started walking again. "I'll miss you. I've gotten used to going on these trips."

I put my arm through hers. "Same."

Isabella was excited to go on a weekend trip, but also clearly worried about what it meant. Heather still came, too, because Isabella wasn't old enough to manage if we had some sort of accident, although I was feeling more and more confident that I had this. While Isabella was a child of the Family and I trusted her not to expose Family secrets in general, she'd also shown she wasn't exactly to be relied on regarding secrets in her inner circle. We decided not to tell her exactly why we were going to the camp. We let her believe what the rest of the Family thought, that we were up there to do a little maintenance. We did let her in on the secret that we weren't working very hard at it. We didn't want to spend all weekend mulching fallen wood and spreading it on the trails or anything.

We decided to try a new approach and just did kind of normal around camp stuff. We walked around, goofed off at the playground, played games, watched movies, did a little camp maintenance stuff. Sometimes someone would take a break for themselves, like Isabella taking some time to play her violin. However, Sabrina took to just walking away from me without notice. She'd grab Isabella's hand (if she was with us) and just book it away from me with the agreement that she'd turn right back around if there was any bleeding at all on anyone's part. Heather bravely stuck by my side after she followed the first few times and it went well. Isabella thought this was hilarious and giggled as they ran away, like we were playing hide-and-seek or something.

During one of the times Isabella was practicing, Heather, Sabrina, and I were sitting at a well-scarred picnic table. Heather had just come back from a walk on her own and was looking a little down.

"Is something wrong, Heather?" I asked.

She sighed. "Yeah. I think so."

"What do you mean you think so?" Sabrina asked without looking up from the carving she was doing on the picnic table.

"I think Maria is going to break up with me."

"Oh, no! Why?" I asked.

Sabrina paused in her carving to examine Heather. "Did you do something stupid?"

"If by something stupid you mean trying to have a girlfriend, then yes," Heather snapped.

It hit me. "Oh. You read her mind and it wasn't good, right?"

Heather sighed, fight gone. "I did a couple of times, but it wasn't exactly bad. She was just thinking normal shit, but I don't want to read her mind, so mostly I don't touch her unless we're with you guys."

Sabrina sighed this time. My guess was that she was thinking about how there were so many people she needed to protect from their powers that it was overwhelming.

"So she thinks you aren't interested?" I asked.

"Yeah. She said something about how I run hot and cold, and of course I couldn't explain, so she just kind of walked away. That was Friday. Hell, maybe we're already broken up and I just don't know it yet." She paused, then continued, "Actually, we never officially were girlfriends, I guess. I mean, we never had that conversation. Now I'm pretty sure we won't."

I patted her hand. "Sorry. That really sucks."

"Yeah. I like her a lot. And I'm not sure I'll ever be able to date anyone, unless I can somehow explain about my power."

I knew all too well what that was like. "What about the guys you dated before? Did you have the same trouble? I mean, of course you did. Unless you only read women. Do you only read women?"

She laughed. "That'd be a solution, wouldn't it? But no. It was the same issue. When Preston kissed me, I could hear all his thoughts about me, and what he wanted to do to me, and it was disgusting." She shuddered and I was reminded of when she first told us about that kiss. She shuddered then, too.

I got up and moved about the picnic table to sit next to her. "Is it okay if I put my arm around you?"

"Yes. Thanks for asking. I actually like touch when it doesn't come with mind reading. But I usually avoid it."

I put my arm around her and pulled her close. "I'm sorry that happened with Preston. Would you like me to practice on him?"

She laughed. "That's not a bad idea. You'd probably be saving other women from him. His mind was a cesspool, seriously."

"I wish I were cut out for being an Avenger. I don't think I could purposefully hurt anyone. I'm sorry."

Heather patted my knee. "It's okay. I wasn't serious. I know you're a lover, not a fighter."

Sabrina, who'd gone back to her carving, said, "I'd do it. I mean if our powers were reversed, I think I'd be okay with punishing people who hurt people I love."

Heather and I both stared at her. She looked up. "What? I would."

"Okay, then," I said.

Isabella came skipping up to the table just then and said, "What're we up to now?" So that was the end of that conversation.

❖

On Sunday, we tried leaving me with a mouse and then getting surprised, but that was hard to do while I was more or less on the lookout for it. I tried thinking of things to make me anxious or sad, which wasn't hard, considering. If I got worked up enough to focus on the negative feelings and ignore my surroundings, the mouse did start to bleed, but when I calmed myself, I could stop it. In fact, it stopped so suddenly that I had an idea.

When we got back home, well, actually Monday morning, I started doing some research in my anatomy and physiology textbook. If Gamma could manipulate mood (still presuming I was even actually related to her), my mom could manipulate metal, and Neil could manipulate wood, what was it that I was manipulating?

Was it cells? Blood itself? It was when I came across cell adhesion in my textbook that I felt a click, like sliding in a puzzle piece. This was it. I was sure of it.

"Sabrina, check this out," I said.

She looked up from the graphic art project she was working on. "Whatcha got?"

"This is about my power, okay? So I'm going to talk about cells and stuff, but it has a point."

"Okay," she said warily.

"Okay, so, because I come from a line of people who can manipulate things, it makes sense that I am manipulating something, right?"

"Yeah. Provided you really do come from that line, but you probably do. You look a lot like your mom."

Isabella whipped her head around. "What?"

Oops. "Sabrina's teasing," I told Isabella, then fixed Sabrina with a look. She had the grace to look contrite for speaking about things Isabella didn't need to be worrying about yet. Her thoughts had echoed mine, though, which didn't eliminate the possibility that my mom wasn't related to Gamma. I wanted to ask Sabrina if she thought I looked like Gamma. Did she? I looked at her for a moment before deciding to put that aside and going on with the topic at hand. "So, I think I'm manipulating the proteins that hold cells together. It must be pretty specialized because if I just manipulated proteins, that would be...well, almost everything has some protein in it. Plants and stuff." I thought again. "Maybe if I...okay, that's a way off maybe. For right now, I'm almost certain that's what I'm doing. Does that make sense?"

"Proteins hold our cells together? Like steak?" Isabella asked.

"Specialized proteins," I clarified, "but yeah. I mean, we're animals, too. It's different than the proteins in our muscles. The purpose of these cells is to form what's called a tight bond, which keeps cells close enough to be watertight. Apparently they're selectively permeable, so some things can get through, like certain ions." I paused again, referring to my textbook. "Actually, it's probably claudins specifically. If I understand this correctly, they're close cells, and they're found in all creatures, which explains my range."

"Do you suppose there's something specific in metal that makes it so your mom can manipulate it? Like some basic component that's equivalent to these claudins? And something like it for Neil with wood?"

I shrugged. "Maybe. I don't know. It doesn't really explain Gamma, though." Then I regretted saying that because it brought up the topic we weren't supposed to be talking about again.

Sabrina said, "No, true, because emotions are amorphous, not physical things." She gave me a significant look.

"Right," I said, but then had a thought. "Actually, think about endorphins and what a mood boost they are. Maybe that's how she controls mood, even if it's subconscious. For that matter, what if Family members all produce some chemical that normal people don't, and that's what gives us our power, and you're a manipulator of that chemical? That would make sense, seeing as how we're related and all."

She gave me a dark look as if to say, "Are we really?" What she said aloud, though, was, "My dad is a precog, though."

I got her point. Okay, now we just really needed to discuss everything. "Isabella, earbuds."

"Aw," she said. "Why?"

"Because Sabrina and I need to talk. Or you could go out to the living room. Your choice." She didn't have much distance yet, so if she was sitting out in the living room by herself, she wouldn't be likely to hear anything.

She crossed her arms. "My mom is a precog, too. Whatever you're going to say about precogs, I should hear it."

"We're not going to say anything about precogs," I said. "This is actually about Heather and it's private," I improvised.

She scowled. "You shouldn't be talking about Heather behind her back. Mind readers have feelings, too!"

Sabrina and I looked at each other. I, for one, was sure that Heather hadn't told Isabella. She was nine, and keeping secrets was hard at that age, or who was I kidding, any age. I was over here telling secrets left and right, but that didn't seem to stop me from collecting more. What a mess.

"Why do you think Heather is a mind reader?" I asked Isabella.

Her face crumpled and she put her hand over her mouth. "Oh. I shouldn't have said." Exactly my point. "I heard her think about it this weekend." She looked near tears.

Sabrina stood up from her desk chair and gathered Isabella up in her arms. "Don't worry. We already knew, but you are right. That's Heather's secret and we need to keep it for her."

"Why hasn't she told anyone? I don't get it." But her face told me that she probably did.

"How has it been since you started reading minds?" I asked her gently. "I mean, have people taken that well?"

She shook her head and looked down. "But I can't hide it! If it weren't for Sabrina, I'd hear everything, and it's really hard! How does she hide it?"

"She has to have physical contact with someone to hear them, so it's a little easier for her. I'm sorry it's been so rough." Sabrina sat down and pulled Isabella onto her lap.

"Have you been practicing your meditation?" I asked.

She shook her head and looked down, looking miserable.

"Isabella," I said softly, trying to get her to look at me. "I was lucky that Sabrina and I were contemporaries. Wait, do you know what contemporaries means?"

She shook her head.

"I was lucky that Sabrina and I were the same age and came into our powers at the same time. Most people with problematic powers aren't so lucky. I'd have had to go into isolation at the least, otherwise. You know that, right?"

"Yes." We learned some difficult stuff in Sunday school.

"Mind readers have different problems. Without going into isolation, they can lose their grip on reality because hearing everything all the time is hard, right?"

"Right."

"Either way, we're both very lucky Sabrina is around. But

here's the thing. Because she's around, we get breaks, and I don't hurt people, and you don't end up going crazy. What this means is that we get the opportunity to practice. Well, only recently for me, but you're getting time apart to practice already. You know what I've figured out lately?"

She looked up. "What?"

"Most everyone does practice. They have minor powers that they can't control at first but that aren't very harmful, so it doesn't matter. As they grow and their powers develop, they've had a chance to practice with them, whether they know it or not. I think it's some of both. That's why we learn all this focus and meditation and stuff. It's to help with our powers. For people whose powers are easy for them, it's a natural progression. For me or Linda, we didn't have the chance to practice at your age. I'm figuring it out now, and it turns out that I do have some control. I think you can practice, too."

"How?"

"Practice your meditation. Practice it when you're in a calm easy place, like hanging out with us while we're doing schoolwork, but also practice your meditation when it's hard. When there are thoughts that you're hearing. Just see if you can start to muffle them."

She sighed. "I don't really like meditating, though."

"I understand. You know what I hated when I first tried it?"

"What?"

"Synchronized swimming."

"Really? But you like it now."

"I know, but at first, I wasn't good and it was hard. I did it anyway because it was important to Sabrina and she was doing so much for me, you know?"

She turned to give Sabrina a hug. "Thanks for doing so much for me, too, Sabrina."

Sabrina hugged her back. "I want you to be safe and happy."

Sabrina and I exchanged another significant look over Isabella's head. Sabrina meant what she said, but it also required so very much of her. I went on. "So, I get that some things are hard to do. But which would be harder? Working on your meditation and learning to control your power, so you can do whatever you want with your life, or having to either stay next to Sabrina forever or go into isolation?"

"Isolation would suck, but I like Sabrina. And you. Why is it so bad if we all are just together all the time?" She'd unwrapped her arms and now slumped against Sabrina.

"It's pretty hard," Sabrina said. "With just the two of us, Joan and I, it's hard. We three, well, we haven't really had to do that much yet, because you aren't with us all the time, but that would be so hard that it probably wouldn't work."

"Why not?" Isabella asked plaintively.

"For one, it's hard to navigate New York and always stay close to two different people. We've struggled with two sometimes. We'd have to give up synchronized swimming. You'd never be able to play in a symphony or orchestra. Also, Sabrina and I are getting to the point where normally we'd go away to college. We couldn't take you in a college classroom when you'll only be ten or eleven," I said.

Sabrina picked up the thread. "Yeah, I mean, that's one thing. It was easier for us because we were the same age, but even now, Joan and I don't want to do the same things with our lives. I want to study languages and she wants to be a doctor. What if you grow up to want to, I don't know, be a teacher or something. Would we just go into your classroom with you?"

"I want to be a violinist with the New York Philharmonic," Isabella informed us.

And of course she did. "That's a great goal, but how would you do that if the two of us had to trail along with you?"

She sighed. "Fine. I'll start practicing my meditation."

"Just give it a try," Sabrina said. "Let us know how it goes."

We didn't try to kick her out again. Instead, we went back to ostensibly doing schoolwork, me at my desk, Sabrina at hers, and Isabella on my bed. Instead of working, though, I texted Sabrina.

Joan: *What if your dad isn't really a precog?*
Sabrina: *Like Heather?*
Joan: *Exactly.*

Sabrina: *Possible.*
Joan: *Do we look alike?*
Sabrina: *(shrugging emoji) who knows? Do cousins always look alike?*
Joan: *Do Megan and Todd look alike?*

Sometimes it was easier to use our parents' names rather than going into all the your dad and my mom stuff.

Sabrina: *(thinking emoji)*
Joan: *Who looks more like Gamma?*

I heard Sabrina shift in her chair and turned to look at her. She was examining my face closely. And I looked closely back at her for a few moments. Then I turned back to my computer and pulled up pictures. We spent the next who-knows-how-long sending pictures back and forth and comparing them side by side. What we decided was that it was hard to tell, but that Todd and Sabrina probably looked more like Gamma than Megan and I did.

After a while, a text came in from Ellie and I responded, telling her my theory about claudin manipulation. She thought it was sound and agreed I should experiment with it. Then she got down to the really important stuff.

Ellie: *Also, when can I see you? Movie night tomorrow night?*
Joan: *Sounds great. I'd say tonight, but we've got synchro.*
Ellie: *I've got the community center today anyway, so no worries.*

Finally, I told her I had to get some work done and pulled out my flashcards for my upcoming A&P test. The term only had a month left, and finals were fast approaching. Even with everything else going on, I couldn't let school slip. If I could control myself, I was going to medical school.

CHAPTER SEVENTEEN

That weekend, Isabella stayed home. After all, she was still only nine and missed her parents sometimes. The good news was that meant Ellie could come again. We decided to leave on Friday afternoon to give us more time for practice. I was really excited about trying out my control. So, on Thursday Isabella, Sabrina, and I visited our mouse supplier. That makes it sound a little like a drug deal, but it was really just a pet shop that specialized in reptiles, so they sold feeder mice. This time I thought I might be hurting them, but hopefully healing them too, and none had died for the last couple of weeks.

Friday after school, Ellie met us at the Complex and we took off from there. It was a rainy drive up, so there wasn't much traffic, because people weren't trying to escape for a fun weekend away when the forecast was for rain all weekend.

I peered out at the rain. "So, I could maybe be in the cafeteria by myself to practice?"

"Yeah, that sounds good," Sabrina agreed from the back seat.

"The rest of us will hang out in the cabin, I guess," Heather said.

There was one common building with the cafeteria, theater, and indoor game area.

"Or, and hear me out here, Joan—who will just be sitting there thinking with a mouse—could be in the cabin, while the rest of us have access to the cafeteria and other entertainment," Ellie suggested.

Sabrina snapped her fingers and pointed at Ellie. "See? I knew I liked you. Always thinking." She tapped her head.

Instead of the traditional stop for snacks, we stopped to eat at an Italian restaurant we sometimes ate in on the way to camp or back, when we were with parents. I needed a real break from driving with the rain.

While we waited for our food, I said, "If you guys could do anything, no worries about what other people need, what would you do after high school?"

Ellie said, "Go to college and major in computer science."

Heather said, "Really anything without expectations?"

"Like, none," I said. "Just what you'd really want to do."

She said, "I'm torn between thinking ahead and going to college, versus something like backpacking around South America for a year, then seeing what I feel like from there."

Sabrina said, "I'm between college to double major in a couple of languages, or going to volunteer in really any non-English speaking country. Maybe working with kids doing art or something."

"How about you?" Ellie asked. "I'm guessing finishing college and going to medical school?"

"Definitely." That was what I wanted for sure. "Okay, then, what about in, say, ten years? What do you hope your lives look like then?"

"I want to be working on a cool project for a company with a short workweek policy. And I want to use my downtime for volunteering with kids still, because that's super fun. Or maybe parenting. I mean, I know it's the thing to wait until you're in your thirties these days, but I want kids, and I'd like to have them young." She gave me a bit of a shy look.

"I can see that," I said. "I want kids, too, and don't see a problem with starting young, at least once I'm past my residency, because I wouldn't have a lot of time to spend with them before that."

Ellie smiled at me and I grinned back, both of us clearly thinking it was nice that we were compatible in that way. Ellie asked, "And where do you want to live?"

"Here in New York," I said, meaning the city even though we were not currently there. "I'd have to, if I had kids."

Ellie looked at me blankly. "What?"

The three of us Family members exchanged a look. Then I answered softly. "My kids would have powers and they might be dangerous, so I'd have to live in the Complex with Family support."

"But they could be adopted? Or your partner's biological kids?" Heather put in. "They could be, sure, but that's not how the Family works. If you and Joan get married and have kids together, Joan has been indoctrinated that they'd have to be her biological kids, and they'd have to be raised in the Complex."

I sighed. That was true. It was indoctrination. With my power, it might be better for me to not have biological children. Although they'd probably end up having other powers, maybe powers that weren't so deadly. It's just that the Family strongly encouraged us to reproduce and supported that fairly intensely. "There are other possibilities," I allowed. "It may take me some time to work out what I really want versus what the Family wants."

Sabrina said, "Yeah. I mean really, I can go anywhere and do anything, right? Because the Family doesn't stop us unless we're dangerous and I'm kind of the opposite of dangerous, but at the same time, I know I'm very useful, and how would I just abandon Isabella? I'd say you, too, J, but you're going to be all independent soon. If I up and left, and Isabella doesn't find some level of control, she'd end up in isolation. How could I do that? I think I'll have to stick around, at least until she's older." She looked a little bleak.

"If I could help, I would," I told her. "I'm sorry."

She shook her head. "You don't have anything to be sorry about. And I know you would."

Heather said, "And I wouldn't be too confident about them just letting you go live your life, Sabrina. They'll want to protect Isabella and keep both of you as useful tools."

"That's true," I said, "but they let Desiree go live her life, and she'd be pretty helpful to the Family in certain circumstances."

Heather looked thoughtful.

Our food came then, and we were quiet as we started to eat. When conversation started again, Sabrina resolutely changed the subject to music. She'd recently started to listen to a group Paul had recommended to her and was super into it. It made me wonder if there was more there with Paul than she wanted to admit. I got it if she was scared to get too involved for fear that it would hurt all the more when he realized he'd really never get to see her without me—or unbeknownst to him, Isabella—by her side all the time.

Or maybe she just liked his taste in music. What did I know? I wasn't a mind reader.

CHAPTER EIGHTEEN

Once we got to the summer camp, we were all tired and decided to call it an early night. However, instead of sleep, we ended up talking late into the night in our bunks. We told Ellie stories about our childhood, trying to embarrass each other. Of course, that was hardest on me because I was the one dating her. She just laughed and told me it was cute that when I was two I'd kicked my paternal grandmother in the shins because she wouldn't let me do something or other that I'd wanted to do. Side note, it was one of the last times we saw her, because she wasn't a nice woman and my dad decided it was easier to just cut ties. By the time we fell asleep, she hated Travis as much as we did, without ever having even met him, and knew probably too much about the details of Sabrina's early food allergies, which included milk and strawberries, and made potty training difficult.

As a result of the late-night girl talk, we slept in the next morning. The ambient sound of rain and the accompanying dimness made sleeping in easy. It was nearly noon by the time we made our way over to the common building for what we ended up calling brunch. We had veggie sausages just warmed up in the microwave (classy, I know) and served in hot dog buns with chips, and bananas (an apple instead for Heather, who was not a banana fan) that we'd intended for breakfast. We were trying to be at least a little better about our eating choices.

When we finished up, the others shooed me away to go practice and said they'd clean up. It was a sign of everyone's trust, including mine, in my control that I just walked away, trusting I wouldn't hurt anyone. I stopped off in a different cabin to pick up a sedated mouse (we'd opted to store them away from us, both because they squeaked at night and because no one wanted to get attached), then went to ours. I could have used any cabin, but ours had comforts like sleeping bags, and it was cool out with the rain.

I settled in, sitting cross-legged on a top bunk, my sleeping bag under me and a little over my legs, considering. The mouse was sleeping in its cage next to me. I'd made mice bleed before by being anxious or mad and somehow working myself up. I knew I'd like several things to happen. One, I'd like to be able to turn my power on or off, just by thinking about it without having to get worked up. I mean, I'd like to never make anyone, or any animal, bleed again, really, unless I was in some sort of life-or-death situation, the specifics of which were eluding me at the moment. So, I'd like to be able to have a shot of adrenaline course through my system without that also endangering the living beings around me.

That made me think of my conversation with Sabrina about how powers work, where we'd decided that hers was like breathing, although so far, she'd shown no ability to hold her breath in regard to her power. What if mine weren't so much like walking, but like talking or making sounds? When the power first came it was like a baby crying. There was no real control. As a baby develops, there is babbling that develops into talking, over which there is more and more control. However, if surprised, most babies, or people, yell or at least gasp, but that could maybe be trained out of me. So I needed to develop skills that would let me really control this power, so I couldn't be scared into losing control.

Okay, so back to what I wanted out of this practice session. I wanted to only make beings bleed intentionally, and also to be able to do the opposite—to be able to stop the bleeding. What I was really hoping I could do was repair cell connections. That might even have some exciting medical applications. That was what I wanted to experiment with today. The control when surprised or excited or anxious was something I would need to work on in different circumstances, probably.

The bad part about this was that first I needed to injure the mouse, and it might as well be with my power, if I was going to learn control by using and not at will. Could I do it while staying calm?

It didn't work the first time I tried. However, I was eventually able to only get a little worked up, and I paid close attention to how I felt. There was a section of my brain that felt different than usual. It was like how doing mental math felt different than thinking about a song I liked. It was like flexing a muscle. I relaxed that part of my mind, and the trickle of blood from the mouse's nose and mouth slowed. I really concentrated and thought about what I knew about how cells connected. The bleeding stopped. Was that because it had healed itself, now that I wasn't causing ruptures, or because I'd actually bonded the cells back together? I wasn't sure. I went again.

After a few hours, during which I took breaks to stretch and walk around the cabin, I was to the point where I could make the mouse bleed by thinking about it, and I was pretty sure I was also repairing it. I decided to take a longer break, and to give the mouse a break, too.

I put the mouse back in the box with the others and gave them some food, then went in search of the others. I found them sitting around a table in the common area playing a card game. When I sat down next to Ellie, they set their cards down and looked at me expectantly.

"I can turn the bleeding on and off at will," I said.

They all cheered a little.

Ellie squeezed my hand. "That's really awesome."

"It is really good. I think that I can also repair the cell junctions. I'm not sure, though, and I'm not sure what to do to test that."

"What if one of us cuts our finger and you see if you can fix it?" Ellie asked.

"I can't stand the thought of one of you hurting yourselves," I said.

"It'd just be a small cut, like what people get all the time, but what about cutting a mouse instead?" Heather asked.

"Ugh." I shivered. "I hate hurting them."

"But better them than us?" Sabrina asked.

"I mean, when it comes to possible systemic bleeding, yes, but when it comes to cutting, a small cut for us would be a big cut for them, and what if I can't fix it?" I shook my head. "I can't do that." I paused. "I'll just cut my own finger. I'm worried that the stress of seeing one of you cut yourself would make my power trigger the wrong way."

Sabrina cocked her head at me. "Will that work? You've never made yourself bleed."

That was true. It was also true that I felt tired, hungry, and grumpy. "I don't know. What I do know is that I'm hungry. Maybe we could have a bite to eat and keep brainstorming? Or better, I'll join in on the card game while we eat and then come back to it. I need a break."

"We made cookies. Want to start with one of them?" Ellie asked.

She and I went to the kitchen, and it wasn't until we were there that I realized Sabrina hadn't followed. I was alone with Ellie, outside my usual range for the first time ever, and she wasn't bleeding. I hoped.

"Do you feel okay?" I asked.

"Sure. I'm having a nice time. I like both Heather and Sabrina." She was leading the way to a cooling rack of cookies and answered a little absentmindedly.

"But, like, you don't have a nosebleed or anything, right?"

She turned around and saw we were alone. She smiled, then moved her hand in front of her face like she was doing a reveal. "Nope." She moved back toward me.

I gathered her in my arms and kissed her. She kissed me back, moving forward until my back was against the work island in the middle of the kitchen. The short, but really alone, make-out session did a lot to improve my mood. But when my stomach growled, we separated.

"I guess I really do need to eat," I said sheepishly.

She gave me one more quick kiss. "Yes. You must keep your strength up."

I felt a near snap as the sugar in the cookie hit my bloodstream. Apparently, working with a power really took it out of a person.

"Good cookie, eh?" Ellie was staring at my lips.

"Um, yeah? Did I take too big a bite or something?"

"You moaned."

I blushed. "Did I? I think I really needed the calories."

"Uh-huh. I don't mind the moaning."

And the look she gave me was some extreme motivation to get my power controlled. But it also brought up another question I considered as I finished my cookie.

"Okay, now you look worried. Too much? I'm sorry. I probably came on too strong there."

"No. I mean, I, no. You didn't come on too strong." I told her about my babies learning to talk analogy, and how I thought that maybe my power worked like making sounds. There was anything from involuntary to complex speech, or singing. "So, I just started worrying about how people, you know, make noises during, um, sex, and then I was worried about, well, having sex and hurting you." I blushed super hard.

"Oh. Well, yeah, I guess that's an extra concern for us. Gives safe sex a whole new meaning. I suppose we'll have to take it slow?"

"Yes. I'm sorry."

She shook her head. "Don't be. We'll find the right speed for us, even if it's a little extra complicated."

"You are amazing. I can't believe how lucky I am that we found each other."

She gave a little curtsy. "I'm pretty awesome."

"You are." I gathered her up in my arms again for some more kissing.

"I think I need some more food," I admitted when we came up for air after a while. "Are you guys hungry enough to make the spaghetti, or should I have a sandwich or something?"

"I could eat, but let's go ask the others," Ellie suggested.

We came back out, hand in hand, to knowing smirks from the other two. I hastily spoke first. "I'm hungry for food-food. Are you guys ready for spaghetti or should I have a sandwich or something?"

"I'm hungry," Sabrina said. "I say let's start dinner."

Heather agreed, so we all trooped back to the kitchen, even though it was about a two-person job at best. We'd gotten a bagged salad, so Ellie worked on assembling that while Sabrina got the water boiling and Heather got the spaghetti package and the jar of sauce out. I lifted myself up on a counter to sit and watch. "I'll supervise," I said.

Sabrina rolled her eyes at me. "Yeah, okay."

"How do people train to be quiet?" I asked. "Like, soldiers, I guess, or at least the ones who sneak up on people and stuff."

"Like how people learn to walk through the woods without making a sound?" Heather asked.

"No, more like how, say, John Wick is sneaking into a house to exact revenge for them killing his dog and he gets surprised, but doesn't want anyone to know he's there, so he doesn't make a sound anyway. Like that."

"First of all, you know that he's an imaginary character, right?" Sabrina faced me and put her hands on her hips.

"Sure, but you know. People do have to learn that sort of thing, like spies and stuff, right?"

"Sure. Why are we talking about this?" Sabrina asked.

I realized I hadn't told them about my learning-to-talk analogy, so I explained. "So, I need to learn not to gasp or, in my case, instinctively make someone bleed, if I'm surprised or something."

"Well, I think you practice by being surprised and trying not to react," Ellie said, reasonably.

I nodded sagely. "That does make sense. So, then, I think I have two things to work on. One is healing cuts or any type of bleeding, really, but the other is staying calm when surprised or whatever. The second part, though, I should do when Sabrina is around so that I just practice the staying calm without killing the person who surprised me, you know."

"Yeah. No one wants to be suddenly bleeding from everywhere," Heather said helpfully.

Sabrina said, "If your power is like talking, and mine, like we said before, is like breathing, I think I should also work on mine. I'm curious if I can hold my breath, so to speak."

"I think figuring out all limits and abilities is good. It helps us to know what we're working with," I said.

"So, maybe you and I spend some time alone with a mouse. You try to make it bleed and I try to not stop you."

"Or hear me out, we try that with something that doesn't hurt anyone. Like, Heather tries to read my thoughts," I said. I was clearly the most sensitive about hurting the mice, but of course, I'd been the one doing that.

"That can hurt," Heather said softly.

"Point taken. I'm sure you've heard some stuff you'd rather not have," I said.

"It's one thing that I just don't have to worry about with you guys at all, and it's hard to think of giving that up, you know?"

"I really do take your point." I sighed. "I'm just tired of hurting mice, but I think we're coming back to that being where we are."

Everyone agreed with varying degrees of sympathy and reluctance.

Eating salad and spaghetti was yet another good mood boost. I was reluctant to go hurt more mice, but Sabrina and I decided to do a little practice together, and I had to be honest with myself that that was unlikely to cause any damage. Unless we somehow got carried away, and Sabrina really did turn off her muting and I hurt her, but I could quickly course correct if that did happen. We left Ellie and Heather to do cleanup, picked a mouse, and went back to the cabin.

"So, what should I do here, even?" Sabrina asked when we were settled on a bunk, backs against the cabin wall legs in front of us. The mouse was in a cage between us.

"For me, I just really paid attention to my thoughts and actions while I was making the mouse bleed. Like doing a movement meditation. I don't know if that'll work for you because it's kind of always there, but maybe?" I shrugged.

She sighed. "Okay. Just try to make the mouse bleed."

I didn't actually know how to try to make just one being in my vicinity bleed. Apparently that was another skill to work on. Instead, I just let the cell loosening flow, but nothing happened. I stopped.

"Did you feel anything?" I asked.

"Um, no. Did you try?"

"Yes."

"Try again but tell me exactly when you start."

We worked for a while but didn't make a lot of progress. After a couple of hours, Sabrina said she could maybe feel a slight pressure at the back of her skull when I was trying to use my power, but she couldn't do anything to change it.

"Well, it's something to keep trying," I said. "But for now, how about popcorn and a movie?"

We did just that, choosing to watch a comedy. I sat next to Ellie, brushing hands over popcorn and touching legs off and on. When we set the popcorn aside, we held hands. After a while, our hands drifted over to settle on my lap. The feel of her hand in mine and on my lap, even over the joggers I was wearing, was very distracting. After the movie, we begged off and went to have a make-out session back at the cabin while Heather and Sabrina decided to watch another movie. The make-out session wasn't really that hot and heavy because I was very aware of maintaining control, but it was still nice to be alone with Ellie. After a while, we just cuddled and talked.

It was amazing how free I felt, really. How much hope I had for myself, at least. How pleased at my progress. I knew I could conquer this with more practice.

We fell asleep before the others got back.

CHAPTER NINETEEN

I broke down and used a box knife on a very sedated mouse the next morning. All I'm going to say about the actual inflicting of the tiny wound is that it took me a long time to work up the nerve to do it, and I cried a little. I probably would have cried more, but I had to calm myself and try to stop the bleeding. I looked away and steadied myself, then felt for that part of my brain that knew what to do. It only took a moment to feel like I engaged. I looked at the mouse to see if it was working to discover that it was bleeding more. Crap. I closed my eyes and centered. I was able to turn it off. I looked down, and the bleeding was slowing, but hadn't stopped. The mouse didn't look good. It lay even stiller than I'd come to expect from the sedation. I was able to keep the bleeding turned off. I reached again, trying to knit vessel walls together. I felt it. It was working, but then something changed. I looked down at the mouse again. The wound looked much better, but it was too late. The mouse was dead.

I got up, turned my back on the mouse, and cried. Then I opened the cage, went outside to bury the mouse, and then went for a walk by myself. The rain had sort of stopped. It was either raining really lightly or misting very hard, so I still got soaked, but I had to clear my head. I wasn't keeping track of where I was going, just wandering. It was an odd thing, to be alone, particularly wandering around by myself. I wished I could enjoy it, but I was mostly thinking about having to cut another mouse. Because the thing was that I did it. I knit those cells back together and stopped the bleeding. If that was a skill I had, it was a skill I had to cultivate, both because I needed to fix any accidents I might have and because the possibility of structurally healing people was too much a positive to not pursue.

"Are you okay?"

I started a little. Ellie was suddenly beside me. I must have walked past the cafeteria and she'd seen me. I breathed, then felt for my power and it seemed to be under control. Only then did I look at her and verify that she wasn't visibly bleeding.

"You probably shouldn't surprise me like that."

"I'm sorry. You've gotten so much control that it didn't even occur to me to be worried. Are you okay, though?"

"I just killed a mouse." I laughed hollowly.

"I'm sorry."

"Yeah. I'm sorry. I'm being difficult. You shouldn't have to apologize twice in ten seconds."

"Nor should you have to apologize for having feelings or for wanting me to be safe."

She tentatively touched my hand. I grabbed on like a lifeline. I stopped walking and looked at her. "I guess the mouse shouldn't matter. It's not like it's the first."

She turned and looked at me. "But it was the first that you purposefully hurt that died, right? I don't mean that to be accusing. It's just that this one was different, and you did care about the others, too. I think it's admirable that you care."

"Thanks. I think I may be joining you in the world of vegetarianism."

"It's a good world for the sensitive-to-animal-pain crowd."

"Indeed."

"Do you want to talk about what happened?"

"I don't know. I mean, briefly, I cut the mouse, then made the mouse bleed more, then started sticking it back together, then it died."

"It worked, though? Mending?" Her eyes lit up in excitement, which brought me back to the win of it all.

I grinned. "Yeah. I...I have to do it again. I'm just out here working up to it."

She hugged me. "You are brave and strong and you can do this. I'm really proud of you."

I buried my nose in her damp blond hair, breathing in the scent of her shampoo. It was citrusy, and I realized that the comfort I'd lately been taking from my morning orange juice was probably tied to the fact that it bore similarities to Ellie's scent. I pulled back, ready. "Okay. I'm going to go try again."

"Let me walk with you. I'll put the mouse in the cage and get it tranquilized."

I squeezed her hand. "Thanks. I want to say no, that I can do it, but the fact is that it would help a lot."

Once Ellie had me all set up, we hugged goodbye and she whispered more affirmations in my ear. Then it was just me and the mouse. Knowing I couldn't save the last one made things harder, but also knowing that the mending worked gave me some hope. As I contemplated actually picking the mouse up and cutting, I wondered if having done it the once would make it easier or harder. On the one hand, we get inured to things. Like, changing a baby's poopy diaper for the first time is so disgusting that many people feel like they're going to puke—but do it enough, and it's still gross, but you just do it. On the other hand, I now knew the visceral feel of the cut and the mouse's reaction, which was slight because of the drugs, but there. Ugh.

I took a couple of moments to center myself, then I just did it. And then I reached and made the bleeding stop. Yes, just like that. I'd found the switch the once and didn't have to fumble for it now. I knew where it was. I just flipped it. I didn't even have to look at the mouse to know it was working, but I did, seeing the blood slow. I kept going and watched the skin knit together.

Holy shit. I had the ability to help people, not just hurt them. I was not just a destructive person who had to be corralled at all times to keep other people safe. I ran out of the cabin, whooping. I ran all the way to the cafeteria where my friends came rushing out to see what was going on.

Ellie was in the lead, coming down the stairs, looking like she was puzzling out if this was good or bad news when her foot slipped on the wet stair and she went down, hitting her head hard on the banister on her way down.

"Ellie!" I was running before she stopped falling and was at her side by the time she was lying awkwardly on the stairs, blood starting to flow on her scalp.

"Get back!" Sabrina yelled. I didn't realize she was yelling that at me until she added, "You might make it worse!"

"No! I can fix this!"

"You have to back up! We have to call 9-1-1!" Sabrina was sobbing.

"Sabrina! I can fix this! Back up yourself so I can!"

"No! No! You might make her bleed more. You're so upset." She was choking the words out between sobs.

Heather was kneeling by Ellie's head, feeling for a pulse. Holy shit, did she really think Ellie was dead? I looked away and took Sabrina's hands in mine. I took a deep breath. "Sabrina," I said calmly. "I know I can do this. I need you to believe in me. Breathe with me. Breathe in for one, two, three, four…"

As I counted, she turned wild eyes on me, and I wasn't sure this was going to work. First I had to get her calm enough to back up and let me do this. Then I had to actually do it. I pushed that aside. Right now, I'm just breathing, I told myself. Sabrina shakily started to breathe in with me. I squeezed her hands. "Now out. Follow me."

It was on our third breath in that I felt a shift. I reached for my power and found the switch. I felt Ellie's wounds start to close. She was bleeding in her head, too, but I was able to really feel it and know where I was sealing the cells together. It was so much clearer than with the mouse. Was that because she was human? I had to assume that Sabrina was doing the gift equivalent of holding her breath so I could do this, but it felt like more. It almost felt like she actually amplifying my gift rather than muting it.

Ellie started to stir and Heather gasped. Our concentration broken, Sabrina and I dropped hands and turned to them. I knelt down beside Ellie. "Are you okay?" I choked out. Now I was crying. Now that the danger seemed to have passed, tears were streaming down my face.

Ellie sat up and looked around. "What happened?" She touched her head with her hand and then looked at it. "Whose blood is this?"

I laugh-sobbed. "Yours, love. It's yours, but I think you've stopped bleeding now. How do you feel?"

She moved her head slowly from side to side, bemused. "Fine. I think. Really, though, what happened? And did you call me love?"

"Um, yeah?" Now I was worried about that.

She smiled. "I love that."

I smiled, relieved again. "You were coming down the stairs and you slipped. You hit your head on the banister and just went down."

"Really? But I'm not bleeding now? Did you heal the wound?"

"Yeah, and some bleeding in your brain, too."

Sabrina broke in at this point, "Really? How do you know?"

"Something happened when we were breathing in sync. I don't know what, but I could see what I was doing. Sabrina, do you think maybe you can also boost powers?"

She looked shocked. "I…I have no idea."

We were all still standing on the stairs, partially on different levels. Heather spoke up, "This is all wild and exciting, but I think we should take this inside. Ellie needs to clean up at the least."

"Maybe a shower and clean clothes?" I suggested.

"Yeah, actually, that sounds good," Ellie said.

We all seemed to want to be together to keep talking about what had happened, so we trooped back to the cabin together. I explained my experiment with the mouse. We told Ellie in detail what had happened in the brief period of time she was out of it. It took much longer to tell her than it did to live it, because each of us had to tell it from our own perspective. We kept cutting in on one another to emphasize certain points, and to tell what we were thinking in the moment.

The cabins had attached bathrooms (it was a fancy camping experience), so Ellie gathered her things and disappeared into the bathroom while the rest of us settled on a bunk. We were quiet for a moment and could hear the mouse scrabbling around in its cage.

"This is huge," Sabrina finally said. "You really have control now. You can go to medical school. If you weren't going to make everyone bleed when you were so distraught about Ellie, you're not going to make people bleed when you're stressed. That was seriously intense."

"Yeah it was," Heather said. "And you totally handled your shit."

"I know. I…I don't know how to feel. I'm excited and also a little scared and I'm—" I burst into tears.

"Are those happy tears?" Sabrina asked.

"No!" I sobbed. "I'm going to miss you so much!"

Sabrina started crying then, too, and we fell into each other's arms while Heather sat by, awkwardly patting first my shoulder than Sabrina's. After a minute or two, she said, "You guys are ridiculous. Just because you can be apart doesn't mean you have to be. You're allowed to still hang out."

I pulled back and wiped my eyes. "I know, but it'll never be the same."

Sabrina got up and went into the bathroom, coming back with a wad of toilet paper for each of us. There were two shower stalls in there, so she wasn't walking in on Ellie or anything. We sat there, blowing our noses and wiping our eyes.

"It's not going to be the same with Isabella," Sabrina said, then started crying again. "Sorry. I'm really happy for you, but I wish it actually meant I was free, too."

I teared up again. "Me, too."

"Maybe Isabella will learn control," Heather suggested half-heartedly.

Sabrina took a deep breath. "What is really cool is your ability to fix wounds. Let's concentrate on that."

I brightened. "Yeah, that's pretty cool, huh?"

Heather cleared her throat and we both turned to look at her. She said, "I hate to burst your bubble, but you know that your ability to actually use that power will be seriously limited. You can't just go to work in an ER and start healing people who are bleeding. You'd give away that you have a power. That can't happen. The Family's rule about keeping our powers secret is one of their good ones."

"Yes," I said slowly, "that's true. However, if I did become an ER doctor, I could at least stop some internal bleeding before any tests showed that there was internal bleeding. I could just boost things a little." I worried the problem over. "Maybe I can figure out what I can and can't do later. For now, I feel good about my control and incredibly happy that I was able to heal Ellie."

Ellie came out of the bathroom then, in yesterday's dress and hair wrapped up in a towel. "Me, too." She set her stuff down and came and sat on the bed next to me. I held my arm out for her to cuddle under and she burrowed in.

"I'm so glad you're okay," I murmured.

"Thank you."

"You wouldn't have even been hurt if it weren't for me."

Heather and Sabrina got up behind me and walked out. I noticed, because I'd spent nearly a decade noticing Sabrina's every movement, but I ignored them and kept my attention on Ellie. I felt more than a little scandalous about ignoring Sabrina leaving, but I did it anyway.

Ellie scoffed a little. "Please. You had nothing to do with me falling."

"Other than being the one who dragged you out here and then making such a fuss that you felt you had to fly out to see what was going on."

"I can take responsibility for my own actions, thank you very much," Ellie chided.

"You're right. You're an independent person fully capable of making your own choices and I'm sorry that I implied otherwise."

She nodded, head moving on my shoulder. "Remember that." Now her tone was playful, though.

"Yes, ma'am!"

She turned her head slightly so that her face was half hidden on my chest, and I hoped like heck that all of the stress of the day hadn't broken through my deodorant. "Joan, when you called me love...did you mean that...what I mean to say is...Joan, I love you."

Her voice was muffled, but the words were music to my soul. I squeezed her closer. For a half a moment, I couldn't say anything. But I knew how worried I'd be if I'd put that out there and she hadn't said anything back, so I started talking. "I did mean that. I mean, I love you, too, Ellie."

She pulled back and looked at me. She was smiling really big and that drew my attention to her lips. I glanced down at them and licked my own, watching her smile slip away. When I looked back up at her eyes, they'd gone a little dark and she was looking at my lips. In nearly the same movement, we leaned in and started kissing, shifting so that I was lying on my back and she was on top of me. The weight of her felt so good that I moaned a little.

"Am I too heavy? I can…"

I cut her off with a kiss and put my hands on her hips, holding her in place. Against her lips I said, "You are perfect, and don't you ever forget it."

She sighed and kissed me back. I trailed my hand up her side and pulled the towel that had gone rather catawampus fully off her head, tossing it to the side so I could thread my fingers in her damp hair. I was only distracted for a moment by feeling her head to reassure myself that it was intact. Meanwhile, her hand trailed down my side to my hip, then back up under my T-shirt. I moaned again.

When I was brave enough to run my hand under the skirt of her dress, I encountered the boy shorts I'd gotten a peek of when she'd explained to me before how dresses really were practical. I was surprised, though, to find that the black boy shorts had a rainbow band. I trailed my fingers along it. "This is awesome."

"Thanks. You should see the matching bra," she hinted broadly, and I helped her out of her dress.

I lost myself in her for I don't know how long, but I can tell you that I enjoyed every moment of that time, even if there were moments where I was unsure of myself. We figured it out together, and that was part of what made it so good.

We were cuddled up together, my fingers trailing patterns on her side, when she said, "It's getting dark."

I sighed. That meant our time was up. It probably should have been earlier. The days were getting long, and we had the drive back to the city yet to do. The clouds and mist made it seem dark earlier than it would have been otherwise, but we still needed to get going.

I buried my face in her neck, making her giggle and squirm. It was funny how when I was kissing her neck while making love, she'd thrown her head back to give me room, but now she was ticklish. I laughed a little and she pushed on me. "Stop!" She put a hand over her neck.

I pulled back and smiled. "You weren't ticklish there a little bit ago," I told her.

"Well, I am now." She kept her hand in its protective position.

I kissed her. "I'll be good. You can lower your hand." Then I sighed again. "We should get dressed and get going, though."

She echoed my sigh. "I know."

Neither of us moved, though. "I do love you, Ellie, and this was…" I didn't know how to describe my feelings about what we'd just done. "This was really wonderful."

"I'm glad. It was for me, too. And I love you, too."

We kissed again, then finally got up, dressed, and fetched the others so we could pack and start the drive home.

CHAPTER TWENTY

We'd gotten home late the night before. Ellie and I had endured the teasing of the others before anyone could be bothered to pack up for the drive back. We'd stopped to let the rest of the mice free and had a little ceremony in which I thanked them for their service. Ellie said she hoped they made it out in the wild and the rest of us seconded the sentiment. We had a moment of silence for the mice I'd killed, even though Heather rolled her eyes a little about that. Then we'd stopped for dinner again, so by the time we'd gotten home, Sabrina's parents were in their room, seemingly asleep, and we'd just gone in quietly and gone to bed. So, I wasn't too surprised when I felt a little strange waking up. What surprised me was when I fully opened my eyes and looked around. I was in a strange room in a double bed. I sat up, panicked. What the fuck? Had I been kidnapped? I considered unleashing my power, but then it came to me in a flash. I knew where I was.

I was in isolation. What the hell had happened?

I took a deep, calming breath, closing my eyes and focusing on the feel of the bed underneath me and the sound of my own breathing. I was safe and I knew it, really knew it. The ability to control my powers had been seriously tested just the day before and I had faith. Still, I was now in a really stressful situation and it wouldn't help to be freaked out, so I centered myself. I could work this out. Sabrina would tell people I was safe. Gamma would fight for me. I just needed to stay calm. I could do this.

When I felt my heart rate slow, I opened my eyes again and

looked around. I was in a room that looked a lot like a generic hotel room. While video chatting with Linda, I'd seen her living room, but not her bedroom, so I wasn't sure if this was the same, but I imagined hers had more personality than this one since she'd lived there most of her life. In the room was the bed I was in, which was bigger than the singles I was used to sleeping in, but not as big as my parents' queen, I guessed, so a double? There were two nightstands, which struck me as funny because when would there ever be a second person to use the second nightstand? There was a lamp on each of the nightstands. I looked for my phone, on each nightstand and in each drawer, but aside from the lamps, there was nothing on or in them. Against the wall past the foot of the bed was a dresser. To my left was a closet with sliding doors, and further down the wall was a closed door. I presumed that opened to the rest of the apartment. To my right were curtains and I could see some light at their edges, so I assumed there was a true window behind them.

I threw the white duvet off and stood. I felt a little dizzy. They must have drugged me to move me in my sleep without me waking up. Why, though? What had happened that made them think they needed to isolate me? Why had Gamma allowed this? I steadied myself with a hand on the bed before moving to the window and opening the curtains. The view outside was different than either my room or Sabrina's. It was most similar to the view out my living room, but higher. So, yeah. I was definitely up on the eleventh floor.

I opened the door and saw a room that contained a couch, a coffee table, a bureau with a television on it, a small table with two chairs (again the absurdity of needing more than one) and a small kitchen area. On the table was a plate with two muffins, a note, and a laptop. That's where I went.

The note said:

Hello Joan,

    I imagine you're feeling rather discombobulated this morning. Sorry about that. Sorry for sending you to isolation in this manner, but while you and Sabrina were away for the weekend, things became untenable for Isabella. I'm not going to go into the details in this note, but it's become necessary for her to spend all of her time with Sabrina. As a constant threesome is just not possible and with your power being what it is, the Council has determined that you will need to move to isolation. Of course, Sabrina and Isabella can visit you. And of course, we will do everything in our power to keep you comfortable. The laptop has been set up to allow you intraFamily communication and one-way internet. That is to say, you can surf all you want, but you won't be able to post anything anywhere or communicate with people outside the Family in any way.

There is orange juice in the refrigerator, as Andrea told us it's your favorite morning beverage. Lunch will be delivered at noon. Please give Andrea a list of any foods you may want, as well as anything else that you'd like to make you feel at home. She is our primary contact for Linda's and your needs.

I know this will have come as a shock, but I also know you are a rational and levelheaded young woman and will do your best to adapt to your new circumstances.

Sincerely,

Fred

Fred? Fucking Fred? Gamma couldn't even be bothered to write me the note herself? That seemed highly unlikely. Maybe this had been done without her knowledge.

I opened the laptop. It was not my laptop. When I opened it, I was greeted with an icon that was captioned Joan. When I clicked on it, I was taken to an interface that didn't look like a regular Windows interface, but I didn't know what it was. There was a Firefox icon and a FamilyChat icon. I only knew what the Firefox icon even was because of having used a Family computer in the teen room before. I clicked on the FamilyChat icon and logged in. As I did so, I wondered how robust the system was for keeping the internet one-sided. Maybe that was part of why they'd given me Firefox.

Had they been able to put some sort of admin lock on it, making the internet read-only for me?

There were messages from each of my parents, each of Sabrina's parents, Neil, Gamma, Fred, Andrea, and Linda. The lack of a message from Sabrina made me think she was still sleeping. They'd probably drugged her, too, so she wouldn't wake up when they were taking me out. I sent her a message first.

> **Joan:** *I'm in isolation. You probably know this. I'm okay. Text me as soon as you're up.*

Only then did I open any of the others. I started with Gamma's.

> **Gamma:** *I'm so sorry, my girl. The rest of the Council did this behind my back. We'll figure this out. Message me as soon as you get this. I want to tell you to be of good cheer, but I feel that might not ring true right now.*

I felt a flood of relief that she had my back and hadn't been part of this. I wrote back.

> **Joan:** *I'm up. I'm okay, a little freaked out, but okay. I am doing all my calming exercises. Can you video chat?*

She responded by calling me.

"Joan!" she said when I clicked Accept. "How are you, my girl?"

I started crying. God, I was doing a lot of crying lately. "I'm okay. I really am," I said, dashing my tears away. "I've been very calm."

She looked sympathetic. "It's okay to have feelings. This is scary. I wish I could make you a cup of tea."

"I'd really like that, too. Gamma, you should know that my range is…beyond isolation. And the fact that no one is being hurt right now proves I'm safe."

She looked a little shocked, and I felt guilty for not keeping her more up to date on what all we'd learned over the last few weekends, but if she knew and had told the Council, I might be in an even worse situation right now.

"I need to check on Linda," she said, turning.

"No, Gamma. It's okay. I've got it under control. I have control. No one is bleeding right now."

"How can you know?"

"I can tell when I'm using my power now. Also, Gamma, I can stop bleeding even if I didn't cause it."

"Tell me everything," she instructed, so I did, even the part about Ellie going to the summer camp with us. I guess I could have lied and said that it had been Heather who'd had the accident, but I'd just gotten into the groove of telling the story. She interrupted at that point. "Joan Elizabeth! You told your girlfriend our Family secrets? That will have to be addressed, but for now, keep telling me what happened."

I hung my head and murmured, "Sorry, Gamma, but I love her."

She sighed exasperatedly. "Everyone thinks they love their first girlfriend or boyfriend. This is why we have rules in place for telling people! But this is a problem to deal with after we get you out of there. Right now I want to know every little thing you did up there."

While we were talking, Sabrina woke up, or rather messaged. I suppose I didn't know for sure if she'd woken up earlier without checking her phone, but it seemed unlikely. I sent her a quick message back explaining I was talking to Gamma and would call her as soon as I was done.

When I'd told Gamma all, she said, "I'm so proud and pleased that you have gotten your power under control, my girl. I am going to go convene the Council and get you out of there. Don't you worry."

We hung up and I called Sabrina. She answered with Isabella by her side, face tense. Isabella looked ashamed. She spoke first. "Joan! I'm so sorry! I didn't ask them to do this!"

Sabrina put her arm around Isabella and said, "We know. You're not to blame here."

"Isabella, Sabrina's right. I don't blame you. What happened this weekend?"

"I couldn't block anything out! I'm so sorry! I tried to meditate like you guys suggested, but the thoughts just kept coming, from everyone. Finally, Mom took me to Jenny, and Jenny said I should go into one of the isolation apartments until Sabrina was back from summer camp. It was so good not to hear anything, but then I was alone and scared. Mom stayed on a video call with me all afternoon and evening until I went to bed, but that was really scary, too. Mom came up with a pill and told me it would help me sleep. I was so glad to see her, but then I heard her thinking about how much she didn't want me to hear her thinking about me and about how"—she sobbed—"she was scared of me but also scared for me and it was awful. I took the pill and fell asleep. When I woke up, I was in your bed, Joan. I'm sorry!"

"Shh, shh, it's okay," I tried to comfort her. Sabrina had better luck, being physically there with her.

"Hey," I said. "The note I got said you two could come visit. Do you want to come up?"

"Do you think they'll let us?" Sabrina asked.

"Why not? They said it was okay and they're not monsters." I paused to consider. "Not complete monsters. Gamma is meeting with the Council and is going to get stuff sorted, but you guys should come up."

While I waited for Sabrina to either call back or show up, I responded to the others who had messaged me, all except for Fred. He was obviously busy with the Council meeting, but also very much on my shit list. Sabrina's parents were very apologetic about letting the middle-of-the-night kidnapping happen. They'd been told to go stay in guest housing for the night, so they hadn't been in bed sleeping after all when we'd gotten home the night before. They'd spent the night restlessly worrying about how Sabrina and I would deal with this situation and assured me of their love and support. My parents said the same. I guess whoever had actually moved us hadn't known for sure where we would sleep, so they'd asked both sets of parents to clear out. It was a sign of how much we all bowed to what the Council said the Family needed that they'd just done it. I couldn't find it in myself to hold it against them, but

I did think again that something needed to change. It also validated my early impulse to not tell them what we were up to. I loved them, but I couldn't completely trust them.

Neil had heard from our parents what was happening, and his text was concerned and outraged about it.

Linda's message was welcoming me to the eleventh floor, but as much as I liked her, it was a welcome I did not want.

Andrea's message had offered sympathy about my new living situation, mentioned she missed our chatter in the kitchen, and reiterated that she was happy to help procure anything I needed. I replied to her saying thank you for her kindness and I would get back to her. I was hoping I wouldn't have to get back to her, or at least not until I could do so in person.

Sabrina finally called back to explain that the visit would have to wait. It turned out it wasn't that easy to just go to the eleventh floor. You needed a key to make the elevator go all the way up or to open the stairwell above tenth, and no one had given Sabrina one yet. She and Isabella had gone down to the caf to ask Andrea if they could use her key, but Andrea said she wasn't supposed to let anyone else use it. She'd have gone to Gamma, but Gamma was meeting with the Council.

"Although maybe you'll just be free before we get it figured out," she said optimistically.

"We can hope." I held up my hand to show my fingers were crossed. "So, there's something else."

"What more could there possibly be?" she asked.

"They know about Ellie or, at least, Gamma does, so I imagine everyone else will soon."

Sabrina glanced at Isabella, clearly wondering if we should be talking about it in front of her. She had a point, actually. It was possible Gamma wouldn't tell that detail, or that if she did, it wouldn't make it past Council. They wouldn't want to give anyone any ideas.

I shifted gears. "Would you text her for me? I don't want her thinking I'm ghosting her after yesterday."

Sabrina got a sly look. "Right. That would be bad. What do

you want me to say? You're grounded and your parents took your phone?"

I shook my head. "No, she'd just wonder why I wasn't using yours then. Tell her…" I stopped, looking at Isabella sitting there next to her, following along in the conversation. I'd been going to tell her to tell the truth, but there was the same problem with encouraging rule breaking. "I'll send you a text to forward to her."

"What will you say?" Isabella asked.

"Something like what Sabrina said, but at least it'll be from me," I said distractedly while I typed out a message to Ellie.

Joan: *Things are happening around here. I think it'll all be okay, but I'm in isolation right now. I love you and I'll get in touch as soon as I can.*

Sabrina read it and said, "Aww," then did stuff with her phone that I presumed was sending it on.

"Shit," I said, then looked at Isabella again. "I mean, shoot. I just realized I can't do school. I guess they figured that if I'm going to be here for the rest of my life, I don't really need to finish the semester, but now I'm going to get behind. I've already been taking the weekends off of homework and studying."

"You can still study, right? You just can't upload assignments and stuff like that. So, study, then."

"I haven't checked out how much I can do online yet. I think nothing except navigate around. I think I won't be able to log into my school account. And they didn't send any of my schoolbooks up, at least not that I've seen. So, no. I don't think I can study."

"Man. That all really sucks. I'm so sorry."

If I got out today, I'd be okay. I tended to keep on top of things generally, but there was an assignment I needed to submit by the end of day tomorrow. "If I'm not out by tomorrow, will you submit my essay for Gender Studies? It's done, it's just sitting in Documents on my laptop."

"Um, your laptop isn't here."

"Is it up in my room? You can just go get it."

"No…mine was up there, so I went to get it for this, and yours wasn't. I think maybe the Council or their minions have it."

Well, shit. If they did, they were probably scouring it, which meant that they would know that I'd told Ellie because I had the messaging app on my computer and used it to text as often as my phone, which they probably had, too, I realized. So, it didn't matter if Gamma didn't tell about Ellie. They'd know. Great. Another thing to worry about.

"Ellie just texted back," Sabrina said. "I'll forward it to you."

It occurred to me that if they were going through my stuff, they would potentially be monitoring my FamilyChat texts, too, but either way the cat was out of the bag, so I just said, "Thanks."

Ellie: *Are you okay? If you need any help, let me know. I don't know what I can do, but if there's anything…I hope you get out soon. I love you, too.*

I didn't know how to reply to that or really what to say to Sabrina, especially with Isabella there. "Listen, you guys should really be doing school right now. I'll go, um, do something."

They both protested, saying that they couldn't possibly concentrate on school considering the circumstances, but I insisted I was fine and it was just a matter of time and signed off. I clicked on the Firefox icon to see exactly what limits I had. Indeed I couldn't log in anywhere or create an account. I could use some strange search engine I'd never seen before to find websites and go there. I could click on links. I couldn't do anything else. If I was going to be here forever, that would have freaked me the fuck out. I couldn't even be able to stream anything without an account. How did this work for Linda? I clicked around on files and settings on the computer. I couldn't change anything. I didn't have admin privileges. That wasn't super surprising. I did find a file that contained movie titles. I clicked on one experimentally and the movie started playing. Great. I had access to about ten movies.

I slammed the laptop shut and concentrated on my breathing.

I did a yoga routine.

When I was done, I checked messages again. Gamma had texted.

> **Gamma:** *My girl, it seems that this might not be as easy as I'd hoped. The Council isn't convinced that you're as safe to be around as you're claiming. They want proof. They are also frankly concerned that I'm manipulating things to help you and have insisted on Sabrina being present for all further discussions so they can be sure their moods are their own.*

I'd told her about Sabrina being able to amplify as well as dampen, and the lack of reference to it here made me feel fairly certain they were indeed monitoring conversations. I wondered if that was someone's job, to watch over all of us like Big Brother. Was it one of the tech people, so helpful if you needed computer help, but actually a big creep spying on us all? Or maybe just people of interest, like me.

> **Gamma:** *It may take a few days to convince them and set up a demonstration, so do make sure you tell Andrea what you need to be comfortable.*

I put my head down on my arms and cried a little. Okay, a lot. I'd truly thought once they heard I had control, I'd be out, certainly in time for dinner. But now it looked like I was going to be here by myself for a while. Going from being with someone literally always, to this, was hard. I was lonely already. Going from the weekend of connectedness with Ellie to nothing? It was more than hard. What if she gave up on me? What if I never saw her again?

When the tears mostly stopped, I went to the sink in the kitchen area and splashed water on my face, then dried it with the dish towel. I realized that I was still in my pajamas, hadn't needed to go to the bathroom yet, and was super thirsty. I went to the fridge for the orange juice I'd been promised and saw a whole carton of it. Of course, if I was living here and wanted some every morning, that made sense. Tears threatened again, but I took some deep breaths and tried to keep them at bay. I was so tired of crying.

I got out the OJ and opened cupboards until I found one with glasses. I opened the carton and started pouring. The citrus smell at first comforted me, but then made me wonder when I'd see Ellie again, if ever. What if I really was here for the rest of my life? I didn't know if I could even get the OJ down, but once I started drinking, thirst took over and I drank the whole glass in one go. I poured another and sipped it more slowly. I didn't think I was up for eating, but getting cleaned up and dressed might help me feel more in control, so I put the carton of orange juice back and went to see what supplies I had.

The shower was stocked with Sabrina's shampoo, my conditioner, body wash, and the face scrub we both used, none new. I wondered if she was now stuck with my shampoo and no face scrub. I showered, toweled dry, wrapped a towel around my hair and one around my torso and went back to the bedroom to see if I had clean clothes or if I was just going to be wearing the same pair of pajamas every day all day. They were comfortable, sure, but they'd start to stink and wouldn't make me look very put together if I was trying to convince people I was okay and in control.

All the clothes from my room were there. Not just all of my clothes, but all the clothes we kept there. Because we mostly slept in Sabrina's room, most of the clothes either of us wore regularly had made their way to her room, so this was B-team stuff, but at least there were clothes. I ignored Sabrina's clothes. She was at least a size smaller than me, and these, being castoffs, were mostly things even she hadn't worn in a long time. I pulled on a pair of underwear that had little pictures of Princess Amidala on them that Sabrina had gotten me as a joke, followed by jeans that were too long and frayed at the bottom from me dragging the ends on the ground when I walked. On top was a bra that had lost its underwire, and a T-shirt that had a hole in the armpit. Great.

I sighed and went back to the laptop, thinking I'd message Sabrina and have her pack up some of my current favorite clothes to bring up. Just the thought made me want to curl up and cry some more, but enough was enough. I also needed books or something to entertain myself with. She could bring those, too.

What I found was another flood of messages, one of which was from just moments ago, and was Sabrina saying that Gamma was going to meet her at the elevator to let her up to eleven and she'd be up in about five minutes. I jumped up and down a little. Seriously, we hadn't been apart this long since we were eight. I did quick replies to the various parents, assuring them I was fine. I mean, I was, sort of, and then there was a knock on the door.

That door knock set off a rapid set of thoughts. Was the door locked? How had I not tried it? Could I have just walked out this whole time? If I did just walk out, would that signal cutting ties with the Family? If it was locked, could Sabrina unlock it? I went to try to open the door, not sure what to expect. It wasn't locked. Well, shit, that right there was a psychology experiment, wasn't it?

The thought was pushed out of my head, though, when I opened the door to see Sabrina and Isabella standing there. Behind them was a kind of open, almost warehouse-looking area. I knew that the four corners were the isolation units with dead space in between that was almost never used. The delivery systems for the apartments were via dumbwaiter. I hadn't yet found mine, but I hadn't looked for it.

That was all one quick flash, though, before I pulled Sabrina in and hugged her. Sabrina hugged me back, just as fiercely. Isabella hung back, looking unsure until we both reached out and pulled her into the hug to make it a three-way.

"Are you okay?" Sabrina asked, muffled by my shoulder.

"Are you?"

"I'm not locked away up here," she protested.

"Apparently neither am I, unless you somehow unlocked the door before you knocked?"

"No," came Isabella's voice, also muffled, but by our sides. "We didn't do anything to the door, right, Sabrina?"

"That's right. You could have left at any time?"

I finally pulled back and shrugged. "I guess. That would

probably prove I was safe, right? If I just walked into the caf at lunch time and no one bled?"

"It's past lunch now," Isabella pointed out.

"Maybe at breakfast tomorrow, then," I said.

Sabrina looked worried. "What do you think they'd do then?"

I wasn't sure how to answer in front of Isabella. "Let's sit down," I suggested.

Only then did I notice that Sabrina had brought a canvas bag. It sat on the floor just inside the still open to the odd dark beyond. I pulled the door closed. "What's in the bag?"

"Just some clothes and stuff."

I picked it up and took a peek. I saw my favorite jeans and T-shirt, the book I was currently reading, and a bag of black licorice on top. "Thanks, Sabrina. This is just what I needed."

"Obviously," Isabella said, eyeing my outfit.

I rolled my eyes. "Okay, fashionista, go sit down and make yourself comfortable." She strutted over to the couch in an imitation of a fashion model.

Sabrina put her hand on my arm and said, "I'd have snuck up your phone if I could have."

"Do you have yours?" I asked.

She shook her head. "Gamma took it at the elevator. I guess I won't just be given a key."

We moved over to the couch and sat next to Isabella. It was really more of a love seat, so it was a tight fit for the three of us. For all that there were two nightstands and two chairs, the people who furnished these places must not really have expected the occupants to have company.

I pulled out the licorice and offered it around, but no one else wanted any. Now that Sabrina was here, I felt a little more settled, and I popped a piece of candy in my mouth. It was the first thing I'd eaten aside from the orange juice and it didn't exactly settle well in my stomach. I got up and went to the kitchen area to start opening doors.

"What are you doing?" Isabella asked.

"I'm looking for the dumbwaiter."

"Oh! I'll help!" She jumped up and beat me to the kitchen. It was a small area, so she found it on her second try. "Here it is! Oh, look, food."

"That's what I was thinking," I said. "I was told lunch would be sent up, but I hadn't checked for it."

Isabella pulled the tray out. It contained a sandwich, an apple, and some chips. Sadly, the sandwich was turkey and I'd just sworn off eating meat that weekend. Andrea would have had no idea, so I didn't blame her, but it was still disappointing. Again, I needed to message her. I wondered what was going to happen at dinner time. The caf didn't have a dinner service, and no one had given me any food. Of course, I'd been told to ask for it and I hadn't.

"Can I have one of these muffins?" Isabella asked, standing by my little table.

"Sure, knock yourself out," I said, lightly tossing the apple from hand to hand as I went back to the couch to flop back down next to Sabrina. "This sucks."

"I say, if they don't have a plan by lunch tomorrow, you just come on down to the caf," Sabrina said.

"Maybe I can't call an elevator from up here without a key, either," I suggested. "How are you supposed to get down? Did Gamma say?"

"No." She shook her head. "I'm assuming I can just call the elevator. If you couldn't, then what would happen in case of a fire?"

"You're not supposed to take the elevator in case of a fire anyway," I pointed out.

She pointed at me. "True, but then you'd have to be able to access the stairway. I suspect that they think you'll stay up here just because you know you're dangerous, or that other people are dangerous to you, in the case of someone like Linda. If you were dangerous and being up here would protect people, you'd totally stay. Any of us would."

I groaned. "This is just stupid. If they trust me to just stay up here, then why didn't they just talk to us and tell me this was what was happening? Also," this just having occurred to me, "how did they get me up here? If they think I make people bleed when I'm away from you, then they couldn't have just picked me up and brought me up here unless they somehow know that my power doesn't work when I'm asleep."

"Maybe that's part of why they drugged me, too. Maybe they brought us both up and then me back down to bed."

"Maybe. Also, who the hell is doing all of this? Like, who is the muscle for the Council?"

Sabrina shrugged. "One of the many people who is employed by the Family, I guess."

"I guess. I suspect that someone is monitoring FamilyChat, too."

"Really? That's super Big Brother."

"Maybe not all the time, but I bet they're looking at everything I've texted since I got up here, and are probably looking at my phone and laptop now. Gamma strategically left out something we'd talked about when she texted."

"So they'll not only know about Ellie, but that I helped you send her a message today," she said.

"Yep. I think we're going to be in trouble. What do you think they'll do?"

"Why will you be in trouble?" Isabella asked around a mouth full of muffin. "What did you do? Are you not supposed to date?"

"I shouldn't have sent her a message today." I left it at that. I sighed and tried to change the subject. It was hard to find anything innocuous to talk about with everything looming over me, so we ended up just watching one of the movies on my laptop. Then they had to go because Isabella had her violin lesson. She used to go out for her lessons, but now it had been arranged to have her instructor come to her apartment.

"How are you explaining being there?" I asked Sabrina.

"I'm not explaining anything. Lynne told her teacher that I was going to be there, but I'd stay quiet and out of the way. Apparently the teacher protested, saying she didn't allow people to sit in on lessons and asking why this was happening. Lynne doubled her fee and that was that. Of course, the Family is paying."

"Of course. Okay, well, come back tomorrow." I was already dreading the hours alone all evening and going to sleep for the first time in eight years in a room all by myself.

"Or we'll see you tomorrow down in the caf," Sabrina said back.

"Will you text Ellie again for me?" I stopped to gather myself. I couldn't believe that I was expected to just drop her like this. Of course, when they put me up here, no one knew how important she'd become to me. At least no one who was in on the decision, since they'd excluded Gamma. What if I never got out of here? I fought down my panic at the idea. I finally said, "Just tell her you saw me and I'm okay."

"I will."

We all hugged again, and I don't think I was the only one who was close to tears. Well, Isabella seemed miserable about having come between us, but not near tears. That was Sabrina and me.

CHAPTER TWENTY-ONE

I was less disoriented when I woke up the next morning. Whether because it was the second morning, or because I didn't have any lingering drugs in my system, I wasn't sure. Maybe both. After Sabrina and Isabella left the previous night, I'd messaged with Andrea a bit and we'd settled on takeout from my favorite Thai place for dinner that night. I'd finally been hungry enough to eat and I couldn't pass up Pad Thai, which I'd ordered with tofu rather than the chicken I'd gotten before the mouse experiments. I'd tried to watch a movie, but I couldn't get into it. My mind just kept going elsewhere. I'd finally texted with Neil for a while, which was helpful, and then with Heather, which was also helpful. She'd had some choice words to say about the Family. Gamma messaged to say that the Council was meeting with Sabrina in the room in the morning and to sit tight.

Sabrina stayed up late to text far into the night, which made me feel less lonely. She'd sent along Ellie's love, which was good, too, but not nearly the same as actually being able to contact her. Aside from generally being alone, the part I felt the worst about was being suddenly cut off from Ellie. Because of the structure of my life with Sabrina, all my other friends were Family, so I still had access to them. Ellie, though…my gut twisted at not being able to contact her.

Then it had finally been time to sleep. I'd meditated before bed, trying to really just stay calm about the whole thing. It wouldn't do to get worked up. I'd promised myself I'd be patient and wait this out. It would be a growth event for me.

Then I woke up and decided that was all bunk.

I wasn't going to just sit up here like a helpless person. I had control and I'd just show everyone. Sabrina was right. I should just walk into the caf. I dressed in the jeans and T-shirt Sabrina had brought for me, went out the door and walked to the elevator.

I was looking at it, deciding if I should push the button to call it or if that would somehow alert someone, and I should take the stairs, when Linda opened her door. I turned, shocked. I'd never seen her in person. Sabrina and I could have visited, but she preferred not to be around people.

I was sure she was going to stop me somehow, but instead she said, "Go get 'em, Joan."

"Thanks, Linda. You're not going to turn me in?"

She leaned against her door jam. "Honey, I can tell you're safe. You're broadcasting loud about how you're safe, and how if you weren't, I'd already be dead."

"Well, thanks. Do you, um, want anything? I mean, Sabrina would still be happy to accompany you places or to come visit..." I trailed off, fairly sure she didn't want that.

Indeed, she shook her head. "No, thanks, just go and stop yelling at me like this." She gave a slightly pained smile.

"Sorry. I'll just..." I trailed off, pointing to the door to the stairwell and made my way over to it.

"I know you are," she said, turning to go back inside her apartment.

I opened the door to the stairwell and started down. My heart was hammering. I was probably going to be in big trouble here, but at least I wouldn't be in isolation anymore. I took the stairs all the way to the ground floor because I felt like I needed the time to gather myself. I tried to treat it like a meditation, just paying attention to how I set my foot down on each step. I wanted to be fully in control when I saw people.

It was only when I was about to exit the stairwell that it occurred to me that Sabrina might be in the caf, in which case everyone would assume I wasn't killing them because she was there. The thought gave me pause enough that I stood and dithered in the stairwell for a few minutes. I wanted to text Sabrina and ask where she was, but of course I didn't have my phone.

Finally, I decided that if Sabrina was there, I'd signal her to walk away. She'd know what I was talking about and why. I opened the door, wondering if I'd run into anyone between there and the caf.

I did. There was a group of six of the elementary school age kids and one parent, Elaine, coming out of the caf all together, presumably on their way to school. At first, the kids looked at me and smiled in greeting, but then they realized I was alone and their eyes went wide and panicky. Elaine put herself in front of the kids like I was some sort of mad bomber and backed up, looking quite panicked herself. "Why, Joan? What are you doing?"

I put my hands up. "Elaine, I'm fine. I've been practicing control and I'm fine. I won't hurt you or the kids. You know I wouldn't. I care about you all."

She still backed up quickly with the kids, not knowing that if I didn't have control, they were all well within range. I didn't want to stress her or them out, so I let them back up, which gave me pause about this whole plan yet again. I would be stressing people out, but just for a moment, and then we'd all be fine, right? There was no real point in just stressing the kids out. There would be a more mixed crowd in the caf, more adults to see and understand. I took a deep breath as they all went around the corner toward the youth center rather than the front door, wondering if I was making them feel like people in a building with an active shooter. Fuck. Maybe I should just go back upstairs. Too late now, though, really. They'd already seen me, and if I didn't get it cleared up that I was safe, I would probably be in isolation for a long, long time.

I moved forward and into the caf. There was a ripple effect. A few people saw me walk in and did double takes before talking to someone next to them or just touching their arm. I saw the awareness that I'd just walked in spread from the door to the far side of the room that was accompanied by silence, and a look of panic, some people going so far as to rise in their seats, as if preparing to run. No, not as if. They were preparing to run. When no one started bleeding, there were looks of bafflement. Lots of people started looking around to see where Sabrina was, probably assuming she was coming through the door behind me. I stepped in a little more so they could see I was alone. I had also scanned the caf and had not seen Sabrina's bleached blond pixie cut, so this was happening.

It wasn't everyone in the Family by far. Some had come and gone, some would come later, and some skipped breakfast in the caf for whatever reasons, but this was peak breakfast time and there were probably around seventy people in the room. Some people were just sitting, some were now standing and yelling. Some were shrinking back. Even though it was only about twenty percent of the people present who were vocally reacting, when those twenty percent started yelling in fear and anger, it was loud.

My dad showed up from a table off to the side where I hadn't noticed him sitting. He walked toward me, only looking a little worried about his safety. After all, I was less than ten feet away from some people and no one was bleeding.

"Joan?" he asked. "Are you…do you really have this under control?"

I was probably the only one who heard him over the ruckus. "I do."

He came to me then, and gathered me in his arms, which felt really good. I might have missed Sabrina and Ellie the most in my one day away, but there was something about a parent's hug that settled the scared kid inside me. I was working to stay in control, and that helped it not be quite so much work.

When the people immediately around us saw this, they looked even less scared, and they started pointing out that Dad was fine to the people around them. Again, there was a ripple effect. This time it was people settling down.

"I think we should call Gamma," Dad said, arm still around me. "The Council should probably come down. They're having a meeting right now."

That explained why none of them, nor Sabrina, were present. "I don't have my phone."

He whipped his out and called. He had to call, get sent to voice mail, then call again to break through the Do Not Disturb Gamma probably had on her phone for the Council meeting. Meanwhile, people around us had chilled out enough that they were going back to talking to each other, and some were even eating. Dad led me to his table to sit down after he dialed the second time. He'd been sitting with Sabrina's parents, I now saw.

I asked, "Where's Mom?"

"In her studio," Todd told me. "How did this happen? How did you figure this out? Is this what you and Sabrina have been doing up at summer camp?"

"Yeah. I, um, had an accident at Central Park a month or so ago." I blushed as they all took a hard look at me. "So, Sabrina and I decided to try to test things out and figure out where limits were and stuff."

"The things you girls keep to yourselves." Sarah shook her head at me.

Dad started talking. "Jenny, hi. So, Joan is down here in the cafeteria and everyone is fine, but you should probably come down." Pause. "Yes." Pause. "No bleeding at all." Pause. "Okay." He turned to the rest of us. "They're all coming down." Then he turned to me. "I'm going to call your mom."

It was only about five minutes before the Council in its entirety showed up, Sabrina and Isabella preceding them. When Sabrina came in, I stood and waved and she made a beeline for me, Isabella trailing in her wake.

"Are you okay?" she asked.

"Fine, but a little scared about what they're going to do." I jutted my chin at the Council who were coming over a little more slowly. "You?"

"Fine, but same."

Past the Council members, I saw my mom slip into the caf, looking a little frantic.

"So, Joan, I see you've decided to take this matter into your own hands," Gamma said as the Council arrived, with maybe a hint of pride in her tone.

Fred grimaced. "Perhaps we shouldn't be encouraging this reckless behavior. Joan, it's best if you come with us and we'll discuss this in private."

Sabrina, though, climbed up on the table and said loudly, "Hi, everyone!"

Everyone was looking in our direction anyway, but now they gave up any pretense of not looking, and the speculative chatter that had been happening died down.

"Yes, hello! Good morning. I think now is a good time to bring up something Joan and..." She paused to look around. I wasn't sure what she was looking for, so I looked with her until my eye landed on Heather, who was behind the serving line, but gave Sabrina a thumbs-up. "Heather and I have been talking about. There are some problems in the Family that are best aired publicly. I mean, within the Family, that is."

At this, some of the Council finally seemed to get an idea that this was something they might not want to have happen. "Now wait a minute, young lady," Fred said.

"No! No waiting until we're old enough to have a voice or even a minute," Heather called out. "This is too important! There are things that are going on that everyone should know about and decide on!"

Some of the adults looked amused. I climbed up on the table with Sabrina. "I know many, if not most, of you know some of the things that the Council gets up to, but I wonder if you all know that they are basically running a breeding program, trying to get the powers they want more prevalent." There were a few surprised looks, but mostly people seemed to know that. "Or that sometimes that's unbeknownst to the parents?" Now some people gasped. "Or even that sometimes the babies they mix have two Family members as biological parents?" At this, there were a few exclamations from the crowd.

"Now, now," Fred tried again to interrupt. He turned to Gamma and hissed, "Do something!"

The something he spoke of may have been to get us, her

granddaughters, into line or it may have been a request to modify the crowd's emotional reactions to what we were saying, but Gamma just shrugged at him.

Heather had made her way through the caf and now climbed up on the table beside us. "It's not right what they do! We should be able to make our own choices about our children!"

"Yeah, that's true" and similar sentiments were being spoken now.

"I think we can all agree that being members of this Family, born or married into, is pretty great in a lot of ways," I said. "We have real community, real support. But these things should not come at the cost of basically having changelings for children, or locking people up who don't need to be imprisoned. All we're saying is that the Council needs to be more transparent in their dealings."

Gamma finally spoke up. "I think that these young ladies have a point. Not only that, but Joan here was indeed isolated without any sort of due process. Perhaps there are cases where that might be necessary, but in this case, she and Sabrina should have been consulted because, as you can see, she is perfectly safe."

"So why did you lock her up, then?" someone called.

Gamma shrugged exaggeratedly. "I'll be frank, I was not consulted." She turned to the other council members.

"It was for the good of the Family," Fred said. "We all know how useful mind readers are. Can you imagine how useful it would be to have a mind reader who can handle being around people? If we can keep Isabella here sane and socialized, that is a huge boon to the Family."

Isabella, who'd been standing next to our table, flinched at being called out. Then she squared her little shoulders and climbed up on the table, too. "I wasn't asked, either, though! Maybe I'd have chosen to go into isolation rather than have Joan go. Or maybe we'd have chosen to all three stay together." She took my hand on one side and Sabrina's on the other. "And that's all if Joan still needed Sabrina, but she doesn't, and no one bothered to find that out or believe her when she told them!"

Sabrina gestured at her. "And this is exactly what we mean. The Council shouldn't be making these decisions in secret without listening to anyone about it. It's wrong!"

Gamma spoke up again. "I think these young ladies raise some very good points. I'd like to suggest that we have a Family-wide meeting where we vote on some of these issues, including a possible change to the way the Council works."

The other Council members looked mad, worried, or just outraged, but most people in the caf were nodding in agreement.

"We'll let you get back to your breakfasts and we'll send out information on this meeting." Gamma turned and gestured at us to get off the table.

I climbed down, feeling a little silly, and like this had been rather anticlimactic. Nothing had really happened. Other than, I suppose, the fact that I wasn't in isolation anymore. I started to shake. It was a huge deal that I wasn't in isolation. That wasn't nothing. I'd been isolated without consent. Locked away from the person I'd spent every minute with since I was eight, locked away from my family and friends. Not only locked away from but had contact cut off from the person I loved. Now that I was out, I wanted to stay out. They weren't going to make me go back, were they? How could they? I looked warily at the Council. Gamma put her arm around me. "No one is going to send you back up. People wouldn't stand for it now. I'm so proud of you, my girl. All of you girls." She pulled in Isabella, Heather, and Sabrina for hugs.

"These girls aren't getting off scot-free," Fred put in. "There is still the matter of telling Family secrets."

"What?" Isabella asked, eyes wide. "Is that what you guys did?" She looked up at Sabrina and me. "Is that what you were talking about?"

Fred looked smug. "See, even little girls know that's wrong."

Gamma chided him. "Little girls who may now have ideas they didn't before you spoke."

Isabella put her hands on her hips and said, "Little girls who are right here, you know."

Fred said, "I thought we were just telling secrets now."

"Then I guess it's not a problem," I tried for jaunty and earned looks from both Gamma and Fred. I wilted. "Look, I'm really sorry about that. It was a one-off thing."

Gamma sighed. "We will still have to address that. Probably the best thing to do is just to start in-processing."

"Jenny, be reasonable. This girl should be brought in for some adjustments, and then Joan should never see her again," Fred protested.

"No! I love her!"

Fred looked smug. "It doesn't matter. Your punishment should be losing her."

My mom joined my side and put her arm around me. "This is exactly the sort of thing that the Council should not be making unilateral decisions about. My mother is right. If we bring Ellie in and have her interview with Linda and she passes, there's no reason not to allow the girls to date. Joan shouldn't lose the girl she loves as punishment. I'm sure we can think of something else."

"Yeah, like being locked up for thirty-six hours," I mumbled.

"It is possible that time served should be on the table," Gamma said. "But first, let's bring Ellie in sooner rather than later and go from there."

Fred frowned at us all. "You think you get to just say it and have it be so. It's not up to you. It's up to the Council." He pointed at me. "This young lady needs to answer for her crimes against the Family. The Council will convene and send you notice of when you'll come in to face the repercussions of your actions."

The remaining three members of the Council had been following all of this with what seemed to me differing levels of agreement with what Gamma, Fred, or I had been saying. When Fred stormed out, Gamma stayed with me. The other three looked between them.

"We're going to have to meet about this," one of them finally said.

"Yes, I see we will," Gamma said. She gave me one last squeeze, then left with the others.

CHAPTER TWENTY-TWO

I watched them walk out with my heart in my throat. Were they going to take Ellie away from me? I had to go see her.

I grabbed Sabrina's arm. "I need to go see Ellie."

I said it softly so our parents wouldn't hear. They were standing near us, talking among themselves. I was worried they'd—I don't know—ground me or something. Sabrina looked around as if for escape routes.

"Come on," Heather said. "Let's just all leave while they're talking. Ask forgiveness, not permission."

That was as good a plan as any. The four of us made for the exit. I expected someone, one of my parents, most likely, to stop us. To call out. But no one did. They must have thought we were just going up to one of our apartments to talk and that they'd catch us there later. Instead, we walked right out the front door.

As soon as we did, Isabella said, "Where are we going?"

"Let's just...let's get away from the building first," I said.

A couple of blocks later, we finally slowed and stepped off to the side to hold a conference.

"What's happening?" Isabella asked.

"We're...I don't know." What was the game plan? We were a couple of blocks away from the Complex. No one seemed to have come after us. I had nothing with me aside from the clothes on my back. Thankfully, the rain from the weekend was gone and it was a lovely spring day. I looked at the others. They were just as unprepared to suddenly be on the streets of New York as I was. Heather was still wearing her apron. What were we doing here? "Don't you need to get to school?"

Heather looked down at herself. "Well, I'm still wearing my apron and I don't have my school bag with me, so I'm going to go with no. Or at least that that's not the priority today. The priority is preparing for the Council meeting, right?"

In long-term thinking, yes. But in short-term thinking, I wanted to see Ellie. Right now.

"Joan needs to see Ellie," Sabrina said.

"Okay, but if we actually prepare you for the disciplinary Council meeting, doesn't that increase your chances of being able to see her all you want?"

She was right, of course. "Yes, but I need to see her. Sabrina, give me your phone."

Sabrina handed it over, no questions asked.

"Don't you think you'll get into more trouble if you run off?" Heather asked.

"What does it really matter at this point? Trouble is pretty maximized. If this is Joan's only chance to see Ellie before… whatever happens happens, she should do that," Sabrina said.

My stomach clenched at that. That was the very problem right there. I needed to see Ellie again while she was still my Ellie. "I need to see her before they change her memories. While she's still the Ellie that loves me."

The phone in my hand buzzed. I looked down at it. "Your dad is asking where we disappeared to," I said to Sabrina. "Maybe Heather is right. We should just all go back."

"What will they do to you?" Isabella asked. I'd nearly forgotten she was there. I looked down at her to see that her face was fearful.

I put the phone in my pocket and looked at her. "I believe it will all be fine, Isabella. I really do. The Family…sometimes they make choices that aren't the best."

"Like locking you away?" she said.

"Exactly like that. But the Family is good. Look at the four of us. Look at your friends. At our parents. I believe they'll make the right choice."

I pulled Sabrina's phone out of my pocket and sent three messages. It took a few minutes, although one was nearly a copy and paste. Then I handed the phone back to Sabrina, who looked at what I'd sent and nodded. Heather took her own phone out of her pocket and read the message that had just come through on the teen-wide FamilyChat. She typed out a message of her own. I took Isabella's hand. "Let's go home."

We walked the couple of blocks back and went inside. Nearly all the teens were standing in the atrium, waiting for us.

"We've got you, Joan!" one called, and several echoed similar sentiments.

"Thank you, everyone. I know I've messed up a little, but so has the Council. We need to stand up for what we believe, what is right. I'm grateful for you all coming to bear witness, to hold them accountable. There should be no more decisions that affect us all made in secret!"

There was a ragged cheer and we moved to the elevators. A few more kids came in as we waited for the elevators. They'd clearly turned back from heading to school. A couple were out of breath. Family business was more important, and everyone who could had turned up.

We rode up to the third floor where the Council offices were. The sight that greeted us warmed my heart even more. My parents, Joan's parents, Heather's mom, and several other Family adults were there waiting.

"Thank you guys for coming. I need to talk to the Council and face up to the choices I made, but I also need—" I broke off as I choked up with a swell of emotions. I was feeling so many things. Thankful for everyone who turned up with only a few minutes' notice. Scared of what was going to happen next. Proud we were standing up for what was right. The scene in the caf was only a start. As much as I'd broken Family rules by telling Ellie our secrets, they'd broken rules with what amounted to their breeding program.

They'd locked me up against my will without even talking to us about what we wanted or were willing to do. There needed to be changes. It was time to shine light on it all and make the Family what it could be instead of the compromised entity it had become. "We all need to make the Council live up to the morals and ethics of the Family."

A few people called out, "Yeah!" A few just nodded. The group parted to allow me to lead the way back to the Council room, where presumably, the Council was meeting. I was surprised to see an assistant on the other side of the room. I hadn't noticed him there behind all the others.

"I told them you were coming in," he said and stepped aside.

"Thanks."

I went down the hall, opened the doors, and stepped inside.

"Joan. Good. Saves us the trouble of sending for you," Fred said from the head of the conference table the Council was sitting at.

I stepped aside and people started filling in after me. It wasn't a huge room, and most of the space was taken up with a large table. People were packed in on the sides and a few stood in the open door rather than making it all the way in.

As he watched everyone come in, Fred's face changed from satisfied to angry. "What is this?"

"This is the opening up of Council business we just talked about in the caf," I said. "Did you think we weren't serious about it?"

I snuck a peek at Gamma. She had a ghost of a smile on her face and gave me a slight nod. When I looked back at Fred, he looked like he'd just sucked on a lemon.

"Well, I don't see why this has to change anything. We were just discussing your punishment, young lady," Fred said.

"What exactly is she being punished for? Leaving isolation without permission?" one of the teens asked.

Fred's expression shifted back to pleased with himself. He leaned back in his seat. "Do your little friends not know what you did?"

I looked around. "I did break a Family rule before I was put into isolation without any consultation." I took a breath. "I started dating

a girl. Because Sabrina and I couldn't be apart, it was challenging."
I looked down and gathered myself. It was a big deal I'd told her.
At the time, it had seemed like the thing to do, and I didn't regret it.
If I hadn't told her, we'd have never had the opportunity to fall in
love. But it was a big Family no. "Ellie and I became very close, and
in order not to lose her, I told her about my power. And Sabrina's."

Some people gasped and exchanged looks. A few shuffled their
feet as if they were suddenly uncertain about being there.

I spread my arms and held my hands up. "I know I did things out
of order, but with my power, there seemed to be no other way. Ellie
and I love each other and are willing to go through in-processing."

"Yes, well," Fred said. "That's all lovely, I'm sure, but you did
break the rules and the right thing to do is to undo this. We can't
have others getting ideas. We'll bring this young lady in and make
sure she doesn't have any knowledge of the Family or you."

Gamma cleared her throat. "No."

"No?" Fred looked at her. "What do you mean, no?"

"I won't do it. Not unless Linda says she means the Family
harm. It's only fair to give her the chance."

"Only fair?" Fred sneered. "Only fair would be if this girl
followed Family rules in the first place!"

Okay, that was true. But my crime was small in comparison.
I'd shuffled around the order of things, sure, but there was a process
for bringing people into the Family. What they'd done was not
only taboo, but also just wrong—and not only for the Family. It
was wrong to force women to carry pregnancies that they didn't
know weren't biologically the children they thought they were. It
was wrong to imprison people needlessly.

"Only fair would be if you hadn't locked me up!" I said.

"Well, if you hadn't been sneaking around without telling
anyone what you were up to, we'd have been able to make a better
decision about that," Fred said.

"Like you'd have let us practice? When you wanted me to be
your human tool?" Sabrina asked.

The look on Fred's face spoke to what the true answer was.

"We needed to get Joan sorted before we came to the Council.

And we were going to this week, but instead you isolated Joan. And drugged us to make it happen." Sabrina looked around. I could see the flash of hurt in her eyes as she scanned our parents. They'd let this happen.

"Not only that, but when the Family helps people have babies, you've been lying to them about whose babies they are," I said. I was being a little vague, not wanting to out Heather. Also, I didn't know if her mom knew. This would be a rough way to find out that Heather wasn't biologically hers at all.

Heather looked at her mother, who nodded, then said, "I know because I'm one of those kids. My mom, while she will always be my mom, is not my biological mother. And she had no idea until I told her. Both my dad and biological mother are Family born." She pointed at the Council sitting at the end of the long table. "They were trying to breed the power they wanted."

Fred stood, slamming his hands down on the table. "Not that it worked! We wanted a mind reader!"

I think that was the moment when the assembled Family members realized it was all true, that it really sank in. That the Council had been going against Family principles and had, in fact, forced pregnancies on people without full knowledge of what they were getting into. People gasped and started speaking to one another in low grumbles. I watched as speculation, fear, and anger spread in the tightly packed room, unsure what to do in the moment. I was just about to try standing on the table once more when Gamma stood up and spread her arms.

"You all have every right to be outraged. May I propose a way forward?"

She couldn't be using her power on the room because Sabrina was standing there next to me, but it was as if she were. Perhaps it was simply how she carried herself, assuming that everyone would calm down and pay attention, that resulted in everyone doing just that. But then I looked at Sabrina, who had a look of concentration on her face and knew. She was holding her breath, so to speak.

"I have long thought that it was time to shake up the Council and bring more light to some of the choices we've been making on behalf of the Family. There have been reasons for the choices, but that doesn't make them all right," Gamma said.

Fred pointed at her. "You! You have been as much a part of this as anyone." He wasn't as angry as he'd been when he'd slammed his hands down on the table moments ago. Gamma was definitely calming the room, and Sabrina was either helping or at least blocking, because I would have expected him to be more angry, not less. I took a moment and let my awareness of my power come to the front of my mind. Everything was enhanced with Sabrina's amplification. No one in the room was actively bleeding, but a couple of people had minor scratches from one thing or another. I closed them up with a moment of concentration, then let that all fade to the back again.

Gamma tilted her head down in a gesture that suggested she agreed she was at least partially culpable. And she was. Even if she'd voted against some of these actions, she had let them happen. She hadn't brought it to the attention of anyone outside of the Council. "You're not wrong. While I've argued against some things—"

"Like your granddaughter being put in isolation," Fred said. "You argue against things when it's convenient for you."

Gamma ignored that and continued, "I have allowed them to happen by and large. I think my place on the Council has helped prevent some even worse things from happening over the years." She shot a look at Fred. "However, I think we should all step aside and have new elections with all of this out in the open so that everyone can make an informed decision. Fred, you should feel free to campaign on a policy of doing what's best for the Family, if you so choose. But know that I will be telling people about your desire to breed dangerous powers into our children, the fact that you have overseen some questionable egg and sperm harvesting, and"— sparks flared in her eyes and I felt the mood of the room shift from calm and collected to angry—"that you wanted to kill Joan when she was a child, even though there was an alternative right there in front of us."

The anger swelled. I wanted to attack someone. Fred, probably. And then all of a sudden, it subsided. I was still angry and sad, but it wasn't the same. I looked at Sabrina. She shrugged a little at me. "It seemed time to dampen again," she said.

I couldn't have agreed more. Still, the room was now a jumble of people talking over one another and gesturing. Fred was calling for order and yelling at Gamma. Gamma was now sitting quietly, looking away, clearly composing herself once more. Other Council members appeared to be trying to explain themselves, but I couldn't hear them clearly because the teens were calling for them all to resign immediately. My parents worked their way to me, and each put a hand on my shoulder.

"We didn't know," Mom said in my ear.

I believed her. There was no doubt in my mind that my parents loved me. I also would never quite trust them the same way after they just cleared out and let me be taken.

I stepped up next to Gamma and held up my hands, hoping people would fall silent. It took a few moments, but they did. "I agree with my grandmother. I think the Council should resign immediately. An emergency election can be held soon. I suspect the Family will survive a few days or a week without a Council."

"I suspect we will," Gamma said.

Fred yelled, "You just want to get away with your own misbehaving! If there is no Council, who will punish you?"

Gamma stood up. "I believe that there is no need to punish Joan. She did things out of order, yes, but she loves Ellie. If we bring Ellie in for evaluation and she passes, there is no reason why they can't continue on as we all do when we find our special someone."

"And if you're intent on punishment, you can count time already served." Dad glared at Fred.

Which seemed fair enough to me. Fred was lucky no one was calling for him to be punished. A small part of me wanted to see him imprisoned in an isolation unit, but there was no need. If he wasn't on the Council, he'd have no power. I didn't have to hang out with him.

Gamma looked around at the Council members. "Are we all in agreement that our last order of business is to order Ellie brought in to be examined after which we all step down?"

Most of them didn't look happy about it but indicated their agreement. One person looked relieved.

Fred was the last holdout. "No. I certainly do not agree."

"Well, Fred, I think you're outvoted." There was something in Gamma's tone that didn't sound like her usual self. It made me think she was echoing something Fred had said to her. The glare he sent her way confirmed it for me.

CHAPTER TWENTY-THREE

Joan: *Is it lunchtime for you?*

I knew it was. I knew her schedule by heart, so I wasn't sure why that's the message I sent. I blamed nerves.

Ellie: *Joan! Are you okay? Are you out? What's happening?*
Joan: *Come outside and I'll tell you everything.*

When the meeting adjourned, Fred had stomped out while the others started on the bureaucratic work of announcing their resignations and putting Family staff in charge of setting up new elections. Gamma had taken a moment to let the IT people know I could have my electronics back. I'd taken a moment to submit the Gender Studies essay I'd been concerned about, but then I gave into what I'd been dying to do since I'd been locked away and went to find Ellie.

Navigating the streets of New York alone was a strange and disorienting feeling, but Sabrina had to stay at the Complex. She and Isabella had school, and Isabella's classroom hours were closely monitored. Not to mention that I no longer needed to have her there all the time, and I needed to get used to that. I was excited, but a little freaked out.

It was moments later that Ellie burst out of the doors. I only had a moment to take in the fact that she was wearing the same dress as the first day I met her, the dress I'd loved so much, before she was in my arms. I threaded my fingers into the back of her hair to hold her while the other hand went to her lower back. I breathed in the scent of her citrus shampoo and let myself sink into the comfort of having her in my arms.

"Joan. Are you okay?"

"I'm okay. Are you?"

"I've been losing my mind, but I'm better now. What's going on?"

There were other students passing us, sometimes shooting curious looks our way. I didn't want to get into talk of escaping, powers, and Family with an audience. "Do you have time to go for a walk?"

Ellie looked thoughtful for a moment. "I can skip my next class, but I have to be back for the one after. There's a test. So, I've got about an hour and a half. I want to know everything."

We linked hands and walked down the steps. "Do you mind if we pick up some lunch? I haven't eaten today and I'm starving."

She looked around and stopped walking. "Wait. No Sabrina?"

"Did you just notice?"

"I was pretty focused on you."

I pulled her in for a hug again. "Just me. I missed you so much."

"Me, too."

I pressed my lips to hers, wanting more connection. She parted her lips, inviting me in. I did my best to show her with my kiss how much she meant to me and how much I'd been missing her. I'm not sure how long I was lost to the sensations of her before there was a wolf-whistle that brought me back to my surroundings.

"We could go back to my place," Ellie said. "I mean for talking privately. Not that I don't want to…I really want to. But I need to know what's happening."

I grinned at her. "I want to, too. Hopefully we'll have all the time for that."

"Hopefully?"

"A lot has happened this morning."

"Okay, well, talk while we walk." She laced our fingers together and turned to start walking toward her apartment.

I told her the story of the morning while we walked. We picked up slices of pizza on the way, too. I hadn't eaten at all yet today and I'd pulled her away before she'd gotten to her lunch. We finished the slices in her living room as I finished the story.

"Joan, I'm so proud of you. That's amazing. I'm so impressed that you took charge of your own destiny and walked out and that you stood up to Fred. You've made a real difference in your Family."

"Thank you."

Love, pride, and affection were radiating off her. It made me feel so good, but also a little guilty. I hadn't told her yet about what happened next. She needed to come in and be interviewed. I believed it was important. While I could look at us and think, *Ellie loves me and it's fine*, I recognized that people in love weren't always thinking clearly. It's why there were rules. I'd had good reason for breaking them. I had to tell Ellie early about my power so I even had the chance to get to know her. But I also realized that I'd gotten very lucky that she was who she was and, presumably, the Family secret was still safe.

"There's a but, isn't there?" she asked.

"Yes. I...do you remember that I told you there was a way that we brought potential spouses in, to an extent we could start telling them some Family secrets?"

"I believe you said something about that the night you told me about your power, yeah."

"Well, that should have been done before I told you anything and now...now we need to rectify that situation."

I held my breath. Was this the point at which Ellie would decide she wanted nothing to do with me or my wild Family? I had high hopes she wouldn't turn and run, but I couldn't be sure. And I felt awful because if she did turn and run, the Family would no longer let that happen. They'd bring her in and modify her memories.

"What exactly does that entail?"

"Usually, I'd invite you to come over without telling you

anything or even letting you know that anything was happening. We'd have a conversation up on that same floor where Sabrina and I spoke to you that night. Linda would listen in. She'd read your thoughts as I brought up various topics that would give her an idea of how you might react to the Family secret. If you passed that test, I'd be cleared to tell you a little bit. Maybe show you, if it was that sort of power. But we'd only go that far if we intended to eventually marry. I'm not asking you to marry me," I hastened to add. "I know that's ridiculous. We're super young."

"Wait. You don't usually tell people until you're thinking of marrying them?"

I blushed and looked down. "Um, yeah. I jumped a lot of steps."

"So, basically, if I don't bug out now, we're engaged?"

"Um…kinda? But it could be a really long engagement and people do break up even after this step, so…but yeah, if you decide that you're okay with all this, it's a commitment?" I couldn't help the upspeak at the end. I was hearing myself say what I was saying. We were seventeen. Getting engaged now was not something that seemed at all reasonable. But the truth was that Family didn't tell their beloveds about powers unless they were planning on getting married to the person.

"Well." Ellie sounded a little brusque and my heart sank. "It's fast and we're young, but I think you may be the one, so I guess we're doing this. Whatever this is."

My heart soared. "Really? You mean it?"

She put her hand on mine. "I mean it. What do I have to do?"

"Okay, well, like I said, we're skipping a few steps here because of my choices. I am sorry. But you'll need to come in, and we'll have a conversation on the tenth floor where we're just open about what you know so Linda can read you. Then my grandmother will talk to you alone. As long as both of them feel your intentions are true, that's really it. Then you'll be considered more or less Family and expected to keep Family secrets like the rest of us."

She started giggling. "My intentions are true? What is this, some sort of nineteenth century throwback?"

I couldn't help but join in. "Yes," I gasped out between giggles. "It's a lot like that. The Family is old fashioned in some ways. But I meant more specifically what your intentions regarding the information you have are. Although, yeah, they'll want to know if you're serious about me."

She said she was, but after the interview, Linda would know for sure. My heart was on the line here. I believed Ellie, but I was nervous.

She sobered. "Well, there's nothing to worry about, then, if that's all it is. I don't intend to tell anyone anything, and I do love you."

"I love you, too."

I pulled her close and melded my lips to hers. We lost track of time and she was nearly late for her test.

❖

"So, what else do you want to do with yourself on this, your day of freedom?" Sabrina asked. I'd found her and Isabella in Sabrina's bedroom when I returned to the Complex. I'd already filled them in on how it went with Ellie. I did leave out a few things. Sabrina had shot me a look indicating she was aware I was leaving stuff out and would be demanding more details another time.

"I've got a lot of homework to catch up on."

Sabrina and Isabella shot me twin looks of disbelief and disappointment.

"I'm sorry, but I do! Don't you guys have school anyway?"

Isabella put her hands on her hips. "I'm done for today."

"But you do have your violin lesson in a little bit," Sabrina reminded her.

Isabella pouted. "It seems like we should be celebrating."

I'd had a celebration of my own already with Ellie, but I got her point. "How about we go get juices before your lesson?"

Isabella crossed her arms. "How about ice cream?"

We agreed.

We were sitting in a park, ice cream in hand, when I remembered something. "Hey, Isabella, I had a thought while I was up in isolation working on my meditation, and I have a question for you."

"What?" she asked, suspicious. "I mean, I did try, but working on meditation seemed to just make it worse this weekend."

"That was my thought exactly. But I was wondering, when you play violin, do you hear thoughts?"

She took a bite of ice cream and appeared to consider the question. "I don't...I don't think so."

"Maybe that's something to test out," I said.

Now she looked excited. "Yeah! I mean, that would be great, right?"

Sabrina said, "Not that I don't adore you, of course, but if you could manage even a little on your own, that would be pretty awesome, right?"

"Right! When we're done with the ice cream, we could try it out before my lesson, if there's time."

Sabrina pulled out her phone. "I think we're going to be tight on time as is. I could just step out for a few minutes during your lesson and see what happens."

The responsibility Sabrina had for Isabella now was more than just a babysitter. Seeing her manage Isabella's schedule made my stomach clench for her. I vowed to myself I'd do as much as I could to make it easier for her.

Isabella looked worried. "I don't know that I want to hear what my violin teacher thinks. Maybe we could try it with my dad after?"

Sabrina agreed to that plan, and we all went back to the Complex, finishing our ice cream as we went.

I buckled down and got a couple of hours of homework done, but eventually my thoughts strayed more and more to six o'clock when Ellie was coming over after her Starbucks shift. We'd decided all around sooner was better than later for her evaluation.

I texted Gamma, asking if she was available to talk. A few minutes later, I knocked on her door.

"It's been quite a day. I've got water on for tea," Gamma said by way of greeting.

"Thanks, Gamma. That sounds perfect." I went to sit at the table. When I'd laid eyes on Gamma, I'd realized that I'd messed her life up a little. "I'm sorry about losing you your Council seat."

Gamma set the tea tray down on the table. She waved off my apology. "The Council needed shuffling up. My losing my spot is a small price to pay." She sat down kitty corner from me. "Besides, I may run again."

"I think people would vote you back in," I said.

She patted my hand. "We'll see. If not, that's okay, too. It might be time for a younger generation to take over."

"It's a little weird that even though you're not on the Council and you're biased in my favor, you're coordinating Ellie's interview." I took a sip of my tea. It helped to calm my nerves.

Gamma pinned me with a look. "Joan, my girl, as much as I love you and hope that things will work out for you and Ellie, you have to know that I will put the Family first if there are any questions about if she will keep our secrets."

Oh, right. If it didn't go well, if Linda decided that Ellie was a poor risk, Gamma would take her back up so that she and Linda could work in tandem to adjust Ellie's memories. I knew that.

I didn't realize I'd slumped until Gamma patted my shoulder. "Shoulders back, my girl. You have to believe your Ellie will pass with flying colors or you wouldn't have told her in the first place, right?"

That was true. I straightened and took another sip of tea. "She will. It's all going to be okay."

Gamma smiled her approval at my optimism. She glanced at her wall clock, then said, "There's over an hour until she's due to arrive. Why don't you tell me about school? What are you planning for your life now, or have you gotten that far?"

Gamma and I hashed over my plans, which I certainly had, because I'd been dreaming of medical school since long before it was feasible. We managed to make the time go, along with three cups of tea. I felt comfortable and relaxed, as I often did around Gamma. Finally, it was time to go meet Ellie, and I excused myself to the bathroom before making my way to the metro station. It wasn't until I was out of the Complex that it occurred to me that I was probably calmer than was warranted given the situation, and I wondered if Gamma had been using her power on me. It was something I hadn't had to consider when I only visited her with Sabrina. It gave me new insight as to why people were hesitant to voluntarily spend time with her. Not that I didn't understand it intellectually before, but this visceral feeling of maybe having been messed with was unpleasant.

I shook off the artificial-feeling calm and bounced anxiously on the balls of my feet, waiting to catch sight of Ellie. I was a whole mix of emotions— excited to see her, nervous about how this evening would go, and worried that she'd be upset with me for putting her through this.

When she did come into sight, we moved toward each other like magnets. Did I run? Maybe. I'm not really sure. All I know is that I went from seeing her to wrapping my arms around her in very quick order.

"Hi," I breathed into her hair.

"Hi," she said back against my neck, sending shivers down my spine.

I shifted so we were side by side, took her hand, and started walking back to the Complex. "How are you doing? Any questions I can answer?"

"Tell me everything you think is going to happen when I get there."

She sounded nervous, and the least I could do was walk her through what was going to happen, even though we'd talked about it earlier.

I couldn't help teasing a little bit, hoping it would put her more at ease. "Okay, so we're going to get to the Complex and then I'll open the door for you. You'll walk through and then I'll hold your hand as we walk to the elevator. I'll push the button for the tenth floor…"

She interrupted with a short, fake laugh. "I see you think you're cute, but move on to the parts that matter."

"Okay, yes, I get it. Sorry. Okay, the big thing is that I'm going with you to the tenth floor. We'll just sit there and have a discussion. Then you'll have to meet with Gamma. Then that's it."

"Wait. What do you mean by that's it? What will happen in this meeting with your Gamma?"

"Well, that's kind of dependent on Linda's report." I didn't want to lie to her. "I'm hoping what will happen is that Gamma will serve you tea and be the typical parental-type figure while she interrogates you about our relationship. Then I'll get called in and we'll retire to my bedroom to get some time alone together and maybe celebrate with cookies."

"Or?"

"Or I won't see you again," I admitted. "If that's what happens, you'll leave thinking you and I broke up, but that it was never very serious, and you'll just go on with your life." I couldn't help the catch in my voice that betrayed how hurt I would be with that outcome.

"That's horrible."

"It would be for me," I said, "It wouldn't really be for you because you wouldn't remember me to be sad about it."

"I just can't believe it would work, considering how I feel about you."

"Well, I think it's true that it works best when feelings don't run deep. I seriously don't know that it's ever happened that someone was truly in love and then had the modification done. The thing is that if someone is truly in love, they tend to pass the *will you keep the secret* test." An icy hand gripped my heart at the thought that Ellie didn't truly love me.

She stopped dead on the sidewalk, pulling me to a stop next to her. "Joan, I love you. If that's all it takes, we'll pass with flying colors."

She sounded so confident that it helped ease my fears. Some. I kissed her, hoping it wouldn't be the last time. "Okay, then. Let's do this."

We held hands as we rode the elevator up, not talking. On the tenth floor, I led her to the area directly beneath Linda's apartment and indicated a couch to sit on. There was no need to signal to Linda that we were there. She'd have heard us by now.

"So, where do we start?" Ellie asked nervously.

"Um, let's talk about meeting on the High Line?"

She smiled, a little nervously, but gamely said, "Well, I saw you there, crouching in the bushes, and couldn't help but go over and see what was going on. And then you stood up and were so cute. What could I do but hit on you?"

I touched the fingers of my free hand to my chest. "Me? You were the adorable one."

We talked for an hour, just going through the beats of our developing relationship, including my decision to tell her after the incident at Central Park. We got up to the accident at summer camp when my phone chimed. I'd turned on Do Not Disturb with an override for Linda, so I knew who'd messaged. I pulled my phone out and, sure enough, there was a FamilyChat message from Linda just saying, "That's enough. Take Ellie to Jenny."

That was dismayingly sparse. I put the phone away and stood up, holding a hand out to Ellie.

"Is that it? What's happening now?" she asked.

"Let's go get on the elevator," I said, wanting to clear out of Linda's space.

Once we were riding down to Gamma's level, I said, "Linda felt like she got enough of a read, and now I'm delivering you to Gamma's to meet her."

Ellie searched my face for clues. I smiled reassurance I wasn't feeling. "Gamma is great. You'll like her."

"Will I have a choice?"

I flashed back to my earlier concern, but I did love and trust Gamma. Well, unless she really felt like the Family was in jeopardy, in which case I did still trust her. I trusted her to do the right thing, which would be heartbreaking, but would also mean that my judgement was fucked up and Ellie wasn't what she seemed. That couldn't be. I shook it off. "I think you will."

"Convincing." She turned to face the elevator door again.

We held hands all the way to Gamma's door. When I knocked, there was a brief pause before she answered. "You must be Ellie," she said, smiling warmly.

"Gamma, this is Ellie. Ellie, Gamma, I mean Jenny," I said, falling back on manners.

"It's so nice to meet you. I wish we were meeting under different circumstances. Come in, come in. Can I offer you tea?" Gamma opened her door wider and put her arm out, indicating the inside of her apartment.

Ellie looked at me nervously, then stepped forward while I stood awkwardly at the door.

"Joan, I'd tell you to go relax until I call you to let you know, but I assume you'll be sitting outside the door waiting?" Gamma asked.

I nodded.

"I'll take good care of your girl." She squeezed my arm, then shut the door.

I sat down next to the door and texted Sabrina.

Joan: *Ellie is with Gamma. Come keep me company?*
Sabrina: *You know I can't come near Gamma right now. Meet you by the elevator?*

That would be far enough away that Sabrina wouldn't dampen Gamma's powers, although it was tempting to have her come to the door and try, if I were honest. I replied with a thumbs-up, and in minutes, Sabrina, Isabella, and I were sitting in the hall just next to the elevators.

"So, how'd violin practice go?" I asked, fiddling nervously with my fingers.

Isabella was bubbling with excitement. "Good! Afterward, we tested your idea by me playing while Sabrina left and it worked! I couldn't hear Dad!"

"Isabella, that's awesome!" I high fived her.

"I know! Now Sabrina can have breaks."

Sabrina patted her knee. "It's good for both of us, right, squirt?"

When had Sabrina started calling Isabella *squirt*? I was missing everything. This whole separation thing was seriously bittersweet.

Sabrina put her hand on my knee, and only then did I realize I'd been bouncing it up and down. I tried to stop. "So, um, talk to me. Just tell me anything."

Isabella started telling a story about learning to play a piece and I took in none of it, but just having them there and having someone talking to me was helpful. I watched down the hall like a hawk, waiting for Gamma's door to open. Why was it taking forever? That was bad, right? But if they were going to modify, Gamma would have to take her up to Linda, and that would also mean opening the door. I cut Isabella off.

"Sorry. Um, Gamma doesn't have a secret way out of her apartment, does she?"

Sabrina looked at me sharply. "Not that I'm aware of. We'd know, right?"

"I mean, we've spent a lot of time there, but I've never gone digging in the back of her closets or anything. It's possible, right?"

Sabrina rolled her eyes. "Don't get caught up in unlikely scenarios."

"Why would she have given me approval to wait in the hall if there was a possibility she'd have to bring Ellie by me on the way up to Joan? Like, seriously. Maybe there are secret passages. Is it that wild to think the Family has secret passages built into its custom-built building?"

"Whoa!" Isabella said, looking excited, which was a far cry from my emotion of near terror.

Sabrina didn't speak up right away, but she put her arm around me. I shrugged it off. I stood up.

"What are you going to do?" Sabrina asked, worriedly.

"I don't know." I started pacing. "But I can't just sit here anymore. I've got to…"

A door opened down the hall and I whipped around. Ellie came out and walked toward me, smiling. Oh my God. Was everything going to be okay? Was that possible?

When Ellie saw my face, her smile fell a little. "Are you okay?"

I hurried to her. "Are you?" I examined her face, looking for evidence this was a casual goodbye.

"I'm fine!" She wrapped me in a hug and whispered in my ear, "I love you."

That was when I knew we were in the clear, and I started sobbing. I choked out, "I love you, too."

EPILOGUE

I exited the building that contained the cadaver lab to find welcome sunshine, rare for fall in Seattle, and Ellie waiting for me. I smiled. "This is an unexpected surprise. Sorry, though, I probably smell bad." I usually went home immediately after lab and took a shower.

"I don't care." She hugged me. "But yeah, a little unpleasant."

We turned and started walking home, just off campus. It was a big campus, but my classes were closest to the apartment. "How come you're in my neck of the woods?"

"Tech writing got canceled and I decided a walk sounded nice."

I smiled at her. "It's lovely weather for a walk, and I'm always glad to see your face."

She laughed. "Same, but you know we live together."

I shrugged. "Still."

"Do we have time to stop for a coffee?" she asked.

I pulled my phone out of my pocket to check. "If we get it to go."

We stopped at our favorite coffee shop by our apartment and left with four beverages. When we walked into the apartment, we were greeted with the sounds of violin and Sabrina, who stood there looking impatient, but softened when Ellie handed her one of the coffees. "Thanks! Gotta run!" She took off.

I went into Isabella's practice room and dropped off her hot chocolate. She nodded her thanks but kept playing. I knew she'd take a break to take sips, but she'd mostly be playing from now until when Sabrina got back from her Russian class in a couple of hours. Sabrina took a lot of her course load online so she could stay with Isabella, who continued to do school online, but language classes were just better in person. The three of us had arranged our schedules so that either Ellie or I would be home with Isabella whenever Sabrina had in-person class.

I took a quick shower, then went back to the living room. We had a nicer than normal apartment for college students. There were three bedrooms, two of which had en suite bathrooms. Ellie and I shared one while Sabrina and Isabella shared the other. The third room was Isabella's practice room. We didn't have to worry too much about her being loud because we lived on the top floor and the couple who lived below us were deaf. That was on purpose. One of the Family secret service, as we'd taken to jokingly calling whichever shadowy people did slightly shady Family business, had somehow figured out an available apartment with a deaf couple living under it. Don't ask me how. Not only was that easier with all the violin playing, but they didn't think in ways that were intrusive for Isabella, which made things easier for her. They were the only neighbors in range for her unless she and our neighbors to the side were within accidental range. This was all paid for by the Family, because that was the compromise. Sabrina got as regular a college experience as possible, and we all did what we could to keep Isabella comfortable and well socialized.

It had been a series of compromises choosing a school that would work for Sabrina, Ellie, and me, but what ended up making the most sense was a large campus that was far away from New York, so we could all have a little independence. Even though the Family had made some changes after the meeting that had taken place after we made our stand and nearly every Council member had been replaced, Sabrina and I wanted to try lives away for a while.

As for Ellie, she was kind of stuck with me. Not that people didn't break up after having been introduced to the Family secrets. They did—Isabella's parents being a prime example. They were divorced, and while both her parents missed her, they also both felt the best thing for her was to get the breaks living with Sabrina provided for her. We were working on her meditation and gave her opportunities to practice closing out thoughts daily. She hated it, but it was worth trying to accomplish the goal and she could see that, so every day she spent at least a few minutes away from Sabrina and not practicing music so she could practice blocking. She said she could kind of mute things if there were a few people so that they jumbled together some, but not more than that because then it got too loud. However, she'd discovered being around one of Sabrina's friends who was an international student from China was almost as good as being around Sabrina. She could hear Sue's thoughts, but they just sounded like so much noise to her because Sue thought in Mandarin. Sue was also an accomplished guitarist and the two had struck up a friendship, which meant we had a babysitter on occasion. That always had to happen at our place, not the dorms, because there were too many people around there.

Back to Ellie being stuck with me, though. Like I said, she wasn't obligated to stay with me forever, but it was uncommon for people not to get married after having done the Family introduction, so while we weren't actually engaged, I'd had to endure a lot of teasing from the family (meaning my parents, Neil, and Sabrina) about having been so judgmental about how young Neil was when he brought Theresa home.

Speaking of which, "Did Theresa text you about the bachelorette party, too?" I asked Ellie. We'd settled in side by side on the couch, laptops open to do homework, coffees close at hand for sipping.

Ellie stopped typing and laid her head on my shoulder. "Yup. Pedicures sound awesome."

"If you say so," I said doubtfully. We were all under twenty-one, so bar hopping wasn't on the table, plus Isabella would be tagging along, of course. Even if we were of age, I didn't drink at all. I wasn't sure what might happen to my control if I got drunk or did drugs. Ellie occasionally got a little tipsy, which was super cute because she got very giggly. Sabrina had gotten falling-down, throwing-up drunk a couple of times, and the third time seemed to have gotten it out of her system. While I was feeling like my world was opening up in the best ways, Sabrina was still feeling hemmed in and I think she felt the need to rebel in small ways. She got some breaks, yes, but she was probably going to be tied to Isabella for life. I hoped the Christmas gift we had planned would help.

It was going to be a pretty eventful December. We were all going home for Christmas and Neil and Theresa's wedding, just over a year and a half after he brought her home. I was excited for all that, except maybe the pedicures, but was so excited about Sabrina's gift that I was having a hard time not letting her in on the secret. We also hadn't told Isabella yet because her secret-keeping skills still weren't great, at least when it came to her inner circle. She was good at Family secrets, but any little thing she found out about one of the three of us, everyone knew shortly.

"Where do you hope we go this summer?" I asked.

Ellie didn't answer right away, and in the pause I noticed a pause in the music, too. Isabella must be drinking her hot chocolate. The next voice to speak wasn't Ellie, it was Isabella, who flung open the door and shouted, "We're traveling this summer? I hope we go to Paris!" There was a brief pause, then she said, "And I can too keep a secret! I won't tell!" She danced around for a bit. "I'm allowed to be excited! This is exciting! We have to go see music wherever we are!" She huffed. "I will keep the secret, just watch. Argh! You two are so annoying!" She went back into her practice room and slammed the door. Soon strains of violin wafted through the air once more. Preteens were fun.

I exchanged amused looks with Ellie. "Guess that cat is out of the bag," she said. "And Paris would be cool, but I bet Sabrina picks something off the beaten path. We should go someplace Russian-speaking for her. I know that's the language she's most excited about."

"Yup. It's not what I'd choose for myself, but we'll have opportunities to travel. This trip is for Sabrina to sow her oats. Paris can wait. Clearly she'll be able to do that with Isabella sometime in the future."

I'd colluded with our two sets of parents, who requested Family funds and got permission for us to have a summer of travel. It would be my last summer off school to go along and help with Isabella, but it was definitely for Sabrina. She'd always wanted to travel. She still would be able to later, so long as she took Isabella and the Family didn't need either of them, but this summer was for her, for whatever she wanted to do. I was guessing she'd find an NGO to volunteer with, teaching art to kids in Moldova or something. Isabella could join in on that, too, but we could also be there to hang with Isabella, so Sabrina could go off and do her own thing sometimes. She'd given up so much for me, and now for Isabella, that she truly deserved this.

I set my laptop aside and pulled Ellie's off her lap. She looked at me questioningly and I answered by cuddling around her. I pulled her legging-clad legs onto my jean-clad ones and wrapped my arms around her. "I'm just so happy and grateful that you came into my life and were the catalyst for so much positive change. If not for you, I…honestly, I don't want to think about it. It might have been bad."

She burrowed in. "I'm glad, but I think I'm the lucky one. You're so kind, thoughtful, and altruistic."

I scoffed.

"What? You are. Think about what we're doing right now. You could have just left Sabrina in the dust, but you're doing everything you can to make it easier for her."

It was the least I could do, and here she was doing the same thing when she really didn't have to, but I wasn't going to argue. I was enjoying cuddling too much.

"I love you, you know," I said. "And I'm so looking forward to our future."

"When we're married and raising little problematically powerful children of our own, back in the bosom of your secretive, supportive, and occasionally sketchy Family?" she teased.

I kissed the top of her head. "Exactly."

"Can't wait," she said.

About the Author

Jordan Meadows has always been a big reader. When her daughter got into reading Young Adult, she read right along beside her, finding a new favorite genre. When her daughter started writing novels, it inspired Jordan to try her hand. Her favorite books involve a capable woman falling in love with another capable woman while they overcome obstacles together. She is doing her best to put more of them out into the world.

Jordan lives in Portland, Oregon, and when not obsessing or agonizing about her writing, enjoys reading, stand-up paddleboarding, hiking, playing board games, and hanging out with her dog.

Young Adult Titles From Bold Strokes Books

Proximity by Jordan Meadows. Joan really likes Ellie, but being alone with her could turn deadly unless she can keep her dangerous powers under control. (978-1-63679-476-1)

A Talent Within by Suzanne Lenoir. Evelyne, born into nobility, and Annika, a peasant girl with a deadly secret, struggle to change their destinies in Valmora, a medieval world controlled by religion, magic, and men. (978-1-63679-423-5)

Take Her Down by Lauren Emily Whalen. Stakes are cutthroat, scheming is creative, and loyalty is ever-changing in this queer, female-driven YA retelling of Shakespeare's *Julius Caesar*. (978-1-63679-089-3)

Two Winters by Lauren Emily Whalen. A modern YA retelling of Shakespeare's *The Winter's Tale* about birth, death, Catholic school, improv comedy, and the healing nature of time. (978-1-63679-019-0)

Boy at the Window by Lauren Melissa Ellzey. Daniel Kim struggles to hold onto reality while haunted by both his very-present past and his never-present parents. Jiwon Yoon may be the only one who can break Daniel free. (978-1-63679-092-3)

Three Left Turns to Nowhere by Jeffrey Ricker, J. Marshall Freeman & 'Nathan Burgoine. Three strangers heading to a convention in Toronto are stranded in rural Ontario, where a small town with a subtle kind of magic leads each to discover what he's been searching for. (978-1-63679-050-3)

#shedeservedit by Greg Herren. When his gay best friend, and high school football star, is murdered, Alex Wheeler is a suspect and must find the truth to clear himself. (978-1-63555-996-5)

The Infinite Summer by Morgan Lee Miller. While spending the summer with her dad in a small beach town, Remi Brenner falls for Harper Hebert and accidentally finds herself tangled up in an intense restaurant rivalry between her famous stepmom and her first love. (978-1-63555-969-9)

Bury Me in Shadows by Greg Herren. College student Jake Chapman is forced to spend the summer at his dying grandmother's home and soon finds danger from long-buried family secrets. (978-1-63555-993-4)

I Am Chris by R Kent. There's one saving grace to losing everything and moving away. Nobody knows her as Chrissy Taylor. Now Chris can live who he truly is. (978-1-63555-904-0)

The Dubious Gift of Dragon Blood by J. Marshall Freeman. One day Crispin is a lonely high school student—the next he is fighting a war in a land ruled by dragons, his otherworldly boyfriend at his side. (978-1-63555-725-1)

Jellicle Girl by Stevie Mikayne. One dark summer night, Beth and Jackie go out to the canoe dock. Two years later, Beth is still carrying the weight of what happened to Jackie. (978-1-63555-691-9)

All the Worlds Between Us by Morgan Lee Miller. High school senior Quinn Hughes discovers that a broken friendship is actually a door propped open for an unexpected romance. (978-1-63555-457-1)

Exit Plans for Teenage Freaks by 'Nathan Burgoine. Cole always has a plan—especially for escaping his small-town reputation as "that kid who was kidnapped when he was four"—but when he teleports to a museum, it's time to face facts: it's possible he's a total freak after all. (978-1-163555-098-6)

Rocks and Stars by Sam Ledel. Kyle's struggle to own who she is and what she really wants may end up landing her on the bench and without the woman of her dreams. (978-1-63555-156-3)